I0661212

THE LONG ROAD
INTO DARKNESS

Also by Michael J. McCann

THE MARCH AND WALKER CRIME NOVEL SERIES

Sorrow Lake
Burn Country
Persistent Guilt
No Sadness of Farewell

THE DONAGHUE AND STAINER CRIME NOVEL SERIES

Blood Passage
Marcie's Murder
The Fregoli Delusion
The Rainy Day Killer

SUPERNATURAL FICTION

The Ghost Man

The Long Road Into Darkness

A Tom Faust Crime Novel

Michael J. McCann

The Plaid Raccoon Press
2019

The Long Road Into Darkness is a work of fiction. Names, characters, institutions, places and events are either the product of the author's imagination or are used fictitiously. Any resemblance to actual persons, living or dead, events, or locales is entirely coincidental.

THE LONG ROAD INTO DARKNESS
Copyright © 2019 by Michael J. McCann

The Plaid Raccoon Press supports copyright, which protects creativity and the right of authors to profit from the fruits of their considerable labour. Thank you for buying an authorized edition of this book and for complying with copyright laws by not reproducing any part of this book, paperback and/or e-book, without permission from the publisher.

ISBN: 978-1-927884-17-1 (paperback)
eBook ISBN: 978-1-927884-18-8 (e-book)

Cover image: Ivan Spasic / Thinkstock. Used under licence.
Author photo: © 2019 by Michael J. McCann

Visit the author's website at www.mjmccann.com

To Lynn, one more time
on this long road

SEVENTEEN YEARS AGO

The house was a ranch-style bungalow on a back country road between the village of Apsley and the Kawartha Highlands Provincial Park. When Ontario Provincial Police Detective Inspector Tom Faust arrived at the scene, it was approaching mid-morning, more than an hour after the 911 call had come in.

Tom parked his motor pool Crown Victoria on the gravel shoulder down at the end of the line of vehicles and walked past the neighbour's house to the barrier marking the outer perimeter of the crime scene. He signed in and was met by a detective constable with the local OPP crime unit who identified himself as Jim Hatton.

"Never seen anything like it," Hatton said.

They walked across the front lawn toward the house. The front door was open. The curtains were drawn in all the windows facing the road. Small numbered markers littered the grass where evidence had been found, catalogued, and photographed but not yet bagged and tagged. Tom stopped at a line of red plastic cones set out by the forensic identification team to prevent intrusion into the area where they were still working.

There were four bodies. The largest, at the far right, was a heavy-set male in his late thirties or early forties. He wore track pants and a T-shirt that were black with blood. He'd been stabbed in the stomach, and his throat was cut. He was lying on his back, with his arms and legs spread out, as though he were trying to make a snow angel in the grass.

Beside him was a smallish woman a few years younger. She'd received the same treatment with the knife, which must have been large and sharp, and she'd been arranged in the same position. On her right were two girls, both pre-teens. All three females wore night dresses that were covered with dark clotted blood.

"Wishart says no evidence of rape," Hatton said, reading his thoughts.

"On any of them?"

"No."

Tom nodded. He'd worked with Dr. Don Wishart, the Peterborough County coroner, several times before. The man was competent and thorough, and Tom trusted his judgment. "Time of death?"

Hatton glanced at his watch. "About nine hours ago, so around eleven-thirty last night."

"How'd it go down?"

"It looks like the man was attacked in the kitchen. The woman was killed in the master bedroom and the two girls in a bedroom they shared. They were all dragged out and arranged here, like a fucking display for us to find."

"Yeah, I see that." Tom looked at the house. "Was the door open or closed when we got here?"

"Open." Hatton frowned. "There's one more bedroom on the main floor; looks like it belongs to a teenaged boy. Trashed up, stuff thrown around, but only a bit of blood spatter and no sign of the kid."

"Oh?" Tom raised an eyebrow.

"Yeah, I know. We're still chasing it all down, Tom. It's

going to take a few more hours before we know for sure who lives here. Lived, I guess."

"Understood." Tom walked away from the bodies, his mind already processing the next steps necessary to get the investigation into full swing. This one was going to be particularly difficult. Mass murders always were, but right away the staging of the bodies was suggesting some kind of religious angle. A complicating factor the press would climb all over.

On his way to the front door he passed two EMS respondents standing on either side of their gurney, waiting for the coroner to tell them what to do. The nearest, a young redhead, caught Tom's eye and quickly looked away again.

"Hang on, Eric," Tom heard the kid's partner whisper. "It won't be too much longer."

Tom took a pair of booties from a box on the step and slipped them over his shoes before walking inside. He took care to avoid the trails of blood smeared across the threshold, knowing that for him it was only just the beginning of something that would not end very soon.

PRESENT DAY

1

When Tom Faust finally rolled out of bed after a long, restless night with little sleep, he felt depressed and hung over. He wandered into the kitchen, threw the empty bourbon bottle into the recycling bin, and put on a pot of coffee. While it percolated, he looked out the window at the morning sky. It was blue and cloudless. A slight wind stirred the leaves of the tree in the backyard.

He decided to take his coffee outside. He poured a cup and sipped. Passable. He picked out a compact disc from the shelving unit next to the refrigerator and put it into the audio player on the kitchen island. The player was one of those expensive mail-order items not much bigger than a box of tissues, with a remote control and wireless speakers. He tapped the touch-sensitive top of the player and the CD—Gentle Giant's *Octopus*—began to play. Turning up the volume, he grabbed a bottle of aspirin from the shelf above the sink and went outside, leaving the sliding glass door open behind him.

The morning was still and warm. The only other

residence in sight was his daughter's, a sprawling, neo-modern monstrosity perched on top of the hill behind his place with a view of the surrounding countryside. Pamela was in Los Angeles right now and her husband, John Marks, was in Vancouver. Their property included most of the drumlin on which their three-year-old home sat, hayfields leased to a neighbouring farmer, and the house down at the roadside in which Tom currently lived.

A former log shanty built by the original settlers of the lot in the mid-eighteen hundreds, the house was small and shabby. Green vinyl siding covered the exterior. The shingles on the roof were lifting badly. The kitchen was its only good feature. The original beams in the ceiling had been exposed and refinished by a previous owner, and an antique wagon wheel had been hung up as a light fixture. Otherwise, the place was a dump. Pamela had intended to tear it down, but Tom convinced her to rent it to him while he fixed up his own place.

The back patio was a small area covered with concrete paving stones. His outdoor furniture consisted of a plastic table with a hole in the middle to accommodate an um-brella, which he lacked, a lawn chair, and a big chunk of wood that served as a footstool. The backyard itself was a patch about one hundred feet across and forty feet deep that he kept separated from the field beyond with the riding lawn mower parked behind the carport.

Home sweet home.

Staring up at Pamela's house as he waited for the aspirin to kick in, he thought about what to do today to pass the time. Since he didn't have anything else pencilled into his calendar, he figured he might as well run into town and order drywall. Pamela's house-sitter, Jade Morgan, was supposed to be teaching him the basics of home renovation. It was as good a time as any to try to light a fire under her feet and get things moving again.

He rubbed his forehead, wishing the headache would ease.

He finished his coffee and went back inside. Turning off the music, he called Jade's cellphone. It went directly to voicemail.

"It's Tom Faust," he said. "I'm going to the Home Depot to order the drywall stuff. Meet me at the church afterward. Try to get there before lunch. I'll bring food."

Doubting that he'd see her before mid-afternoon, he stripped and showered. First cold, then hot. Towelling himself off, he glanced in the mirror at the belt of extra flesh around his middle. Since retiring a year and a half ago, his waistline had expanded from thirty-two inches to thirty-four. He refused to weigh himself but figured he'd put on about ten pounds that he didn't need.

Combing his salt-and-pepper hair straight back, he looked at the stubble on his long, narrow face and decided not to bother shaving. He threw on jeans and a Hawaiian shirt that was mostly blue, stepped into sandals, shoved a pair of reading glasses into his shirt pocket, and considered himself ready to face the world once again.

Outside, he slid behind the wheel of his black Lincoln Town Car and backed out of the carport. Dalton Road was a quiet stretch of hardpan gravel in rural Selwyn Township that seldom saw traffic. After half a kilometre it ended at Sixth Line Road, where he turned left. Five minutes later he took a right onto County Road 29 and was on his way into Peterborough.

He loved driving the Town Car because its power reminded him of the Crown Victoria police interceptors he'd driven during his long career with the Ontario Provincial Police. Some retired guys he knew liked the muscle cars or sports cars. They went for the Firebirds or the Corvettes, they joined collectors' clubs, and they proudly displayed their toys at weekend car shows. Tom preferred a big, imposing sedan. The Town Car rode smoothly, it was safe, and the engine responded nicely when he floored the gas pedal.

At the Home Depot, he pulled out his notebook and went over to the side counter to place an order for drywall and the various supplies Jade had told him they would need. He arranged for everything to be delivered on Thursday.

His next stop was McDonald's, for coffee. The woman who served him was in her forties. She wore her hair in a neat bun at the nape of her neck. When she took his order, she made eye contact and smiled. He nodded politely, his mind elsewhere.

He drank his coffee at a table near the back, watching people come and go. When it was done, he left the restaurant and drove to another fast food outlet, where he ordered two submarine sandwiches to go, one for himself and one for Jade. He threw them into the car and went across the street into the liquor store to pick up another bottle of bourbon.

He left the city on Chemong Road and drove north fifteen minutes until he reached the turnoff onto Cedar Hill Road. Two kilometres later he turned into the wheel tracks that served as a driveway for his home-to-be. He shut off the engine and got out of the car.

Formerly known as St. Mark's Presbyterian Church, it had been built in the late nineteenth century to serve the rural community between Lakefield and Selwyn. A century later when its congregation had evaporated into nothing, it was decommissioned and sold. It changed hands a few times and was used variously as a meeting hall, a storage facility, and a haven for bats and mice until the afternoon in May when Tom Faust drove by and saw the For Sale sign.

He'd been retired for just over a year and didn't know what to do with himself. He was spending a lot of time in the Town Car, driving up and down back roads, trying to work off the free-floating, residual tension that had followed him from the job. Sometimes, after an hour or two behind the wheel, window down, elbow out, a can of beer in his hand, he felt a little better, but he knew he was floundering. According to his daughter, he needed a new focal point in his life. Something to do with his time. New objectives to meet. He was beginning to believe she was right.

He'd never noticed Cedar Hill Road before that day. Seeing the sign for it, he'd slowed on a whim and turned. It was late spring. The fields on either side of the road were already green with new growth. Dust plumed behind him in the rear-view mirror. The sun shining through the back window felt warm on his neck.

He passed the church before the real estate sign registered. There was a quick impression of a stone building with a tower of some sort at the front, weeds sprouting everywhere, and stained-glass windows coated with road dust. He stopped, shifted into reverse, and backed up. He sat in front of the church for a while, taking it in, and then used his cellphone to take a picture of the sign before driving on.

Two days later he was shown inside by the real estate agent, an indifferent middle-aged woman who worked out of Lakefield. It needed a lot of tender loving care, she cautioned, but the foundation and overall structure of the building were sound. The bell, unfortunately, was long gone from the tower, donated to a museum somewhere near Toronto.

Tom shrugged, not caring. He called a retired fire chief

he knew who worked on the side as a building inspector. The report came back glowing. Tom gave the agent a lowball offer, negotiated for a good price, and bought the place.

He pushed away from the Town Car and wandered around the side, admiring the new windows he'd just paid a contractor to install. He'd disliked on sight the original stained glass windows with their religious-themed depictions of suffering and death, so they were gone, sold to a guy who specialized in architectural salvage. He held back only a small peaked window with a floral design that Pamela had admired and wanted for her garden.

Another contractor had come in to cover the roof with stainless steel and to reinforce the trusses and beams in the ceiling. With Jade's help, Tom built a kitchen, a laundry room, and a guest room beneath the choir loft. After that, they roughed in a bedroom and a bathroom upstairs in the loft. He then hired someone to drill a well, install a septic system, and complete all the plumbing. Still to come were new wiring, new interior walls, propane and electrical heating units, central air conditioning, new flooring to replace the rotting and splintered old pine floor, and a new set of stairs leading to the belfry at the top of the square, Norman-style tower at the front where his study was going to be. There was a lot of work to do, but he had nothing but time on his hands and a lot of undirected energy to devote to it.

He strolled around the church until he reached the front again. The side of the tower facing the road was solid stone, but there was an arched opening on the right-hand side. He stepped in, conscious of the ponderous weight of the tower above him. There were two doors, a small one that gave access to the tower staircase and a large, heavy oak door that led inside the church. Both were secured with heavy padlocks. As Tom fumbled for his keys, he noticed that the lock on the big door was hanging loose on its hasp.

Frowning, he opened the door. He didn't like to think he was getting so careless and distracted that he'd forgotten to lock up the last time he'd left. There were a lot of expensive tools and supplies lying around that he wouldn't care to have stolen.

He walked through the vestibule into the nave. All the pews had been removed and sold by a previous owner, and the interior was now filled with work benches, tool cabinets, saw horses, scaffolding, and other renovation paraphernalia he'd rented from a supplier in Peterborough.

He looked up.

Suspended from a beam in the middle of the church was a man, hanging by his neck from a thick nylon rope. His hands were bound behind his back. He appeared to be in his mid-fifties, balding, with thin limbs and a pot belly.

He wore soiled jeans, a blood-soaked golf shirt, and tube socks. There was a plaid carpet slipper on his right foot. The left one had fallen off and lay on the floor beneath him.

He was very, very dead.

2

Tom leaned against the rear fender of the Ontario Provincial Police cruiser and tried again. "The guy looks familiar, yes, but it would be someone I haven't seen for a long time. Not someone who lives around here, that's for sure."

OPP Detective Constable Jim Armour shook his head. "Familiar, but you don't know him. Strung up in your building, which you say you keep locked, but you don't know how he got there. Someone just happened to pick this place at random out in the middle of nowhere to leave a body for you to find?"

"I don't—" Tom bit off a sarcastic reply. Armour's question, while overtly skeptical, was a good one.

"When was the last time you were up here?" asked Detective Constable Patricia Bell, Armour's partner. Unlike Armour, who was unknown to him, Bell was someone he'd bumped into at crime scenes during his career.

"As I said, not for the past three days."

"Did you lock the door the last time when you left?"

"Yes. I'm pretty sure I did."

"Who else has a key to that padlock?"

"Besides myself, just Jade."

Armour grunted. "Your girlfriend."

"God, no. She's my daughter's house-sitter. As I already said, she's helping me renovate this place."

"When was the last time she was up here?"

"You'll have to ask her that question yourself, but I severely doubt she's been up here since I was here the last time. It's like pulling teeth to get her to do anything for me."

Bell jotted something down. Tom knew they'd already interviewed Jade, who sat in the police cruiser behind him. Unbelievably, she'd actually shown up at the church shortly after the arrival of the first responders, clueless as to what was going on.

The provincial constables securing the scene had wasted no time getting her into the back seat of the cruiser, where she'd waited until being hauled out for questioning by Armour and Bell. They'd stuffed her back into the cruiser immediately afterward for safekeeping.

Tom spotted the coroner emerging from the church, followed by Detective Sergeant Bill Gerhart. Gerhart was the commander of the Peterborough County Crime Unit to which Armour and Bell were assigned as investigators. Tom pushed away from the cruiser and began to walk up the line of parked vehicles.

"Mr. Faust! Just a minute!" Armour called after him.

"Let him go," Bell said.

Tom left the shoulder of the road and cut diagonally across the grass toward the yellow tape sealing off his property. Gerhart noticed his approach and snapped his fingers at a nearby uniformed officer, who intercepted Tom just as he was lifting the tape to enter the scene.

"I'm sorry, sir," the constable said, "please remain behind the tape."

Tom swung under the tape. The constable blocked his way, hands raised.

"Hold it right there," Gerhart called out, coming over. "This is a crime scene, Faust. You're a civilian. Get the hell out, right now."

"I've got a few questions for the coroner," Tom said, stepping sideways.

The constable mirrored his movements, staying in front of him.

"Like hell you do," Gerhart retorted. "Now back off before I have you arrested."

They had a history, going back to when Gerhart was a detective sergeant with the Lambton County detachment and Tom worked West Region as a major case manager out of General Headquarters in Orillia. Tom had found him to be arrogant, self-important, and ambitious, and they'd butted heads more than once.

"Was this the primary scene, Gerhart?"

"Bell, get him out of here."

Tom glanced over his shoulder at Detective Constable Bell, who'd followed him in from the road. Moving back behind the tape, he asked Gerhart, "What's the coroner's preliminary finding on cause of death?"

"Take him in for follow-up questioning," Gerhart said to Bell. "We're not getting the full story here yet."

"What about the woman?" she asked.

"She can go."

"Who's been assigned from CIB?" Tom asked. "Elliott? Greene?"

Gerhart was already walking away.

"This way, please, Mr. Faust," Bell said, tapping him on the arm.

Detective Inspector Faust, he almost instinctively corrected her, adrenaline pumping and anger riding high, until he caught himself and kept his mouth shut.

Just Mr. Faust now. Civilian.

And up to his neck in someone else's homicide investigation.

3

Tom waited in an interview room at detachment headquarters in Peterborough for almost two hours before the door opened and Armour and Bell walked in. He immediately sensed a difference in their attitude and manner, a calm focus he recognized from long experience on the job. They knew something he didn't and were about to see if they could use it as leverage to elevate his status from person of interest to suspect.

Armour sat down at the little table and Bell leaned against the wall. Armour opened a file folder and flipped through the pages for a moment before advising Tom of his rights and asking if he wished to speak to a lawyer.

Tom shook his head. "What have you got?"

"I'm asking the questions, Mr. Faust. Do you wish to speak to a lawyer at this time? Please answer yes or no."

"No." Tom glanced at Bell, who watched him without expression. "Have you identified the victim?"

Armour leaned forward. "If you don't mind, Mr. Faust, I'll ask the questions. You answer them. Can you account for your whereabouts yesterday morning?"

"Yesterday morning?" Tom maintained eye contact with the detective, thinking that the coroner must have given them an approximate time of death that was twenty-four hours or so before he'd discovered the body in the church. "I was at home. I didn't leave the house until almost noon."

"What time did you get up?"

"About eight. Eight fifteen."

"What did you do then?"

"The usual. Coffee. Went online to read the morning news."

"How long did that take?"

"About an hour. Then I showered and got dressed."

"Is that when you left the house?"

"No, that would have made it only around nine o'clock, wouldn't it? I changed the oil in my car first."

"You're a do-it-yourselfer, are you?"

Tom smiled humourlessly. "Not for most stuff, no. But I can change oil just like anybody else."

"Can anyone vouch for all this? Your girlfriend, maybe?"

"If you're referring to Jade Morgan," he replied patiently, "I've already told you she's not my girlfriend. She's my daughter's house-sitter. I called her just before I went out to change the oil in my car. She didn't answer, as usual, so I left a message. So there's that. Wait." He thought for a second. "I got a delivery while I was doing the oil. UPS. I ordered a bunch of CDs, and they came while I was out there. I had to wipe my hands before the guy would let me sign for them."

Armour looked at Bell before writing it down in his notebook.

"Mr. Faust," Bell said, "does the name Joseph Kohl

mean anything to you?"

Tom frowned. "It rings a bell." He mulled it over as they stared at him, then shook his head. "I know the name; I just can't place it at the moment. Is that the victim?"

"What can you tell us about your involvement in a multiple homicide case that occurred on August 29, 2002, on Lake Road, east of Apsley?"

In a flash, he had it. The Bush family murders. A husband, wife, and two children brutally knifed to death in their home. A third child, the son, had managed to escape but couldn't identify his assailant.

"Right," he said. "Joseph Kohl was some kind of religious nut we looked at very closely for the Bush family murders. Now I know why he seemed familiar." He took a moment to run it through his head. "Kohl was having an affair with Brenda Bush, the wife, and he mixed it up with the husband. Ended up being alibied by another church member, another woman he was sleeping with." He frowned. "You think he was strung up in my church because of my connection to him through that case? That was seventeen years ago, for crying out loud."

Armour leaned forward. "Are you still angry because Joseph Kohl filed a complaint against you for harassment and unprofessional conduct after he was cleared?"

Tom raised an eyebrow. "Christ, I'd forgotten about that."

"Did you continue to carry a grudge against Mr. Kohl for having damaged your professional reputation?"

"Of course not. Come on, Armour, you've been there yourself, surely to God. It was investigated and dismissed. It wasn't the first complaint filed against me, nor was it the last, and it certainly didn't damage my professional reputation, as you so tactfully put it. So no, I didn't carry a grudge."

"Have you had any recent contact with Mr. Kohl?"

"None. I'd completely forgotten about him."

"Did you know where he was currently living?"

"Nope. No clue."

"Why do you think his body was left in a church that belongs to you, Mr. Faust?"

Tom cocked his head to one side. "What was the cause of death? Ligature strangulation, or something else?"

"Just answer the question, please, Mr. Faust."

He thought for a moment. "Let me guess," he finally said. "His throat was cut before he was strung up. There was no blood to speak of on the floor, so your primary scene is somewhere else. My church was the dump site. Where was Kohl living?"

Armour stared. "Are you saying you have no idea why Joseph Kohl, a person you knew and previously had trouble with, was found hanging in a building belonging to you?"

"That's what I'm saying."

Bell pushed away from the wall and looked at Armour, who stood up. "Please remain here, Mr. Faust." They left the room.

Nearly twenty minutes passed before the door opened again and a uniformed officer looked in. "You're free to leave."

Tom followed her out of the interview room and down the corridor. "Wait a minute," he said to her back as she opened the security door to the public entry area, "I need a ride home. You guys impounded my car."

She held the door open for him. "Please wait out here, sir."

Sighing, he went out and leaned against the wall next to a bulletin board covered with news releases and pamphlets. Two uniformed constables were practising their situation defusion techniques on a stocky young man who was complaining about a neighbour. There seemed to be some kind of problem connected to trespassing and cutting down trees. The man kept stroking his beard and insisting he was trying to keep it civilized, while the cop doing the talking reassured him that he was going about it the right way.

After ten minutes of this, Tom went over to the glass and caught the attention of the civilian receptionist. "I'd like to speak to Inspector Roach."

"I'm sorry, sir, he's not available at this time."

"All right. Could you please call Gerhart up here?"

"I'm sorry, sir. Detective Sergeant Gerhart's in a meeting and can't be disturbed right now."

"Armour? Bell?"

"Same meeting," the woman smiled apologetically. "Someone will be with you shortly."

Tom gave her a little wave and retreated back to the bulletin board. He scanned a news release recommending that motorcycle riders practise increased defensive driving techniques to stay safe on the roads. Behind him, the two constables wrapped it up with the bearded young man, who left. The officers let themselves back in through the security door and disappeared.

Tom was reading about a provincial campaign to increase boater safety when the security door opened again. He turned around. One of the constables who'd been talking to the bearded man nodded toward the front door.

"I'm your ride home, sir. Shall we go?"

4

Jade was smoking a cigarette beside the pool, reading a paperback novel. There was a tall glass of what looked like purple-tinted lemonade on the table by her elbow, along with a pitcher half-filled with more of the same.

Perspiring from the long walk up the driveway to Pamela's house, Tom dropped into the lounger next to her. "You okay?"

"Sure, chief. Why wouldn't I be?"

He glanced over as she turned a page of her book. She held it on an angle six inches away from her gaunt, freckled face. The cigarette found its way back into her mouth.

"Thought you might be upset, talking to the police."

She squinted against the smoke curling up over her cheekbone. "Worried I might have a flashback and burn down the house?"

Jade was thirty-eight and looked fifty. Her bare legs were skinny and her shorts and halter top hung on her body like adult clothing on a child. An alcoholic and cocaine addict, she'd been in recovery for the past four years after accidentally burning down her house in Toronto while under the influence. Her husband, asleep in the bedroom at the time, died in the fire.

Pamela's husband John was Jade's second cousin on his mother's side. A film production manager, John had employed Jade as a set designer on several projects before the fire. He stuck with her during her six-month sentence for criminal negligence causing death, and after her release he shepherded her through a court-ordered rehabilitation program. Although she was no longer able to work in the film industry, he found construction and carpentry jobs for her here and there. This summer, hopeful she'd turned the page on her addictions for good, he and Pamela hired her to look after the house while they were away at work.

Tom had voiced his concerns, but Pamela waved them off. "She needs a break, Daddy. She's had a hard life."

Unimpressed, Tom kept his eyes and ears open. So far, things had stayed quiet. Few visitors, no parties, no trouble.

"Will you?" he asked. "Flash back and burn down the house?"

She glanced at him over the top of her book. "Once a pig, always a pig."

"Did you know the guy? Joseph Kohl?"

Jade put her book face down on the table and drew heavily on the cigarette. "No. Was that his name?"

"Yes. When was the last time you were up at the church?"

Jade took a drink of the purple lemonade. "I don't know. When did I go there the last time with you? To sign off on the windows?"

"Four days ago."

"Then it was four days ago." She tipped her glass at him. "Why don't you have some of this, Faust? It's very calming."

"What's in it?"

Jade ran a hand over her bony skull. Her hair, which she'd shaved off a week or so ago, was showing again in a fine red fuzz. "No alcohol. Just lemon juice, lavender oil, honey, hot water, ice cubes. Reduces anxiety, lowers the pulse rate, and eases depression. I can show you the studies that demonstrate how lavender oil improves mood and increases alpha waves on EEG tests."

"Another time. Where have you been, anyway? I called yesterday morning and left a message. You didn't call back."

"Like I told the *other* cops, Faust, I was in town. I crashed at Paul's the night before, then hung out with him yesterday at the bowling alley." She narrowed her eyes. "I was having a problem, okay? He got me through it."

Paul Bliss was her Narcotics Anonymous sponsor. He managed a bowling alley in Peterborough, and Jade called him whenever she was struggling. Tom hadn't met the guy yet. So far, it hadn't made his to-do list.

"Did you use?"

"No, Faust, I didn't use. And I didn't drink. And I didn't have sex with Paul. Did I mention he's gay? Did I mention I'm celibate? Did I mention I'm not fucking perfect but I'm trying my best to toe the fucking line? Anything else you'd like me to fucking mention while I'm *fucking* at it?"

"All right. Calm down. Drink more of your tea."

"It's lemonade, shithead."

Tom stood up, regretting having badgered her. "I'm borrowing Pamela's Lexus for the next few days."

"Whatever." Jade picked up her book and went back to her reading.

"I left another message for you this morning. Can you go up to the church on Thursday when they deliver the drywall, if I can't be there? I gave them your number as well as mine."

She didn't respond.

"Another thing. When are we going to get a quote for the rewiring?"

Jade's book trembled a few centimetres from the tip of her nose as her lips formed the words *Fuck off*.

"All right. Okay. I'll talk to you later." Tom went into the house and found the keys to the Lexus in the key cabinet in the laundry room.

Before leaving, he took a quick look around the place. The house consisted of three enormous concrete slabs on corrugated steel skirts. The centre slab, which included the living room and kitchen, jutted out into space, affording a spectacular view of the countryside to the east. The slab on the south side contained the master bedroom, the study, and a large home theatre, while the north wing, resting on top of the hill, held the guest bedrooms, laundry room, pantry, and three-car garage. He wandered around, looking into each room. Everything seemed fine.

Jade occupied one of the guest rooms in the north wing. The door was closed. He stared at it for a moment, then went back to the kitchen.

He opened the refrigerator and checked out its contents. It was still reasonably well stocked. Since Jade was a little hit-and-miss in terms of grocery shopping, Tom had promised Pamela he'd make sure she didn't run out of food and stop eating, which had happened before. He grabbed a bottle of water for himself and headed out.

As he walked around the pool on his way to the garage, he said, "Do you need anything, Jade?"

No response.

He backed Pamela's Lexus out of the garage and started down the driveway. A third of the way down he slowed as a car turned in and started up toward him. Instead of edging over to the side to allow the other vehicle to pass, Tom stayed in the middle of the driveway and shifted into park. The other car approached, slowed, and stopped.

Tom got out and went over to the driver's side of the car, a beat-up Honda Civic. Duct tape held the left side of the front bumper in place, and the windshield was cracked from side to side.

The driver was alone in the vehicle. He lowered the window and smiled tentatively. "Are you Mr. Faust?"

"Who are you?"

"Uh, my name's Paul. Paul Bliss? I'm Jade's friend."

"You're her sponsor, correct?"

Bliss nodded. He was a heavy, balding man in his late forties. He licked his lips nervously and tried to keep the smile in place. "I thought I should come out and keep her company for a while."

"When was the last time you saw her?"

"Uh, well, she stayed overnight with me night before last. I mean, I put her up in my spare room. Then she spent the day yesterday with me at the bowling alley. I'm the manager at Central Bowling, on George Street? She hung out with me and a few other friends. Very quiet. I brought her home last night. About nine."

"Is she using, Paul?"

"No. Look, the understanding is that what's said between a person and their sponsor is supposed to be confidential, all right? But I know who you are, and I know this is your daughter's place. I get where you're coming from. She's clean, and she's fighting very hard to stay clean. This . . . thing that happened today, it really threw her. I'm going to stay with her for a while to help her through it. If that's okay with you, I mean."

"Anybody else expected to show up besides you?"

Bliss shook his head. "Just me. Jade doesn't like a lot of people around. She was okay yesterday at the bowling alley, but normally she needs to be alone. I'll probably spend most of the time just reading." He patted a canvas messenger bag on the passenger seat beside him. "I've got my iPad with me. Anyway, if she knows I'm there and we can talk whenever she wants to, it usually helps her a lot."

Tom took out his wallet and removed a business card with his name and cellphone number on it. He'd had them printed up after retiring. He'd handed out so many cards during his long career that he didn't feel right without them. "Call me if anything comes up."

"Yes, sir. Thanks." Bliss tucked the card into his shirt pocket.

Back in the Lexus, Tom pulled over to the side. Bliss edged past, the nervous smile back on his face.

At the end of the driveway, he swung out onto the road and was about to turn into his own driveway when he found a CHAX TV news van parked in the way. Annoyed that he hadn't spotted it from Pamela's house before coming down, he pulled over onto the shoulder and got out.

A woman materialized from behind the van, followed by a chunky cameraman with a portable unit perched on his shoulder. A tired-looking brunette in her forties, she was a veteran of the local crime beat. Tom had seen her often on the six o'clock news.

"Detective Inspector Faust!" she called out, striding down the driveway to meet him. "How do you feel about finding a body in St. Mark's church on Cedar Hill Road? I understand you're the owner of the property?"

"No comment," Tom said, raising a hand. "Please get your truck out of my driveway, will you?"

"Can you tell us anything about the victim? Was he known to you?"

"No comment." He tried to sidestep past them to avoid the camera, but the guy was nimble for his size and stayed in front of him.

"Do you have any idea why he would have been there? In an old church belonging to you?"

"Look," Tom said, trying to keep his voice even, "the case is under investigation by the Peterborough County Crime Unit of the OPP. Please direct all your questions to them. I have nothing to say at this time."

The reporter nodded at her cameraman, who lowered his weapon and turned it off.

"Thanks," she said. "I'm sorry to bother you." She stuck out her hand. "I'm Doreen Lacey, by the way."

He hesitated only a fraction of a second before shaking her hand. "Tom Faust. Not a detective inspector any more, by the way. I'm retired."

"Yes, I know. This is Les Hume, my cameraman."

Hume nodded, stowing his equipment in the van.

Doreen held out a business card. "Since you're not subject to OPP policy any more, if you want to make a public statement at any time just give me a call. Otherwise, Les and I will respect your privacy and keep our inquiries reasonable. Sound okay?"

"I'm still not going to say anything on or off the record about a case in which I'm involved, even as a civilian." Tom took the card and stuck it in his shirt pocket. "Sorry."

"That's okay. Just planting the seed, so to speak." She moved onto the lawn as Hume got into the van and started the engine. Her eyes went up to the house at the top of the hill. "Wow, that's quite the mansion. Who lives there?"

Tom shrugged. "My landlady."

"Looks like it's worth a fortune." She smiled at him in a friendly, harmless sort of way. "So, are you renovating the church as a residence for yourself, or will you sell it when it's done?"

"On the record or off?"

She blinked. "Off, of course. It looks like a neat place."

"You were up there, were you?"

"We shot some footage to go with the report and got a quick statement from Detective Sergeant Gerhart."

"I see."

"He referred us to the media relations officer who's giving a press conference in a couple of hours." She opened the passenger door of the van. "So, will you sell it or live there?"

"Live there."

"Good for you."

Tom watched them drive away, hoping her curiosity about the house on the hill wouldn't lead her to trace its ownership. The last thing he wanted was for the publicity from this thing to splash back onto Pamela. If word spread south of the border and the show business journalists who tracked celebrities like his daughter caught wind of the story, they'd blow it all out of proportion in their search for a sensational angle.

When Tom was still working, his career had been good for a few short background pieces covering her childhood, but thankfully no one had really given a damn what Pamela Faust's father did with his time back in Canada, where bears roam the streets and kids play ice hockey on frozen ponds in July. Now, however, without the protection of his badge and with a victim found on his property connected to an old case in which he'd been the subject of a complaint, Tom was worried that the carnivores would smell blood and come hunting.

As a dark funk leaked into his thoughts like spilled ink, he went inside and slammed the door behind him.

5

Tom sat in the darkness staring up at the house, watching the lights switch on in the big picture windows as someone, Jade or Paul Bliss, moved around from room to room. The ice cubes clinked in his glass as he took a long pull. Crickets buzzed rhythmically and a train rumbled somewhere in the distance, a faint, throbbing sound.

His cellphone vibrated. It was Pamela.

"Are you okay, Daddy?"

"I'm fine, darling." He tipped the lawn chair back until he was leaning against the wall. "No need to worry."

"Well, I am worried. What a terrible thing to happen. Is Jade going to be okay?"

"Her sponsor's up with her right now. Do you know this guy? Paul Bliss?"

"I've met him before. He's all right, Daddy. John checked him out."

Tom switched the phone to his left hand so that he could pick up his drink. "How's the picture coming?"

"Oh, fine. I've only got a few more days and I'll be

finished."

"Is it fun, like you thought it would be?"

She laughed. "Oh, yes. Stephen's terrific to work with, and he's got a great team here. I'm glad I took it."

Pamela was working on an animated feature film in Los Angeles, providing the voice for the lead female character in the picture. It was about a spaceship full of aliens who land on Earth and try to save the inhabitants of an animal shelter from mass euthanasia. Or something like that. Apparently their ship was the size of a mailbox and the aliens were the size of fleas. Pamela's voice, high-pitched and girlish, was ideal for the part.

Despite Tom's best efforts, the ice cubes in his glass clinked again as he sneaked a sip.

"Go easy on that stuff, Daddy. You promised."

He put the glass down again and shifted the phone back to his right hand. "All right. Don't worry; everything's under control. I'm a little concerned, though, that they'll connect me to you and you'll get hit with negative publicity. You don't need that sort of garbage right now."

"Don't worry about it. I'll talk to Colleen. She'll get some kind of statement ready in case we need it. She'll know how to handle it." Colleen Kinney had been best friends with Tom's late wife Linda before becoming Pamela's agent. She was an insider in an industry where 90 per cent of the workforce could only wish they were on the inside.

"Okay."

"When will they let you back into the church?"

"In a few days. Ident has already processed it, but they like to hold off until after the post-mortem in case something comes up and they want to take another look."

"Will you be okay? Going back up there, I mean, after what happened?"

"Sure. Remember, kiddo, I used to do this sort of thing

for a living."

"How could I forget? Oh, just a sec." She covered her phone with her hand for a moment, then came back on the line. "I have to go, Daddy. We're going out for something to eat, then it's back into the studio for another couple of hours. Stephen wants to re-do a few scenes."

"All right, darling. Don't work too hard."

"I won't. Love you."

"Love you, too. Bye."

Tom broke the connection and put the phone aside. He drained the glass and thought about going into the kitchen for more. Instead, he sat there, staring up at the illuminated windows of Pamela's house.

He was intensely proud of her. He loved seeing her photograph on the covers of magazines in the grocery store check-out aisles. Occasionally he bragged about her to former colleagues and friends. Her Golden Globe nomination last year was the high point of her career to date, and although she hadn't won, it had been cause for celebration. Tom was certain that, with the right part, an Oscar nomination was a definite possibility. She was still young and her elfin features, inherited from her mother, made her a favourite of Hollywood casting directors.

She was a celebrity and a star in the most powerful entertainment industry in the world, but she was still his daughter, and Tom missed her on nights like this. She might be thirty and married and very wealthy and surrounded by security personnel, but he continually worried that she wasn't under his roof and therefore under his protection. When darkness fell, he never failed to think of her, wondering where she was, who she was with, and if she was safe.

He knew it was not only paternal instinct but also an unavoidable association with Linda's death. Pamela was constantly in the air, flying from location to location during a project and from event to event in between. She frequently travelled at night on someone's private plane in order to be somewhere early the next morning when the cameras would begin to roll.

When he thought about it, Tom couldn't help but remember the small aircraft which had left Toronto for Orillia late one evening after sunset many years ago with Linda on board as its only passenger. A family of three became a family of two because an air pocket caused a stall from which the pilot was unable to recover.

When it happened, Tom was still a long way from retirement. He was managing Central Region homicide investigations out of Orillia, a territory covering 30,000 square kilometres that extended north and south from Muskoka to Lake Ontario, and west to east from Dufferin County to Northumberland County. The region was divided into fourteen detachments that provided police services to nearly a million residents and a half million seasonal vacationers.

Which meant he wasn't home a lot of the time.

That night, he happened to be there, waiting for Linda to return from a meeting with clients. A partner in an interior design firm, she often flew to Toronto on business, and they never gave it a second thought. As Tom knew from personal experience, having attended so many highway fatalities in his career, flying was much safer than driving.

He wrestled with himself for a moment and then got up and went into the kitchen. The quart of bourbon was sitting on the island. There was about a third of it left. He grabbed it and went back outside.

Just before he fell asleep, the empty bottle on the ground a few inches from his fingertips, he wondered who the hell would bother to slit the throat of a worthless bag of dog vomit like Joe Kohl and string him up in Tom's church, long after that particular set of files had found its way into the cold case archives.

The problem was, he pretty much knew.

The more important question was what he was going to do about it.

6

The next morning he drank his coffee at his desk while searching the Internet for news about the homicide. So far, there was very little. The few reports he could find were virtually identical to the piece filed by the local Peterborough newspaper:

> The Ontario Provincial Police are investigating a homicide after a body was discovered on Tuesday morning in a decommissioned church on Cedar Hill Road in Selwyn Township, north of Peterborough.

> Joseph Kohl, 57, a resident of Bancroft, owned and operated the Rough and Tumbled rocks and minerals store on Hastings Street North.

> Kohl's body was found in the former St. Mark's Presbyterian Church by retired

> OPP Detective Inspector Thomas Faust, who owns the property and has been renovating the church for conversion into a private home.

> The Peterborough County Crime Unit of the OPP has been called in to investigate. They are currently searching the victim's residence in Bancroft to determine whether he was murdered there before being transported to Selwyn. They are also questioning Faust, a former homicide investigator, in order to verify a previous connection he may have had to the victim.

The source of the information was not identified, but Tom suspected it was Gerhart, who would be happy to leak Tom's name and past connection to Kohl. There was no mention of the case manager appointed by the Criminal Investigation Branch to direct the investigation, another common element in OPP press releases. Hopefully Gavin Elliott or Kate Greene would get the assignment.

Tom began a search for background information on Joseph Kohl.

When he retired, Tom had decided not to make copies of his open, unsolved case files to bring home with him. They'd been reassigned, the Bush family murder case in particular being passed along to Gavin. While it was a truism that there were certain open investigations you never forgot and never lost the desire to solve, and that a few old war horses were known to have sneaked files home with them after leaving, the fact of the matter was that Tom was close to burning out when he signed the papers and walked out the door. The last thing he wanted to do was haul away boxes of unfinished business. Not to mention that it also would have been a breach of policy, one he had no particular desire to violate.

Although he didn't have access to the Bush family case file now and would have to start from scratch, he wasn't completely without resources. His account in the Canadian Police Information Centre's central database had been deleted as soon as he was no longer an active law enforcement officer, but over the years he'd subscribed to several privately-operated database services as well. His accounts had been set up to renew themselves automatically on an annual basis with direct withdrawals from his personal bank account. He hadn't bothered cancelling them. As a result, he was still able to log in and run a few queries.

Joseph Kohl was originally from Mississauga, Ontario. He'd been forty years old at the time of the Bush family murders, seventeen years ago. With this information as a starting point, Tom soon tracked down Kohl's date of birth and social insurance number, property ownership history, driver's licence, current address, and business information.

Kohl was fifty-seven years old at the time of his death. He was divorced and had no children. He lived at 81 Bond Street in the town of Bancroft and drove a 2005 Hyundai Sonata. As the news item had mentioned, he operated a rocks and minerals store called Rough and Tumbled and was listed as one of the vendors at the annual Rockhound Gemboree held in Bancroft this past weekend. He'd apparently occupied an outdoor booth close to the front entrance of the community centre.

At the time of the Bush family murders, Kohl had led a small religious group known as The Fellowship. Membership in the group included about twelve families, off and on, and services were conducted every Sunday morning in Kohl's home in Apsley.

Kohl had told Tom during questioning that his group was an offshoot of some sort of millenarian Protestant sect, the name of which Tom couldn't remember. A Google search on The Fellowship led him to Facebook, where he discovered that Kohl had started up his church group once again in his home in Bancroft.

Kohl's problem in the past had been that he couldn't keep his hands off the female members of his congregation. Scrolling through The Fellowship's Facebook page now and looking at the photographs posted there, Tom got the distinct impression that history had been repeating itself in Joe Kohl's little world. The women in the pictures were to all appearances ordinary middle-aged housewives, but Kohl always seemed to have his arm around the most attractive one in the group.

He finished his coffee and decided to go for a drive.

The town of Bancroft was located about one hundred kilometres northeast of Peterborough. With a population of just under four thousand people, it saw a brief boom in the middle of the twentieth century when the Faraday Mine, later known as the Madawaska Mine, was pulling uranium-bearing pegmatite out of the earth. Perched on top of the Canadian Shield, an enormous stretch of rock that gave northern Ontario its barren, mostly flat character, the town and surrounding area survived on mining and mineral-related activities until Madawaska closed in 1982.

As he drove into town, Tom thought it seemed appropriate that the largest employer in the area these days was a long-term care facility. No building along the main street was taller than two storeys, and some still bore old-fashioned false fronts hiding run-down frame structures behind them. The town seemed to radiate exhaustion, age, and the end of things.

Before going to Kohl's house, Tom decided to take a look at the victim's business first. He drove down Hastings Street and pulled into a vacant parking spot a few doors up from Rough and Tumbled. The building, a narrow little two-storey frame structure, was sealed with yellow crime scene tape. The windows upstairs were covered with old newspaper. Tom walked past, looking in the front window, but saw no activity inside. He stopped in front of a bakery next door and looked around. Across the street was another rock shop, Jamieson Minerals. He waited for a pickup truck to pass, then jogged across and went inside.

Expecting a flea-market style place catering to teenagers who liked shiny things, Tom was surprised to find himself in a fancy jewellery store. The walls were painted a tasteful mauve that complemented the natural wood display cabinets and shelving units. The floor was highly-polished hardwood. Glass cases displayed rings, pendants, and earrings featuring a variety of semi-precious stones, and other cabinets held large chunks of beautifully coloured rocks and crystals. The prices were well beyond the means of the average teenager, and certainly a lot more than what Tom would pay for a rock, no matter how shiny and eye-catching, but business seemed to be booming.

A man emerged from a back room. "Good morning, sir. Anything I can help you with?"

"Nice store you have here."

"Thank you. Something in particular you were looking for?" Short and bald, the man slipped behind the front counter and folded his hands. His crisp short-sleeved white shirt had a monogram on the breast pocket. His watch was a Rolex that looked like it might be genuine.

"Actually, I came up here looking for an acquaintance of mine, Joe Kohl." Tom looked out the window across the street. "I see his store's closed up. Do you know what happened?"

The man's smile went away. "It was on the news this morning."

"I must have missed it."

"How well did you know him?" the man asked. "Were you good friends?"

"Not really. I—"

"Well, he was murdered. Down near Peterborough. They found him hanging in an abandoned church. According to the news, his throat was cut at home on Monday, over here on Bond Street, and then whoever did it took him all the way down there to leave him hanging in an abandoned church. The guy who owns the church didn't find him until yesterday. They've got Joe's house here in town sealed off and the CSI people are still going through it. I live the next block down, so I drove right by it this morning."

"I see. What—"

"He was a weird sort of guy, I have to admit. Ran this offbeat kind of church out of his basement. Did baptisms in the river, that sort of stuff."

The man pinched the end of his nose, looking up at Tom. "Didn't think much of his store. I don't suppose you've ever seen the inside of it, but it wasn't anything like this." He waved his hand around. "Just folding tables with table cloths and cardboard display boxes, like you'd see at the Gemboree. Low-end stock at low-end prices. Guess he made enough to pay the bills, or else his Sunday collections would have to cover it."

"Do you—"

"According to my wife, Jane, and this is from her sister, whose best friend went to his church for about a month or so before giving it up, he was mixed up in that killing down in Apsley nearly twenty years ago. Remember that?"

"I—"

"The police questioned him pretty closely at the time, apparently, but he had some kind of alibi. According to Jane, he was seeing a little too much of the wife, the woman who was killed. They—"

The shop door opened and Detective Constable Pat Bell walked in. "Just a few follow up questions for you, Mr. Jamieson—" she broke off, staring at Tom.

Behind her, Detective Constable Jim Armour entered the store. He quickly moved around Bell. "What the hell are you doing here, Faust?"

"Just talking to this gentleman."

Armour turned to Jamieson. "Who'd he say he was?"

"Uh, a friend of Joe Kohl. Didn't get his name. Why, is there a problem?"

"Did he say he was a police officer?"

Jamieson shook his head. "Not at all. Just a friend."

"Acquaintance," Tom offered.

Armour grabbed his elbow and lifted. "Out. Right now." He was about two inches shorter and several pounds lighter, but he held an unfair advantage over Tom in youthfulness, overall physical fitness, and authority.

"Easy does it," Tom warned quietly.

"Jim, I got this." Bell stepped between them, forcing Armour to release Tom's elbow. "Mr. Faust, if you'd please leave the store with me right now I'd greatly appreciate it. Detective Constable Armour needs to ask Mr. Jamieson a few questions. Sound good to you?"

"Sounds good to me." Tom eased around Armour and headed for the door.

Outside, Bell poked a finger on his sternum. "Jesus, I don't know what you're trying to pull, but you need to stand down right now and back the hell away from our investigation. If I catch you fucking around like this again

I'll personally rain all kinds of hell down on your retired, out-of-line ass. Am I getting through to you?"

"Loud and clear, Pat. I—"

"Glad to hear it, because some of us don't like you very much, and some of us still have you on a shit list going way back and would love to have a chance to step on your face now that you're a weak-assed civilian. Still getting through to you?"

Tom nodded. It was safe to assume she was referring to Gerhart.

"Good. Now beat it, for crying out loud. Go have a coffee at the Tim Hortons with all the other retired geezers and stay the fuck out of our case."

"All right." He nodded and crossed the street back to his car. He sat for a moment behind the wheel without starting the engine, ears burning, jaw clenched.

To surrender the authority and power that goes with a badge and a senior position within one of the largest police forces in North America was one of the hardest things he'd had to do in his life. And it wasn't getting any easier. To be dressed down by two young detective constables with only a fraction of his experience was almost too much to bear.

He pounded on the steering wheel.

Thump thump thump.

Eventually he calmed down enough to start the engine and pull away from the curb.

He needed to talk to the detachment commander. Roach knew him well, and knew what he'd accomplished in his career. There was supposed to be a code of honour among commissioned officers at their rank. Tom expected that code to extend to him now, retired or not, civilian or not.

It was time to go up the ladder.

7

Peterborough County OPP detachment commander Mark Roach loved hockey.

Born and raised in Sudbury, he'd played the sport as a kid, but his lack of size and skill kept him out of major junior competition. As a substitute, he'd gravitated to coaching.

While attending college he coached ten year olds at the Atom level. While serving as a provincial constable with the North Bay detachment he coached fourteen year olds at the Bantam level. As a sergeant in Barrie he made the move up to the seventeen year olds. He'd coached at the Midget level now for eight years as an inspector commanding the Peterborough County detachment. His dream was to land a coaching job at the university or major junior level when his law enforcement career would permit the extra investment of time.

Roach firmly believed that coaching ability was a reflection of overall leadership skills. In Barrie he'd reorganized the detachment's community services and auxiliary policing programs, gaining a reputation as someone with strong ideas on how things should be done and the determination to make sure they were done his way.

Given his ability to manage a budget and allocate resources, his promotion to staff sergeant at the Peterborough County detachment was unsurprising, and when the incumbent detachment commander moved on to greater challenges, Roach was the natural choice to move into the vacancy. One didn't need to have a stellar background in investigation or enforcement, as far as he was concerned, to excel as a manager in the field.

Over the years, Tom had heard Roach deliver speeches on the subject of leadership at several professional conferences and public functions. The inspector loved to draw a parallel between coaching children to achieve excellence in sports and managing adults dedicated to preserving the safety of our streets and homes. Tom had found him to be a good public speaker, relaxed and confident, but too slick and superficial for his liking. He'd always seen Roach as a fussy pedant, a little too comfortable with chapter and verse according to the policy manual.

As a result, when he arrived at the detachment office on Lansdowne Street demanding to see him, Tom had thought it through and more or less come to accept that Roach would be unlikely to see his point of view. Just the same, he had to try.

When he was finally shown into Roach's office and invited to sit down, the detachment commander wasn't there. The civilian receptionist explained that Roach would be with him shortly.

Twenty minutes later, Roach walked through the door, closed it, and held out his hand.

"Hello, Faust. Nice to see you again."

"Mark. Thanks for taking the time." Tom shook hands with him.

"Upsetting, this dead guy showing up in your building." Roach settled behind his desk and straightened a pile of file folders in front of him.

"It wasn't exactly my first body, Mark."

"No, of course not." Roach picked up a file, opened it on the desk before him, and frowned at it for a moment before signing the top document.

"What can I do for you?" He closed the folder and set it aside.

"Well, first," Tom said, "you could give me your attention."

Roach had already opened the next file folder. "What? You have my attention. I *am* pretty busy this afternoon, though."

Their eyes met, and Tom fought to keep his expression neutral as he said, "I don't appreciate being pushed around by your detectives like some meathead civilian who doesn't know his ass from a hole in the ground. Thirty-five years should earn me a little more respect than that, Mark."

"They're only doing their jobs. You know how this works."

"I have a ton of homicide investigation experience your people could benefit from."

"I appreciate that. But you have to face the fact that you're out now. When you retired, it didn't exactly leave us completely without expertise in this area." He shrugged, as though trying to soften the sarcasm. "It's a question of roles and responsibilities. Yours as a civilian witness is to make yourself available for questioning if my people need additional information, and otherwise to keep a proper distance from our investigative activities. Correct?"

Tom sighed. "Who's been assigned from CIB?"

"Gavin Elliott." Roach tapped his pen on the document in front of him. In instances where the Ontario Provincial Police held jurisdiction over a homicide investigation, a detective inspector with the Criminal Investigation Branch was assigned from General Headquarters in Orillia to take the lead as major case manager. While the detachment commander—in this instance, Roach—was operationally responsible for the investigation, the major case manager held functional authority for its conduct. It was the job Tom had done for sixteen years. For most of that time, Gavin Elliott had been a colleague of his in CIB, and a good friend.

"Great. He's the best. I'd like to talk to him."

"I'm afraid that's not possible right now."

"Why not?"

"He's not here, Faust. He's still in Orillia."

"In Orillia? Why?"

"Unexpected family situation came up. His daughter broke her leg or something."

"Shit." Tom knew Claire, Gavin's daughter. She was a smart, athletic kid. He did the arithmetic and realized she would have been a high school senior this past year. "That's too bad."

"Yeah," Roach agreed, signing another form and setting the folder aside.

"Look, Mark, have you found anything yet that definitely connects Joseph Kohl's murder to the Bush family cold case?"

Roach set down his pen and folded his hands. "Of all people you should understand the situation. Our investigation's ongoing. We have everything well in hand. If we need you to answer further questions, we'll be in touch. Otherwise, please respect our polite insistence that you stay outside the tape, both literally and figuratively."

"Christ." Tom stared at him for a moment, then looked out the window. "All right. All right." He stood up. "Thanks for your time."

"Not at all." Still sitting, Roach offered his hand. "Thanks for your co-operation."

Outside, there was a small group of people in the parking lot. Tom tried to circle around them, realizing they were reporters, but Doreen Lacey spotted him and stepped into his path.

"What was the nature of the relationship between you and Joseph Kohl?"

"No comment."

"Is it true he filed a complaint against you after your treatment of him in an investigation seventeen years ago?"

"No comment."

By now the others had realized who he was and were crowding around, shouting questions, holding up cellphones, cameras, and other hardware.

"Just a moment, just a moment. Just a moment, please." Tom gave them a few seconds to stop yapping and then said, "I refer all your questions about the case to the official OPP spokesperson. I'm happy to co-operate fully with police in their investigation and have already provided whatever information I can to assist them. I'm always available to them should they require anything further. That's all. Thank you."

He shook his head at the other questions shouted at him and moved away. A couple of them dogged him for a few steps before letting him go, while others grabbed last-second footage of him walking across the parking lot to his car.

He fished his keys out of his pocket, staring at the ground. As he unlocked the car door, he heard the sound of a vehicle rolling to a stop behind him. Reluctantly, he turned around.

The tinted window on the rear passenger side of the black Mercedes S600 limousine slid down, and Tom found himself looking at a woman he hadn't spoken to in quite a few years.

She smiled. "Hello, Tom."

"My God," he blurted. "Natalie Stone. What the hell are you doing here?"

"Get in the car," she said. "We should talk."

8

Natalie Stone's bald, cigar-chewing chauffeur took them into a drive-through for coffee and then headed downtown. As they made their way north through the traffic on George Street, Tom tried to remember how long it had been since he'd last seen her.

"Ten years," she supplied. "At that conference in Chicago. You gave a presentation on major case management. Derek and I had a suite on the twentieth floor. He landed several lucrative contracts that weekend."

"I remember." The night before he'd flown back, Tom had gone down to the hotel bar for a nightcap and found Natalie by herself, nipping at a horrible-looking cocktail with plastic things sticking out of the glass. They closed down the bar together, then sat in the lobby until sunrise, good friends catching up. "Has it been that long?"

"It has."

He smiled at her. She wore a navy skirt suit, a purple blouse with a filigree pattern in it, and plain black shoes. Her shoulder-length hair had been carefully maintained to match the chestnut colour of her eyebrows. She'd always been slightly overweight but didn't seem to have added any additional pounds in the intervening decade, unlike Tom. He was pleased to see her again.

"You haven't aged a day, Nat. How do you do it?"

"Tom, spare me." She looked sideways at him. "You realize I turn sixty next month. I don't like that number very much."

"I'm right behind you, Nat."

"Let's talk about something else. How's Pamela?"

"Great. She's working on an animated feature. Having a lot of fun with it."

"Good for her."

The car pulled to a stop in the parking lot of the marina at Little Lake, not far from downtown.

"Let's go for a walk," Natalie said, opening her door. "Charlie, we won't be long."

"Copy that." The driver caught Tom's eye in the rear-view mirror and held his gaze for a moment. Tom gave him a slight nod and got out.

As they walked along the edge of the water looking at the boats docked in the marina slips, Tom asked, "How long has he been working for you?"

"Who, Charlie? About a month or so. Before that he was assigned to Derek."

"Personal protection?"

She glanced at him. "Charlie's job description is actually rather complicated."

"You didn't answer my original question, Nat. What brings you to Peterborough?"

She stopped and looked up at him, a little shorter than he remembered. "You do, Tom."

"I don't understand."

"Here it is in a nutshell. After Joseph Kohl was

murdered and strung up in your church, we were brought in to consult on the Bush cold case. I was about to drop in to introduce myself to Inspector Roach when you popped up. Good timing, because I'd rather talk to you first."

"I don't understand," he repeated. "Why would Cage Intelligence want to consult on the Bush family murders?"

"Don't forget, cold case review is just one of the many services we offer."

She resumed walking, and Tom fell in beside her, recalling what he'd read in the newspapers and magazines about the Cage Intelligence Group. They were a private investigations consulting firm based in Toronto and London, England. Natalie's husband, Derek Winter, had founded the company as Winter and Stone Investigations fourteen years ago after he'd retired from the Toronto Police Service. A few months later, Natalie left her position as OPP superintendent of municipal policing to join him.

In 2010, they sold a majority interest in their company to Sean Cage, recently retired from British intelligence. Re-branded as the Cage Intelligence Group, the corporation apparently had moved rather quickly into the murky world of international intelligence and security.

As Tom understood it, Derek was president of the company and Natalie was vice-president in charge of investigations, while Cage himself oversaw the entire show from London as chief executive officer. The Canadian operation continued to focus on criminal and civil investigations, case review, security, and threat assessments, while the London office fell under the mysterious shadow cast by Sean Cage and his handful of intelligence operatives.

"And of course," Natalie added, "it helps when the contract's so reasonable it'll pay us little more than our expenses."

"I don't understand."

"Leverage, Tom." She showed him the sad smile he remembered so well. "It's all about leverage."

"Leverage on whom? The commissioner?"

They sat on a bench and watched the Centennial Fountain spray water seventy-five metres into the air.

"No, Tom. On you."

He laughed. "You'll have to explain it to me, Nat. I'm afraid I'm a little slow today."

"Here's my offer. Sign a contract to work with us as a consultant for a year. I'll assign you immediately to Bush, and that'll give you access to the case file. I'm guessing by the look on your face when you came out of the detachment office just now that that's what you were hoping to get from Mark Roach, and it didn't happen. Come work for me, Tom, and all that changes. You're in. Just like that."

"Gavin won't like it. It's his cold case, and Kohl's his, too. He won't stand for the interference. I know I wouldn't. Not even from you, Nat. With all due respect."

She patted him on the knee. "Gavin's an old friend."

Tom frowned, thinking. "You've already talked to him."

"Anything we uncover in our review that impacts the Kohl investigation we immediately turn over to Gavin and his team. We operate without publicity, completely under the radar. In effect, we'll act as Gavin's black box as far as whether or not the Kohl homicide is connected to the Bush case. We'll conduct our cold case review while his team focuses specifically on Kohl and his homicide. If it turns out Kohl was murdered by someone unconnected to Bush, then Gavin hasn't expended a lot of time and resources unnecessarily."

"Okay," Tom nodded. "Makes sense."

"So is that a yes?"

"Not so fast. I'll have to think about it. I'm not really interested in becoming a private investigator."

"I know."

"What do you mean, you know?"

She shrugged. "It's not uncommon for people to put in for a PI licence after leaving law enforcement. I happen to know you didn't."

"You've been checking up on me?"

"*Please*, Tom," she said in mock exasperation. "Would you like to take a look at the contract, or have you decided to sit this one out after all?"

Tom stood up and walked a few paces, thinking about it. He wasn't thrilled with the idea of working as a private investigator after a long career on what he considered to be the legitimate side of the badge. On the other hand, it *was* Natalie. And she was trying to do him a favour. Or was she just recruiting another experienced asset for her company?

In any event, she was opening a door for him to get another crack at the Bush case. And it was, at the same time, a back door into the Kohl murder, which directly involved him and from which he was being completely stonewalled.

"I'll think about it," he said, returning to the bench.

"I thought you just did."

"I'll think about it some more."

Natalie stood up. "Charlie will take you back to your car. He'll give you the contract. Look it over. It's more than fair as far as remuneration's concerned, and I think you'll find the terms and conditions are comfortable enough."

"What about you? Aren't you riding back with me?"

She looked across the lake. "We've set up shop in an office building a few blocks from here. I need the walk.

And I've decided I'd rather hear back from you first before I talk to Roach, so please don't think about it too long."

"I'll call you tonight."

"That'll be fine." She gave him a business card. "I really hope you'll say yes."

"No promises. But we'll see."

"That's all I can ask." She patted his arm and walked away.

9

Greenslade's *Time and Tide* boomed from the audio player in the kitchen as Tom, a full glass in one hand and his cellphone in the other, juked out the sliding door, dropped into his lawn chair, and put his feet up on the chunk of wood. He took a long drink and punched in a number on his phone.

"Trace, it's Tom Faust. How're you doing?"

"Hey, Tom. Not bad. How's retirement treating you?"

"Rough, at the moment."

"So I heard." Tracy Drummond was a former long-time colleague. He and Tom had worked together for several years in West Region when Drummond was a regional intelligence co-ordinator and Tom was a detective sergeant. They'd renewed their friendship at GHQ when Tom made staff sergeant and moved to Orillia, where Drummond was supervising the Strategic Analysis Unit. Drummond was now a deputy director, and very well connected. When something touched the web, he felt it.

Tom heard the sound of a television in the background.

He must have caught Drummond at home. "I hear Gavin's still up there."

"Yeah. His daughter shattered her collarbone playing volleyball. She's pretty upset about it, so he's waiting until tomorrow to get down there."

"That's too bad."

After a pause, Drummond asked, "What can I do for you?"

Tom caught the hesitation in his voice. "Nothing directly related to the investigation, Trace. What do you know about the Cage Intelligence Group?"

"Wait one."

Tom heard the line go mute as Drummond went somewhere he could talk in private. His study, or outside on the deck. After a few moments, he came back on. "You were asking about Cage?"

"Yeah."

"What do you want to know?"

"Whatever you can tell me that I haven't already read on the Internet."

Tom heard a lighter flick in the background as Drummond lit a cigarette. "So I can skim the basics, then. Derek Winter started his company in 2002 with Ted Bundeswal and George Meyers, all from TPS. Natalie came in and took over the investigations division while Bundeswal ran security and threat assessment. They sold a majority ownership to Sean Cage, ex-MI6, in 2010 and re-incorporated as Cage Intelligence Group, based in Toronto and London, England. You're aware of all that, right?"

"Yes. Have you ever worked with them, Trace?"

"Me, personally? No. Natalie did a cold case review for Kate Greene about a year ago, though. Brought in their profiler, Dr. Ryan Baker. It kick-started the case again and she ended up making an arrest that stuck."

"Which one was that?"

"The McGraw rape and murder. Elliott Lake."

Tom remembered the case. A teenaged girl had been found strangled in the back seat of a derelict car in an abandoned quarry north of town. The physical evidence had led them down several blind alleys, and Greene had been pulling her hair out for the longest time trying to generate a fresh lead. About a year before he retired, Tom sat in on an impromptu bull session with Greene, Gavin Elliott, and Ellie March. They rehashed all the old theories, sifted through the evidence, and brainstormed possibilities, but ended up getting nowhere with it. If Natalie and her profiler had managed to put Greene on the correct path, they'd definitely earned their money. The McGraw case had been Kate Greene's *bête noir*.

"Impressive," he said.

"Derek and Natalie have done it the right way," Drummond went on. "They're not pushy, they keep things low key and away from the media, and they deliver results. Completely professional. That's their reputation."

"So why did they offer to review the Bush family cold case?"

Drummond hesitated, then said, "Well, it's my understanding it was Gavin who dropped the dime on that one, not the other way around."

"You're sure about that?"

"Hello, this is Detective Inspector Tracy Drummond of the Ontario Provincial Police. To whom am I speaking?"

"Sorry, Trace." Tom thought for a moment. "What about the intel part of it?"

"Now that's another matter. Cage keeps that side of things very much underground. I know he's really well connected. CIA, Mossad, you name it. He started out in MI5 and transferred to MI6, which is where he earned his chops. Speaks eight or nine languages, always under the radar, has a reputation for handling the spookiest stuff. Not really the sort of thing I could talk about to a civilian."

He sighed into the phone. "Why are you asking, Tom? Thinking of a second career?"

"As a matter of fact, Natalie offered me a contract."

"Uh oh. I'm envious. *Mucho dinero*."

"Yeah. Let's just say it's very generous."

"And you're checking them out with me, why?"

"I don't know. I'm . . . not sure I want to make a commitment at this time."

"It's not as though she's asking you to marry her, Tom. Although word was, at one point it almost came to that."

Tom dropped his feet from the chunk of wood. "Say what now?"

"Never mind. Look, everyone knows you're a stubborn son of a bitch, but so's Mark Roach. You know Gavin can't have you freelancing around on him, and you *do* happen to live in Roach's jurisdiction, if you get my drift. It's better to be nice than to be a prick, Tom, believe it or not. Sign the damned contract and get on with it. That is, if you're asking for my advice."

"I am."

"Then you've got it. Can I go back to my movie now?"

"Sure. Thanks. I appreciate your time. Say hello to Sarah for me."

Tom ended the call and sat in the darkness, staring up at the bright windows of Pamela's house. He'd always had a soft spot for Natalie Stone, although there'd never been anything between them except friendship and mutual trust.

When their paths had crossed on the job they'd always worked well together. After Linda's plane crashed, Natalie spent a lot of time with him, talking about how she'd lost her oldest brother the same way, eight years before. He liked being around her, he'd grown fond of her sad smile and low, quiet voice, and he admired her quick mind and calm decisiveness. She'd been an excellent senior manager and was obviously succeeding in the private sector.

So why was he hesitating?

He pulled her card out of his shirt pocket and punched in the number.

When she answered, he said, "I'm in, Nat."

"I'm glad. We're at 200 Water Street, eighth floor. See you in the morning?"

"In the morning." He ended the call.

Retired, but never out.

10

The elevator door opened on the eighth floor of the office building on Water Street the next morning at four minutes after nine o'clock. Natalie met him in a small, featureless lobby and punched in a number on the security keypad of the only door on the floor.

"We're still getting settled in," she said, holding the door open. "We've taken a year lease, and there are a lot of changes we still need to make, but for now it'll suit our purpose."

Tom found himself in a large space that looked like a penthouse suite in an *Architectural Digest* magazine. There was a seating arrangement on the left by the windows that afforded a picturesque view of the Otonabee River. There was artwork on the walls and discreet lighting from halogen pot lights in the ceiling.

The room was silent. No traffic noise from the street below, no humming lights, no ticking clocks.

A second security door opened into another large space. This one had offices around the edges and a common area in the middle with desks, filing cabinets, printers on stands, and other office furniture.

"When we bring in administrative staff," Natalie said, leading the way to an office on the far side, "they'll be set up out here for easy access to everyone."

Tom followed her into the office where the driver, Charlie, sat reading a newspaper behind a large, bare desk. He lowered his feet and set the paper aside.

"You haven't been introduced," Natalie said. "Tom, this is Charlie Danko."

Charlie stood up to shake hands. An unlighted cigar jutted from the corner of his mouth. His grip was firm and friendly. "Good to know you."

He was younger than Tom had originally thought, somewhere in his early forties. He was short, only a few inches taller than Natalie, but muscular and self-possessed in a way that reminded Tom of cops and military personnel he'd known, people who kept themselves physically fit and mentally prepared for whatever the next moment might bring.

"Tom's decided to join us, Charlie."

"Glad to hear it."

"One more person to meet," Natalie said to Tom, "then we'll set you up in your office and take care of all the paperwork."

"All right."

In the next office a man in his late twenties crouched behind a desk, connecting the cables to a computer with a large flat-screen monitor. Hearing them come in, he stood up and edged around from behind the desk. His beard needed a trim. He wore a denim shirt with the sleeves turned up, khakis, desert boots, and a blue driving cap.

Adjusting his glasses on his nose, he said to Natalie, "Just about ready to go. This is the unit for our sensitive data. External hard drive for backup, UPS in case of power failure, and the best encryption money can buy."

"Tom, this is Jeremy Dunaway. Jeremy, meet Tom Faust. He's joining the team."

"Howdy." He gave Tom a quick nod and rooted around in the debris covering another desk for a manila file folder, which he handed to Natalie. "Everything's here."

"Thanks." Natalie opened the file, glanced at its contents, and closed it again. "Jeremy's my administrative assistant. He's also a licensed private investigator."

"Around here it's important to be multi-functional." Jeremy picked up a connecting cable of some kind and ran it through his fingers. "Anything you need, let me know."

"Thanks."

Tom's office was next door. It was larger than the others. It contained a desk and a big leather chair, two more seats on the other side of the desk for visitors, filing cabinets, a large whiteboard on wheels, a reading area with an armchair and pedestal lamp, and a rectangular meeting table with four chairs.

Natalie slid the file across the desk and sat down. "Let's get the formalities over with. I take it you looked over the contract. Are there any changes you want to make?"

Tom sat down behind the desk and shook his head, opening the filc. "It's more than generous, Nat."

"You'll earn it, believe me."

The contract stipulated that he would provide consulting services that included cold case review, major case review, private investigation services, data analysis, and advice and guidance to Cage Intelligence Group management and staff as required. The contract would run for one year from the date it was signed. He'd be paid a guaranteed six-figure amount in twelve equal payments, plus a five-figure signing bonus that would be deposited in his account the moment he added his signature and initials to all the appropriate blanks. It also included a termination provision by which either party could exit the agreement on thirty days' notice. In the event that Cage was the terminating party, Tom would still be paid the full amount guaranteed in the contract.

He signed and initialled all the copies of the contract, closed the folder, and slid it back across the desk to her. There was a noise in the doorway. Jeremy came into the room with three file storage boxes on a hand jack. He put them on the meeting table.

"What's this?" Tom asked, standing up.

"Thanks, Jeremy." Natalie went over and lifted the lid on one of the boxes. "This is our copy of the Bush family murder case files. I thought you might want to take a look through them." She glanced at him. "To refresh your memory. See if anything new occurs to you."

"This is great." He went over and swung the box around for a look. There were files containing daily activity reports, interview reports, minutes from meetings, and all the other paperwork that had been generated seventeen years ago by the OPP crime unit investigating the murders of the Bush family.

Much of the information in these files, he knew, still lay somewhere within his memory, covered by the detritus of the years, but he was very pleased to have the opportunity to refresh himself on the details.

"I went through it all this morning," Natalie said. "Everything seems to be there."

"You went through it all? When did you get in this morning, Nat?"

She shrugged. "I'm staying here. There's a suite of rooms in back for me, and another for Charlie."

"I'm the lucky one," Jeremy said. "I get to stay offsite."

When Tom looked at him, he shrugged. "Holiday Inn. It's okay."

"You'll want to get started." Natalie moved toward the door. "Let Jeremy know what you want for lunch."

"She didn't tell you I'm also a chef. Charlie's suite has the bigger kitchen, so I've pretty much taken it over."

Tom stared at him.

"No, I'm not kidding." Jeremy cocked an eyebrow. "I also make a killer cappuccino."

"Regular coffee would be great. Black."

"Coming right up."

"Just bring the pot and a cup," Tom said.

"You got it."

Natalie gave him a mock salute. "I'll leave you to it, then."

11

Late one night seventeen years ago, on Sunday, August 29, the Bush family was brutally murdered at their home on Lake Road, a few kilometres outside the village of Apsley, a small community about sixty-five kilometres north of Peterborough.

Responding to a 911 call the following morning from the next-door neighbour's house, first responders arrived at the scene a few minutes after sunrise. What they discovered resulted in a flurry of telephone calls that brought out detectives from the OPP Peterborough County Crime Unit, the coroner, and, ultimately, Tom Faust as well.

Piecing together evidence found at the scene, and after conferring with the coroner, Detective Constables Jim Hatton and Jack Pulver constructed a storyline explaining what they thought must have happened.

Forty-year-old Gregory Bush was surprised in the kitchen of his home at approximately 11:30 PM Sunday night by someone who had gained access to the house through the unlocked front door.

Bush was stabbed in the stomach and his throat was cut. The killer proceeded upstairs to the master bedroom where he cut the throat of thirty-six-year-old Brenda Bush, Greg's wife. The coroner smelled alcohol coming from Brenda's body at the scene, and autopsy results later confirmed a high blood alcohol count and the presence of a tranquillizer, explaining why the killer had been able to attack her husband in the kitchen and then enter her room upstairs without awakening her.

The killer then went into the bedroom shared by the two Bush girls. Cheryl was eleven years old and Donna was nine. Cheryl was murdered while she was sleeping, but Donna apparently woke up and fell out of bed during the struggle before the killer partially decapitated her.

No signs of sexual assault were found on any of the victims.

The bodies were dragged out onto the front lawn and arranged spread-eagled as though they were angels. This kind of staging at the scene suggested advance planning and religious overtones, and Tom knew there was a report on file from the Criminal Profiling Unit in Behavioural Sciences on the subject. He decided to re-read it later.

The only family member to escape the slaughter was thirteen-year-old James Bush. He apparently woke up, struggled with his assailant in the darkness of his bedroom, and managed to get away, fleeing into the woods behind the house. He was found late next morning when he emerged on the highway about four kilometres northeast of his home. He had lacerations on his chest and collarbone area, forearms, and hands, which suggested he'd fought off the attacker and suffered defensive wounds before running away.

Analysis of the victims' lacerations, and Greg Bush's stab wound in particular, suggested that the murder weapon had a long and very sharp blade, likely ten inches in length. Bush had been almost completely run through in the initial blow to his stomach. The blade was 5/32 of an inch thick and had a saw back, similar to a Bushmaster survival knife. It was never found.

Setting aside the report on the murder weapon, Tom poured another cup of coffee and walked over to the window. Staring down at the river, he took a few minutes to clear his head. Reviewing the file on the knife had been a little disturbing.

Six years after the murders, and every year since, Tom had received a card of condolence on November 1, the anniversary of Linda's death, signed "The Bushmaster."

The handwritten signature on the cards had been analyzed, but the forensic documents examiner considered it too small a sample to tell them anything reliable about the sender. The writing was small and compact, she noted, suggesting a reclusive, introverted person, and the letters were straight, without a noticeable slant, suggesting someone who kept his emotions in check. The shapes of the letters were varied irregularly, however, suggesting that the person was deliberately disguising his handwriting. Subsequent cards with slightly different characteristics confirmed this assumption.

To Tom, however, the cards meant two things. One, because there was no doubt in his mind that the person sending the cards was the same one who'd murdered the Bush family, it was clear that he obviously enjoyed the play on words suggesting he had "mastered" the Bush family with a Bushmaster knife. Two, the killer had gone to the trouble, years after the murders, to look up the lead investigator and reach out to him in an obvious taunt.

It's personal for me, Faust, the cards whispered to him. *Is it personal for you, too?*

Forcing his thoughts back to the murder weapon itself, Tom remembered that they'd conducted an extensive search for Bushmaster knives in the surrounding area without much success.

A hunting and fishing store in Apsley carried the knives but had had only one in stock at the time in question. The store owner remembered a local teenager purchasing it that June, two months before the murders, at the end of the school year.

When they followed up, they learned he'd taken it with him when his family moved to Thunder Bay in July. After an inventory, the store owner failed to account for only one other Bushmaster knife out of the order he'd originally received, suggesting it had probably been stolen at some point during the year. The thinking among the team was that the missing knife had become their murder weapon.

Unfortunately, this conclusion led many of them on the investigative team to begin referring to their unknown offender as The Bushmaster. Tom disliked giving killers a nickname and discouraged the practice, but it had caught on and stuck.

Tom paced around his office and then went back to the banker boxes, mentally shifting gears. The first important focus of the investigation had been on young James Bush. The boy was questioned several times, twice by Hatton and Pulver and once by Tom himself. He pulled out the transcripts of the interviews and sat down with them.

James's story remained consistent throughout the process. He told police he'd awakened thinking he'd heard his sister call out from the next bedroom. He lay half-asleep for several moments, not hearing anything else, until a thumping noise in the other room brought him fully awake.

He got out of bed and crossed the floor of his darkened

bedroom toward the door, which was partially open. A shaft of light shone in, presumably from the bathroom at the end of the hall, where the light was always left on. As he neared the door, it flew open.

At this point, an unknown person approximately his own height and weight rushed into the room and collided with him, knocking him backward. As he regained his balance the shadowy figure slashed out with a long knife, barely missing his face. On the return sweep, the knife grazed his right forearm, cutting him. He grappled with his assailant, receiving several other cuts, before he succeeded in shoving the attacker into his dresser.

As the killer fell to the floor, James ran out of the room and into his parents' bedroom. He saw his mother lying in bed, the sheets pulled down. The room was partially illuminated from the en suite door into the bathroom, and he could see that she was covered with blood. The bedclothes beneath her were blackened with it, as well. The attacker staggered to the bedroom door and James ran through the bathroom, down the stairs, and out the front door.

He circled around the house and ran into the woods at the back of their property. He kept going until he was exhausted. Leaning against a tree, trying to catch his breath, he heard no pursuit behind him. Looking around, however, he realized he was lost. There was a moon that night but the sky was overcast, so there was little light to see by in the woods.

He wandered for several hours, then collapsed behind a fallen tree and slept fitfully. When he awoke the sun had come up and there was light to see by, although he still had no idea where he was. He kept moving until he finally emerged onto a two-lane highway, which turned out to be Highway 28, north of Apsley. He walked along the road on the northbound shoulder until a man driving a van stopped and picked him up. After hearing James's story, the man drove him to the hospital in Bancroft, waited until he was admitted for treatment, and then left.

Tom went back to the box for the transcript of the interview with the man. Orel Pilon operated a hunting camp in the Bancroft area and was returning from dropping off his daughter at a coffee shop in Apsley where she worked. He saw James walking unsteadily along the side of the road ahead of him, his back to oncoming traffic, and slowed out of caution.

As he passed the boy, he saw that he was wearing blood-soaked pyjamas, so he stopped. According to Pilon, James told a disjointed story that matched in all the essential details what he told police in later interviews. Pilon said the boy was exhausted and fell asleep during the drive to the hospital.

Pilon's own story checked out. No prior connection could be made between him and the Bush family, and he was never considered a possible suspect. Tom had observed the Pilon interview and remembered it well, even today. The man was clearly a decent human being upset by what had happened to the boy and willing to help as far as he could, which was not very far.

As Tom re-filed the Pilon folder, Jeremy appeared in the doorway.

"What would you like for lunch?"

Tom glanced at his watch and was surprised to see that it was nearly one o'clock in the afternoon. He'd apparently been at it for almost four hours without realizing it.

"Today I can offer you grilled chicken caesar salad," Jeremy said, "a vegetarian salad, if you're that way inclined, or a steak sandwich if you're a confirmed carnivore."

"That sounds good."

"Steak sandwich? Coming right up. And to drink?"

"What do you have for beer?"

"As per company policy, we are alcohol free."

"Bottled water is fine."

Jeremy glanced at the case files and asked, "In here, or would you prefer to eat in the dining room?"

There was a dining room? "In here."

Jeremy waved and disappeared. Tom looked at the banker boxes, his thoughts immediately returning to James Bush.

They'd had doubts about the boy's story at the time and had questioned the doctor who'd treated his wounds at the hospital. Could they have been self-inflicted? Possibly, the doctor had thought, but not likely. The angles on a couple of the lacerations were such that it would have been extremely awkward for James to have cut himself.

On the other hand, a search of the woods retracing James's supposed escape to safety showed only one set of footprints, which were a match to the boy's footwear.

Ever suspicious, Hatton had wondered if the entire story had been fabricated, but Pulver felt it was more likely that the killer had quickly lost track of James in the darkness and hadn't bothered to chase him beyond the house. After much thought, Tom had agreed. Their focus then turned to other possible suspects.

As Jeremy brought in his steak sandwich, a side dish of fries, and bottled water, Tom decided to backtrack on the timeline to the 911 call, which had been made from the home of Gerald Little, the next-door neighbour, before James Bush had turned up at the hospital.

Taking a bite of the sandwich, which he noticed peripherally was delicious, Tom hunted through the boxes until he found the transcript of the interview with Gordon Masterson.

12

Gordon Masterson was a fifty-six-year-old grounds-keeper who worked at the provincial park located at the far end of Lake Road, about three kilometres from the Bush home.

On Monday morning just after sunrise he passed the house on his way to work and saw four bodies spread-eagled on the lawn. The front door of the house was wide open. As he later explained to Hatton and Pulver, he put his foot on the brake after passing the house, thought about what he'd seen, lifted his foot off the brake and kept on going, then changed his mind and pulled into a driveway about a kilometre away. Turning around, he drove back to the Bush house, slowed down on the opposite side of the road, saw again what he hadn't believed he'd seen the first time, and pulled over.

He got out and walked across the front lawn for a closer look. When he saw the dried blood on the clothing, the gaping throat wounds, and the staring eyes of Greg Bush, he ran back to the road and threw up in the ditch.

The closest house was about a hundred metres away, so he got back in his truck and drove over to it.

DC Hatton: What happened next?

Masterson: Well, this young fellow came to the door after I knocked for quite a while. I told him what I seen next door and, well, he didn't believe me. So I told him, come out and look, but he wouldn't. I said, call 911, mister, because they're all dead. He wouldn't do it.

DC Hatton: Did he say why not?

Masterson: Said he didn't want to interfere in other people's business. I said, Christ, man, they're all dead. That *is* our business. But he still wouldn't call, so I asked if I could use his phone to call myself. He showed me where the phone was. So I called.

DC Hatton: Would you say that Mr. Little was acting unusually?

Masterson: I'd say he was a thick-headed, dopey, stubborn son of a bitch. Did say it, as a matter of fact.

DC Hatton: How'd he react to that?

Masterson: He had the nerve to ask if I'd been drinking. I just made the call and got the hell out of there. I figured, To hell with you, pal. Be that way.

Tom couldn't help but smile, remembering Masterson as an unpleasant old curmudgeon in mud-clotted boots and stained coveralls who'd complained bitterly about missing time from work. Pulver checked out his background and confirmed that Masterson had no connection to the Bush family other than being the one who first discovered their bodies.

Tom moved on to the report filed by one of the responding provincial constables who'd spoken to the next-door neighbour, Gerald Little, at the door of his home during the initial response. Little stated he was completely unaware that anything unusual had happened next door the night before. He confirmed he hadn't believed Gordon Masterson's wild story when he'd come to the door first thing that morning. He preferred to keep to himself and not get involved in other people's business, he said.

Hatton was uncomfortable with Little's demeanour and his answers, so he brought him down to the detachment office for a more extensive interview.

It turned out that Little's wife had just given birth to their first child the previous afternoon. He'd returned from visiting her at the hospital in Peterborough shortly after midnight. He claimed he'd looked over at the Bush house after getting out of his car, but hadn't noticed anything unusual. He thought he remembered a downstairs light being on, but wasn't sure. When questioned on the timing of his arrival at his house, Little said he'd stopped off to see friends in Peterborough after visiting hours were over at the hospital. He'd left the city about 11:20 PM.

Hatton checked out his story with hospital staff and the friends he'd mentioned. It held water.

In addition, contrary to what his surname might suggest, Little was a very tall and slender young man, well over six feet in height. If James Bush had told the truth, Little was far too tall to have been the killer.

Tom finished his lunch and took a washroom break. Returning to his office, he pulled over the whiteboard on wheels so that it was close to his desk. A tray along the bottom held dry erase markers, a cleaning brush, and a box of small magnets. He dug into the files for a printout of the timeline of the case. He went out into the central administrative area, found a photocopier, and ran the pages through. He went back into his office and stuck the copies up on the whiteboard with the magnets.

Little had confirmed that the Bushes had a boy in addition to the two murdered girls, and when James could not be found at the scene, an intensive search of the surrounding area began that drew resources away from other investigative work during the morning. As a result, it wasn't until the early afternoon on the first day, after James had been tracked down at the hospital in Bancroft, that Brenda Bush's sister, Cecile Long, was identified and located in Apsley.

With James still in hospital, Cecile was brought in to identify the bodies. Afterward, she was too upset to answer questions in any detail. In addition, she was very worried about her son, Mark Long, who attended high school in Lakefield. There would be no one at home when he got off the bus, she said, and she didn't like leaving him alone, despite the fact that he was fifteen years old. Consequently, Tom recalled as he scanned the timeline, it wasn't until the following day that Cecile was questioned at any length.

He pulled the Cecile Long folder out of the box and put it on the desk. Instead of sitting down, though, he went back to the whiteboard and grabbed a black marker. He stared at the board for a moment, then began to sketch out a basic link chart.

Link analysis was a technique he'd always encouraged younger detectives to use because it tracked associations between individuals, vehicles, and addresses that cropped up during an investigation. Occasionally it yielded surprising results in a simple visual format. The degrees of separation between victim and killer almost always turned out to be much fewer than appearances might have originally suggested.

He began by writing down Brenda Bush's name. He'd always felt very strongly that Brenda, as opposed to her husband, had been the central focus of the murderer on that night. He'd believed at the time that her connection to Joseph Kohl substantiated his feeling, and even after Kohl had been ruled out as a suspect, he continued to be convinced that Brenda was somehow the key. Greg had been murdered first simply because he was awake at the time, downstairs in the kitchen, and had posed an immediate threat to the offender's plans.

He drew a line from her name and wrote down "Greg Bush," followed by their three children underneath in order of age: James, Cheryl, and Donna. He drew a line from James and wrote "Orel Pilon," the man who'd found him on the road and taken him to the hospital. Then he went back up to Brenda, drew a second line from her name, and wrote "Cecile Long."

"Mind if I come in?" Jeremy asked from the doorway.

Tom replaced the cap on the marker and dropped it into the tray. "Not at all."

Jeremy sat down, removed his glasses, and began polishing them with a tissue. "How was your lunch?"

For the first time he noticed that the remnants of his meal had been cleared away, presumably while he was in the washroom. "It was fine, thanks. Delicious."

"No problem. I live to serve. You and Natalie have a meeting at two o'clock in her office. Gavin Elliott."

"Oh." Tom glanced at his watch. It was twelve minutes before two. It surprised him that Gavin, who'd probably only been in Peterborough for a few hours, would take the time to meet with consultants brought in on a convergent cold case when his first priority would be getting up to speed on the progress the crime unit had been making on the Kohl investigation. It was an acknowledgment of Natalie Stone's influence, Tom suspected, and perhaps a gesture of courtesy to him as well. Gavin wasn't the kind of man to feel threatened or pressured.

Jeremy pointed his glasses at the whiteboard before putting them back on. "We have a really good link analysis program on our server. I can show you if you want. Hand-drawn charts are kind of a twentieth-century thing, don't you think?"

"You make it sound like a hundred years ago."

Jeremy snorted, still looking at the whiteboard. "Mind if I ask a few questions?"

"Sure. Ask away."

"I confess I haven't read all the files. I got a good start, but other things intervened. Cecile Long was the victim's sister, correct?"

"Brenda Bush's sister, yes."

"Yeah, right. Was there any evidence to suggest that the killer had to be male? Could it have been a female?"

"Good question, but I don't really think so." Tom pointed at the banker boxes. "There's a profile report in there from our behavioural sciences unit—"

"I know, I read it," Jeremy interrupted. "She profiled a white male between the ages of eighteen and thirty, reasonably good at school but not exceptional, mentally disturbed but probably not diagnosed and treated, somewhat organized, and slightly over-inflated in self-confidence. This last because of the lack of hesitation in the wounds. Like most profiles, it reads like your daily horoscope forecast."

"You're not a big believer in behavioural profiling, I

take it."

"You take it correctly."

Tom was beginning to see that Jeremy had an edge to his personality that he didn't bother to hide.

"Be that as it may," he said slowly, "there weren't any females who jumped out as suspects. Certainly not Cecile Long, if that's what you're driving at. Was there something particular you had in mind?"

"Foot size."

Tom tried to remember the physical evidence collected at the scene. Finally he shook his head. It was too long ago, and there had been too many cases over the years. "Refresh my memory."

"There were no anomalous shoe prints found in the house." Jeremy glanced over his shoulder, as though he'd heard something outside the office. "This lack of physical evidence suggested the killer removed his or her footwear upon entering the house. Rather a tidy thing to do. But Forensic Identification did find foot impressions outside in the grass on the lawn that were probably left by the killer as he or she brought the bodies out and arranged them. They measured ten inches in length. For a male, that translates to about a size eight shoe, or a size nine for a female. The average shoe size for a thirteen-year-old male of a height around five-nine is a size eight. The average shoe size for an adult female? Size nine."

"That's very interesting," Tom said, patiently. "It's certainly a theory. Although, as I say, at the time there were no credible female suspects. If you—"

"Am I interrupting anything?" Natalie asked from the doorway.

"Just brainstorming," Jeremy said, getting to his feet.

"Good. Well, put that on hold for a bit," she said to Tom. "Gavin Elliot's waiting in my office."

13

OPP Detective Inspector Gavin Elliott looked like the man behind the automotive counter at a Canadian Tire store who books you in for an oil change and then gives you the bad news about your transmission.

He was short, stocky, and almost completely bald. When he smiled, he showed you large, yellow teeth that betrayed years of cigar smoking, and when he shook your hand, his grip was firm, callused, but brief. He was careful with his words, he seldom betrayed any emotion, and he looked at you with eyes that seemed to see right through you. He was a cop's cop, and Tom had always liked him.

"How's Christine?" Tom asked, sitting down.

"Well, thanks." Christine was Gavin's second wife, an engaging redhead who wrote historical novels for a living.

"What about Claire? I understand she broke her collarbone."

"She's all right. Thanks for asking." Claire was his only child.

"Will it heal okay, Gavin? Will it affect her scholarship?"

"She had surgery yesterday. They put in a plate and screws. The doctors seem to think it'll heal with no problem by the time she enrols, but it'll sideline her for about twelve weeks. She's pretty much guaranteed to make the team, she's a five-star recruit, but she'll miss games. We're waiting for Waterloo to confirm that they'll still honour her scholarship."

"Hopefully they will."

"Yeah." Elliott glanced at Natalie on the other side of the desk. "You got everything you need on Bush?"

"Yes, thank you," Natalie replied. "Tom's spent the morning going through it."

"Part way through it," Tom said.

"Of course." Elliott shifted sideways in his chair for a better look at him. ""Kind of out of the blue, this guy dumping Kohl's body where you'd find it, wasn't it?"

"A little weird," Tom agreed.

"How are you taking it? Holding up okay?"

"Not my first dance, Gav. Not by a long shot."

"Still, it would have thrown me for a loop, that's for sure. Finally away from it all, trying to make a new start on things, and some wacko invades your place to string up a corpse connected to an old case. Must have been a helluva shock."

Tom maintained eye contact with his former colleague as he replied, "Not really. A surprise, but not a shock. So, was this your idea? Bringing Natalie's company on board?"

"More or less. We haven't had a chance to talk for a while, Tom. Mind if I ask you something before we get on with things?"

"Ask away."

"Why a church? I'm just curious. Is there some kind of

religious significance for you?"

Tom understood that Gavin was feeling him out, wanting to gauge his mental state. Had the air gone out of his tires after leaving the job, or could he still handle the demands of a criminal investigation, even at a consultative level?

"It was there, I thought it looked like an interesting project to spend some time on, so I bought it. More impulse than anything else, I guess."

"The fact that it was a church didn't figure into your decision at all?"

Tom sat forward, clasping his hands between his knees. "You've seen the pictures, haven't you?" Meaning the crime scene photographs, which would have included exterior shots of the church as well as interior pictures of the body and its surroundings.

When Elliott nodded, he said, "It was the tower out front that grabbed me. Solid stone, square, with a top like a battlement or something. As soon as I saw it, I could see myself up there, with a view all around, ready for whatever shit life had left to throw at me. Not religious, though. Not in the slightest."

"A fortress," Elliott said.

"I guess so."

"Must bother you that this guy penetrated it so easily, violated it like that."

"Fucking pisses me off, as a matter of fact."

"How pissed off are you?"

Tom shrugged. "Don't worry. I know how this is supposed to work. I just want a piece of the action, that's all."

Gavin studied him for a moment, then nodded. To Natalie he said, "I can share some of our preliminary thinking, but at this point I'd rather listen than talk."

"That's understandable," Natalie said. "Is there any indication yet of a direct connection between this murder and the Bush case?"

Gavin shrugged, looking at Tom again. "I understand your contract with Cage has a non-disclosure clause. Any information Cage receives from us that you're privy to during the period of your contract is to be held in strict confidence. Am I correct?"

"That's right," Tom replied, not offended. "As I said, I know how this works."

"Okay, then. So what's your thinking on it?"

Tom saw creases at the corners of Gavin's eyes, indicating that he'd passed whatever test his old friend had been administering.

"Has to be a connection of some kind, Gav, don't you think? The combination of Kohl, myself, and a church is just too much to be a coincidence."

Gavin nodded. "Which is why we're looking to the Cage Intelligence Group for fresh ideas on the Bushmaster cold case. Anything yet?"

Tom said to Natalie, "Jeremy asked me just before you came in if we'd considered a female offender, despite the fact the profile had indicated a male. I told him there weren't any credible female suspects at the time."

"It might be worth considering," Natalie said.

Tom looked at Gavin, who'd taken on the file after his retirement. Gavin shrugged. "Not really a female's crime, generally speaking, and as you say, no female suspects at the time. The closest would have been the sister, Cecile Long."

"She was working that night," Tom said. "Confirmed by multiple witnesses."

"Plus, she was a wreck after the notification, wasn't she?"

"Devastated," Tom agreed.

Natalie asked, "Could she have been acting? Putting on a show of grief and instability?"

"Not a chance," Tom replied instantly. "Not as far as I'm concerned. If she was acting, she deserved an Academy Award even more than Pamela does."

Gavin flashed a brief smile. "Wouldn't hurt to run down the female angle though, I suppose."

"We will," Natalie said. "Am I correct in assuming that you've identified Joseph Kohl's home in Bancroft as the primary scene?"

"You are." Gavin touched the sunglasses hooked into the V of his open-necked shirt. "He was stabbed to death in his kitchen. He bled out there, then was transported down to Selwyn and Tom's church."

Tom sat forward. "Are you saying it was the same set-up as Greg Bush?"

"Near enough. Taken by surprise and stabbed in the gut, then his throat was cut from ear to ear."

"Well, Christ, Gav, that sounds to me like a direct connection. The Bushmaster, right?"

"It's still preliminary," Gavin frowned. "You know that. We're still waiting to hear from the lab and the autopsy's still pending, so let's not jump to conclusions, okay? But preliminary indications are that Kohl let someone in the side door of his house early Monday morning. They went upstairs into the kitchen, where Kohl had just about finished breakfast. The stomach wound was almost a replay of Greg Bush's, fast and brutal and right through, as though to catch him off guard, then the throat slash was the coup de grace while he was down on the floor, helpless."

"Okay," Tom said, visualizing it. It did indeed sound very similar to the attack on the father, Greg Bush, seventeen years ago.

"Parts of the house were ransacked, as though the guy was looking for something in particular. A spare bedroom in which Kohl kept a computer and personal papers, and the basement, where he held his church services and Bible study sessions. The computer was left on, with the file manager program open on the desktop."

"What the hell would he be looking for?" Tom wondered aloud.

"Good question. Maybe it was just stage dressing, to give us stuff to waste our time on. Anyhow, once he was done he went back for the body. He brought out a carpet from the spare room, rolled up the corpse, and carried it out through the side door. His vehicle was parked there, in the carport. A van of some kind, from the looks of it."

"Sounds like advance planning," remarked Natalie.

Gavin nodded. "He left bloody boot prints up and down the stairs from the kitchen to the side door and out on the driveway. Work boots. I expect they're long gone. Doesn't look like there's going to be much in terms of trace evidence. Probably wore coveralls and head gear, maybe a baseball cap or something."

"So Locard's principle notwithstanding, he wanted to make sure he left behind the absolute minimum."

Gavin nodded again. Locard's exchange principle, developed by a famous French forensic scientist, held that every contact with another person, place, or thing resulted in some sort of exchange of physical material. It was the reason that the Forensic Identification team spent so much time processing a crime scene, looking for the slightest bit of physical evidence, down to a single hair, fibre, or flake of dandruff. A lack of such evidence strongly suggested that the offender had made advance preparations to safeguard against this kind of exchange.

"What size were the boot prints in the blood?" Tom

asked.

"Elevens." He grimaced. "I know we had nines at the original Bush scene, outside on the lawn. Doesn't rule anything out yet, though."

Tom thought about Jeremy's theory of a female offender but still didn't like it. He thought about James Bush and the fact that teenagers still had some growing to do. Size nines could easily become size elevens, seventeen years later.

"Is there anything else you can tell us that might suggest a parallel?"

"Not in terms of physical evidence," Gavin replied. "You're aware, I take it, that Kohl had started up his church again?"

"Yeah, I was looking at his Facebook page. Once a slimebucket, always a slimebucket, apparently."

Gavin shrugged.

"Are there any carry-overs in Kohl's flock from seventeen years ago?"

"Good question. As a matter of fact, no. Different community, different people altogether."

"He disbanded the Apsley group after the Bush investigation, didn't he?" Natalie asked.

Tom nodded. "Getting cleared of suspicion wasn't enough to hold the flock together after his philandering was out in the open. Everybody headed for the hills, and that was the end of it. Looks like he made a fresh start in Bancroft with a new crop of married women, though."

"So if the motive for killing Kohl now was jealousy," Natalie said, "say, an enraged husband or boyfriend, it would tend to suggest a copycat at the most and a one-off at the least, connected to this new group and not to the Bush murders at all."

"Yeah." Gavin slid out onto the edge of his chair. "The

team's working that angle very hard at the moment. We'll see where it leads. There were twelve families in Kohl's new group, so there's a fair bit of footwork to get done right now. Speaking of which." He slapped his thighs and stood up. "I'd better get back to it, and let you get on with your review of the files."

Tom stood up and shook his hand. "Great to see you again, Gav."

"Same here. Let's have a drink together soon, do some catching up. There are a couple of decent places downtown here."

"Good idea. I'll give you a call."

"How about I give *you* a call instead." Gavin squeezed his shoulder and headed for the door.

"Sure." Tom felt a spike of annoyance, then realized it was Gavin's way of reminding him that things were not the way they used to be, back in the day. They still might be friends, but they were no longer colleagues.

There was now uncrossable ground between them, and Tom needed to accept it and get over it.

14

The moon was down, and Dalton Road was very dark. Tom's shoe heels scuffed against the hardpan surface as he walked away from his house, staring up at the sky.

The Milky Way was a pale smudge overhead. The galaxy, seen edgewise. Millions of stars, too far away to be relevant to the little puff of heat that was the fleeting life of Tom Faust.

He frowned, annoyed that he could no longer remember the names of many of the stars and constellations. When he was a kid, his older brother Rodger, the physicist-to-be, had had an annoying habit of pointing them out, one by one, night after night. Tom couldn't help but learn how to locate Polaris by using the stars of the Big Dipper, or how to find Vega in the constellation Lyra and Arcturus in Boötes. Now, after years of ignoring the night sky during a long career in which his attention had been drawn to much more worldly matters down here on earth, he found that much of what he'd learned from Rodger's insistent coaching in astronomy was gone.

Forgotten.

He'd spent the evening reading the rest of the case material supplied by Gavin Elliott on the Bush family murders and was annoyed at how much detail he'd failed to recall before reading it in the files. He'd been wrong to assume everything was still there inside his head, waiting beneath the silt for him to recollect it. In fact, many important facts had slipped away into the same void that had swallowed up the names of the constellations and God knows what other things he'd once considered important to remember.

He lifted the bottle of bourbon and took a swig. Screw that. It was all back, all of it, right there in his forebrain, already being processed and analyzed the way case information always was when he was on the job.

He took another swig as his thoughts unavoidably shifted to Will Eaton.

Will had been his mentor, a quiet, brilliant cop who'd made it to the rank of assistant commissioner in the OPP before age forced him to pull the pin and walk away. He'd already been showing the indications of early-onset Alzheimer's disease in his final year, although no one had understood at the time what was going on. Once a clever, gentle, brilliant man, he now lived in a long-term care facility in Port Hope, where kind strangers bathed and fed and toileted him.

Will had been Tom's go-to person, the one he would call when he was stuck on something and needed an attentive ear. Day or night, it didn't matter to Will. He was always available, always interested, always ready to brainstorm or just listen.

Tom took out his cellphone, wishing he could call Will now and ask him what it had felt like when the disease first began to erode his mental processes. Confusing?

Perplexing? Frightening?

He thought he still had Will on speed dial, although he hadn't called him in several years. He thumbed the power button on the phone. Nothing happened.

The battery was dead.

"Shit." Tom put the phone away and took another swig. His father, Clayton Faust, had died of a heart attack at the age of sixty-seven, and his mother, Patricia Todd, had passed away from cancer at sixty-nine. His older sister Elsa had been a victim of breast cancer, so cancer and heart disease both ran in the family, but there'd been no trace of dementia that he was aware of, in either his parents' or grandparents' generations.

In fact, they'd all been brilliant. He came from a family of Type-A achiever scientists. His father had had a notable career as a professor of biology at Queen's University in Kingston, where Tom was born and raised. Elsa had been a microbiologist in Halifax, and Rodger was now a nuclear physicist working in the United States. His mother, thank God, had been a librarian and the only quiet one in the family. The rest of them, the father and the two eldest, never seemed to shut up. Dinner was especially tedious.

I read the most fascinating article in Nature *today.*

You can't possibly accept that hypothesis, Rodg, it's just blah blah blah.

What are all these Cs doing on your report card again, Tom? Didn't I tell you—

Tom had always suspected his IQ was up there in the same bracket as theirs, but he was the rebel in the family, the youngest, the one who'd wanted to be different. He'd had little interest in science, disliked school, had gotten into playground fights, refused to submit to IQ tests, and drifted through each grade with mediocre marks, waiting for something to light the fuse.

When it happened, it happened in a big way. Mid-way through the summer before Grade Twelve, the house two doors down from the Faust residence on Earl Street was burglarized. The old woman who lived alone there was bludgeoned to death by the intruder. Tom hung around at the crime scene tape watching everyone come and go. When a plainclothes detective began interviewing bystanders to see if anyone knew what had happened, Tom waited impatiently for his turn and then peppered the detective with so many questions the man gave up and handed him over to the incident commander at the scene.

Sergeant Jack Boal, a seasoned veteran of the Kingston Police Service, recognized genuine interest in Tom's questions and took a liking to him. Later that week he called the Faust house and asked if Tom would like a tour of the police station. Tom jumped at the chance. Boal later arranged for a ride-along, took him to various community events put on by the KPS, and always found time to talk whenever Tom called.

They kept in touch after Tom enrolled at Queen's University to begin a degree in sociology. (*A soft science?* Rodger had sneered. *A soft science? Are you trying to make a statement of some kind?*)

When Tom and his best friend, Mark Marston, both decided to skip their honours year and apply to the OPP instead, Boal stayed in touch. Their friendship continued until Boal passed away two years later from cirrhosis of the liver, apparently brought on by long-term alcoholism.

Tom hesitated, the mouth of the bottle on his lips, and took only a small sip. *Pam's right*, he thought. *I should be more careful with this shit.*

But it took the edge off. Got him down another mile on the long road into darkness. Got him through the nights when he fought the fear and wondered where the hell to turn.

Tom stopped and spat in the general direction of the ditch. He turned around and headed back the way he'd come.

The landline telephone was ringing when he let himself in through the sliding door from the patio.

"Daddy, are you okay?" It was Pamela, sounding a little stressed. "I kept trying your cell but it went right to voice mail."

"Sorry, darling, the battery's dead. I was out for a walk. Just came in. What's up?"

"I wanted to know how you were doing. Have they made any progress finding out who killed the man in your church?"

"It's coming." Tom frowned, hearing an echo on the line when he talked. There was also static he hadn't noticed before. "How are you?"

"Oh, fine. There's a party tonight, but I'm not going to go. I'm just too tired. Colleen's already made excuses for me. I'm just going to call John and talk for a while, read, then get some sleep. I'm exhausted."

"Sounds like a good idea. Don't worry about me, okay, darling? I'm fine."

"Okay, Daddy. I believe you where thousands wouldn't."

After ending the call, he inspected the phone closely. Neither the set nor the receiver showed any sign of having been tampered with. Fighting a bit of light-headedness from the booze, he plugged his cellphone into the charger on the kitchen counter and grabbed a flashlight.

Outside, he opened up the telephone junction box on the wall in the carport and played the light around. He immediately saw a small circuit board, about half the size of his thumb, attached to the coloured wires in the box that connected his landline phone to the outside world. He recognized it right away as a transmitter. It was tapping into his telephone feed and broadcasting to a receiver somewhere nearby.

Given the remoteness of the house, out in the middle of nowhere, it was unlikely someone was sitting around actually listening in on his conversations. More likely, the receiver was a recording device hidden somewhere within range of the transmitter. Whoever planted the bug would probably return for the recording later, when Tom was away from the house.

Adrenaline began to pump into his bloodstream, helping to clear his head. Tom searched the carport, shining the flashlight up into the rafters. Nothing. He emptied the blue recycling bins and hunted through a few cardboard boxes of junk he hadn't gotten around to throwing out. No receiver.

A device like that would only have a range of about fifty to one hundred metres. He walked around the house, playing the flashlight over the exterior, and saw nothing unusual. He couldn't see up into the eavestroughing, but figured it would be too difficult a location for easy retrieval. He walked down the driveway and looked in the ditch, thinking there might be a sealed container of some kind disguised as litter. Nothing.

Giving up, he decided to remove the bug and call the telephone company in the morning for an inspection of the pole and whatever other junction boxes or distribution boxes they kept in the neighbourhood.

He went back into the house and grabbed his digital camera and a portable tool kit. He took several photographs of the bug before removing it. Back inside, he lifted the telephone receiver and listened. No static. He dialled Jade's number and was surprised when she answered.

"Jade, it's Faust. Everything okay up there?"

"I'm trying to sleep. What do you want?"

There was no echo on the line, and still no static. "Did you or what's-his-name see anyone suspicious around the house down here today?"

"No, chief, *Paul* and I didn't see anybody *suspicious* hanging around your place. Goodbye."

"Was anyone at all around today?"

"I don't know, Faust. I don't sit up here watching your fucking dump with binoculars all day like I've got nothing else to do. Christ, leave me the fuck alone, will you?"

"Is Bliss up there?"

"He went home."

"When?"

"This afternoon. Goodbye." This time, she disconnected before he could say anything else.

He cradled the receiver, thinking hard. He didn't know Paul Bliss from a hole in the ground. How far could he trust him? Not very far. Was it possible Bliss had planted the bug for some reason? Was he something other than what he seemed?

Sighing, he grabbed the bourbon from the kitchen counter and put it away in the cupboard. It was remotely possible, but not very likely, that Paul Bliss wanted to listen in on his telephone conversations. The guy came off as a doofus. An amateur. Harmless.

He fixed himself a quick cup of coffee and took it outside onto the patio. He sat down, put his feet up on the chunk of wood, and stared into the darkness. Only an outdoor spotlight glowed from the top of the hill, possibly triggered by a raccoon or a skunk. Jade had apparently gone to bed after all.

An amateur. He mulled over the word. Anyone could buy wiretapping devices such as the one he'd found. They were easily available from Chinese suppliers through the Internet for less than twenty dollars apiece, plus shipping. There were likely a dozen videos posted online that demonstrated how to attach them to a landline phone system and how to set up a receiver or recorder. Anyone could do it.

It had been so easy to find that it came off as rather clumsy.

Or obvious.

He sipped the coffee. Deliberately obvious? Intended to be found?

When his coffee was done, he went back into the kitchen and picked up the phone again. Still silent. He took the transmitter out of his shirt pocket and tossed it onto the counter, then punched in Natalie's number.

"Is that you, Tom?"

"Sorry to disturb you so late, Nat." No echo or static.

"You didn't. I was just reading."

"I found a wiretap on my landline this evening."

Silence.

"Are you there, Nat?"

"That's odd."

"It is. I took it off. I think the line's clear now. It was in the junction box in the carport. I think it was meant to be found. A message of some kind. Any ideas?"

"None. It's very strange."

"Not something Jeremy would do, Nat? Some sort of Cage policy or whatever?"

"No, of course not, Tom. I'm surprised you'd ask that question."

"Too paranoid?"

Silence, then: "A little paranoia never hurts in this line of work, for sure, but Cage Intelligence certainly wouldn't have any need to eavesdrop on your private conversations at this point. What about your cellphone?"

"I don't know. The battery's dead. I'm just recharging it now."

"Check for any apps you don't recognize or remember installing. Sometimes that sort of thing will run down the battery. Would you like Jeremy to take a look at it for you?"

"No, I'll check it out, Nat."

"Would you like him to come up and do a sweep of the house, see if there's anything else?"

Tom hesitated. At the moment he didn't completely trust anyone. "Not right now. Maybe later. I'm just trying to figure out why. What's the point? What's the message?"

"We'll discuss it in the morning at the office."

"See you then." He hung up the phone and looked at the cupboard where he'd put the bourbon.

After a little soul searching, he decided that since someone seemed determined to bring their game right to his doorstep, it was probably a good idea to get his edge back after all, and keep it on.

15

The next morning someone called from the detachment office with the welcome news that his car was being released back to him. Tom hung up and punched in Jade's number. He was surprised once again when she answered before the call went to voice mail.

"What is it?"

"Jade, hi. Can you give me a ride into town? I'm going in to pick up my car."

"Is it okay with you if I finish breakfast first?"

"I thought you'd still be sleeping."

"Yeah, I know. I'm such a degenerate piece of shit. Give me half an hour."

Tom tossed the phone on the kitchen island and went into the bathroom. He showered and shaved off the stubble. In the bedroom, he stared in his closet for a while before selecting khaki trousers and a navy summer suit jacket over a white shirt open at the neck. He was having fun with the loud Hawaiian tops and faded jeans, but it was time for a slightly more professional look.

Jade was quiet on the way into town. She gripped the steering wheel tightly with one hand, her knuckles white and her jaw clenched. She held her cigarette up to the open crack of her window so that the smoke would escape outside. The hand trembled as she pulled it down, shoved the cigarette between her lips, and inhaled deeply. She blew the smoke out of the side of her mouth and held the cigarette back up to the open crack.

"Are you all right, Jade?"

"No."

"What's the problem?"

She flicked a quick glance at him. "Three guesses. Your cop pals were all over me about the dead guy in the church again. Replayed my entire life history for me. Such fun. 'Come on, you're using and dealing all kinds of shit, aren't you?' Thank you very much for helping them dig that up, Faust. When John gets back, I'm outta here. I've had it with your bullshit."

"I'm sorry, Jade. I didn't talk to them about you. They can find out that stuff all by themselves, you know, without any help from me. It's what they do for a living."

"Yeah, well, you're the one who knew the guy. Got jack shit to do with me. But I'm the one gets raked over the fucking coals."

"I'm sorry, Jade. Really, I am."

She said nothing, glaring out the windshield. Her whereabouts had been substantiated not only by Paul Bliss but by other witnesses at the bowling alley and by Bliss's partner, Terry Melvin, who confirmed she'd spent Sunday night and Monday morning at their condo. There was little chance that Armour or Bell would need to interview her a third time, surely, but their aggressiveness had obviously opened old wounds.

"Is there anything I can do to help?"

She snorted.

"If there is, let me know."

She chewed on her lower lip, easing up on the gas pedal to give a red light ahead of them a chance to turn green. As they sailed through the intersection, she looked at him.

"You think those faded good looks of yours will still get you a pass with the women, Faust, but it won't work on me. I'm immune to your bullshit. Go try your crusty charm on some other bitch. This one ain't biting."

They'd never gotten along, but she'd never spoken to him like this before. He decided it would be a good idea to sit there and take it. She was hurting, and he was, at least indirectly, responsible for it.

He gave it a few minutes and then said, "I'm going to make a couple of calls, see if I can get a decent quote on the rewiring."

She said nothing. A tear rolled down her cheek. She put her cigarette hand on the steering wheel to free up her right hand, which she used to wipe her face.

"Jade, I'm sorry this happened."

She stuck the cigarette out the window so that the slipstream would clip off the ash.

Tom got out in the parking lot of the detachment office. She drove away without a word.

He found his car in the parking lot and looked it over carefully. Although it likely would have been stripped down and re-assembled by Ident in their search for physical evidence, it looked none the worse for wear to him now. He went inside and signed for it, then drove to the office.

Charlie was sitting over by the windows in the outer reception area, eating a submarine sandwich. A newspaper was spread out on the coffee table in front of him. He looked up and nodded, then went back to his reading and eating. Tom went through the security door into the inner area.

The workstations in the middle of the room that had been empty yesterday were now filled with people who were typing, reading documents on their computer monitors, and talking on the phone. A young woman got up and walked over to him.

"I'm Kashi Chopra," she said. "I'm Natalie's personal assistant." She held out her hand. Her grip was soft, quick, and polite.

"Nice to meet you."

She looked very natty in her black skirt suit and black high heel shoes. The red tartan scarf around her neck, Tom thought, was the finishing touch. She led the way toward Natalie's office in the far corner.

"I just got here this morning," she said. "Natalie's waiting for you." She stuck her head through the doorway. "Mr. Faust's here."

"Thanks, Kashi."

Tom sat down in the same chair he'd occupied yesterday in the meeting with Gavin Elliott. "She's your personal assistant?"

"Kashi's my right hand. She's an amazing young woman. The intellectual on the team."

Tom said nothing, having thought that Jeremy occupied that niche.

"Plus," Natalie added, "you'd never know to look at her that she has black belts in jiu-jitsu and aikido."

"Really."

Natalie closed the file she'd been reading and moved it aside. "Have you checked your cellphone for malware?"

Tom shook his head. "I will. The phone company's coming out to my place this afternoon to check the landline. I want to make sure there's nothing else on it."

There was a knock at the door and Jeremy walked in. He handed Natalie a piece of paper. "Got her."

She read it quickly and slid it across the desk to Tom. "We've found Cecile Long."

"She was hiding in plain sight," Jeremy said.

Tom scanned the single-page report. Cecile was in Peterborough, living on McDonnel Street in a place currently rented by someone named Mack Kiff, age fifty-three. Also living at the residence were Thomas Kiff, twenty-seven, and Ben Kiff, nineteen.

"Shall we go see if we can have a little talk with her?" Natalie asked.

Tom stood up. "Sounds like a good idea to me."

"Give Jeremy your cellphone, Tom. I want him to run a complete scan and make sure it's clean."

"I'll take care of it."

She shook her head. "He'll take care of it. It's his job."

Tom hesitated, then reluctantly dug out his phone and passed it over, hoping his lack of enthusiasm wasn't as obvious as he thought it was. He took a replacement phone from Jeremy and looked at it dubiously. A number was written on a post-it note stuck on the front.

"A company phone," Natalie said. "Use it for business, Tom. Jeremy will get your personal phone back to you right away, but I want you to use this one while you're working this case."

"If you insist," Tom said.

"I do. Thank you."

A little paranoia never hurts in this line of work, she'd said last night.

Tom was now officially paranoid.

16

Charlie pulled the Mercedes up to the curb beneath a tree at the corner of McDonnel and Bethune Street and shut off the engine. Tom got out and joined Natalie on the sidewalk. They walked down to the middle unit in the two-storey brick rowhouse in which Cecile Long was supposed to be living.

A man sat on the unpainted front steps, forearms on his knees, cigarette held between the fingers of his right hand. Thinking this must be Mack Kiff, Tom walked up to the bottom step of the porch.

"We're looking for Cecile Long. Does she live here?"

Kiff looked up from under the bill of his baseball cap. He slowly stood up, flicked the ash from his cigarette in Tom's general direction, and nudged shoulders with him on the way past. Natalie stepped onto the grass to avoid similar treatment as Kiff walked away, cigarette between his sullen lips.

Tom rapped on the door. Inside he could see a hallway cluttered with footwear, a bicycle, and a skateboard. After a moment the door was opened by a short, heavy-set woman.

"Cecile Long?"

She took the cigarette from her mouth. "Yes? What is it? I've already talked to the police. I don't know anything else."

She was barely recognizable. Seventeen years ago she'd been a slender, thirty-four-year-old brunette with haunted, tear-filled blue eyes and a tentative smile. Time had been rough on her. She'd put on a lot of weight, her hair was grey, her eyes were flat and dull, and her mouth turned down at the corners. The only thing familiar to Tom was the faint French accent that had followed her from her childhood home in west Quebec.

"My name's Tom Faust," he said. "We met when your sister died. I'm not with the OPP any more; I work for a private investigation firm. This is Natalie Stone. May we come in for a few minutes?"

"What for?"

"We're looking into your sister's death. We think what's happened to Joe Kohl may finally help us find out who killed Brenda and her family. We'd like to ask you a few questions."

She looked at Natalie. "I don't want to go over this again. I saw what happened on the news. I haven't seen Joe in years. I have no idea who would do that to him."

"Look," Tom said, "it'd be better if we just come in for a few minutes, then we'll leave. Better than doing it out here on the front step."

Cecile reluctantly opened the door wider and stepped back.

Tom moved inside and almost immediately hit his shin on the pedal of the bicycle. He reached out to steady the bike as Natalie edged in behind him, closing the door. They followed Cecile down the hallway into an untidy kitchen that smelled of bacon fat and toast. She pulled out a chair and gestured for Natalie to sit down.

"Thank you." Natalie gave her a business card. "Our company, the Cage Intelligence Group, assists the OPP and other police departments on a regular basis by reviewing cold cases and hopefully turning up new information to help solve them."

Cecile glanced at the card and tossed it on the kitchen table. It landed on a plate covered with toast crusts and smears of jam. "That's what Brenda is, I guess. A cold case."

Natalie sat down. "She was a person. A sister, a mother, a wife. I worked for the OPP for many years, Cecile, and believe me, we don't forget people like Brenda, no matter how much time passes. Is it okay if I call you Cecile?"

"Fill your boots." She sat down across from Natalie and stabbed out her cigarette on a plate. She lit another one from a pack on the table. She didn't offer coffee or a cigarette, and didn't offer Tom a chair. He leaned against the edge of the stove, moving aside a frying pan filled with congealed grease.

Natalie opened her notebook on the table. "How long were you a member of Joseph Kohl's religious group?"

Cecile shrugged. "Not long. Maybe two years."

"You were living in Apsley at that time, in an apartment above the hardware store, is that right?"

"Yeah. Me and Mark."

"You had a daughter as well, didn't you?"

"Yeah. Megan."

"She was killed in a traffic accident?"

Cecile looked at Tom. "I went through all this with you back then."

"When you get to be my age, Cecile, you start forgetting

things."

Cecile cackled suddenly, a smoker's laugh. "Tell me about it."

"It'll help if you go over it with Ms. Stone, since she wasn't involved with the case back then. Maybe you'll think of something that didn't come up at the time."

She tapped ash on the plate. "What do you want to know?"

Natalie leaned forward, folding her hands. "You and your husband, Chris Long, lived with your sister and brother-in-law for a short while in the house on Lake Road, didn't you?"

"Yeah."

"How did they seem back then, Brenda and Greg? Did they get along?"

"They were okay. They had their fights, same as me and Chris. Well, not nearly as bad as me and Chris. We were at each other's throats all the time."

"Why was that?"

"Oh, Chris wasn't working. Greg was a plumber, and he had a good job. That was what brought the four of us from home to begin with. From Ottawa, I mean. Greg got a job on a big construction project here, and he and Brenda moved right away. James was born here. They talked us into coming after about a year, but Chris couldn't find work. It was pretty bad."

"What did he do for a living?"

"Chris? This and that. Pumped gas, delivered pizza. Stuff like that. Mostly he was between jobs. He was jealous of Greg."

"I see. Why did he leave?"

She shrugged. "You tell me. We were there for three weeks, living in Brenda's basement, and he got in the car one afternoon and I never saw him again."

"Never heard from him again?"

"Never. Not that I ever want to, you know. God only knows why I married him in the first place. I don't really remember, now."

"Did he argue with Greg and Brenda?"

Cecile paused, considering the question. "No, not really. He was too much of a chickenshit. He knew Greg wouldn't stand for it. Greg told him a couple times to stop hassling me. Chris didn't like it much, but he didn't say a word back. Too scared."

Natalie raised her eyebrows. "Was Greg the kind of person who got into a lot of arguments with other people?"

Cecile waved her cigarette in the air. "No no no, not like that. He was a very nice guy. He didn't fight with people, not really. In fact, after Chris left, he kept an eye on Mark. Tried to be a substitute father to him. No, Greg was okay. He just didn't like all the yelling and fighting coming from the basement all the time, that's all."

"I see." Natalie shot Tom a look while Cecile was putting out her cigarette and lighting a fresh one. He gave her a nod, encouraging her to keep going. She turned back to Cecile. "You met Joseph Kohl not long before your sister's death, is that right?"

"Yeah."

"How did you meet him?"

"Through Brenda. She introduced us."

"Where were you working at the time?"

"Oh, let me think. I was washing dishes in a restaurant just out on the highway." She stood up and went to the refrigerator, taking out a can of Coke. "You guys want one?"

"No, thanks," Natalie replied.

Tom shook his head.

"I used to drink like a fish," Cecile said, sitting down and opening the can, "but now it's just this stuff." She sipped the Coke. "That was the problem, you see. That's why I lost poor little Megan."

Natalie waited for her to go on.

"All the time I wasn't working I spent sitting at the bar. It was more what you'd call a roadhouse, I guess, than just a restaurant. I gave them back most of my pay cheque right there at the bar for Crown and Coke. That was my drink, C and C. I came in that day for a lunch shift and spent the afternoon bending my elbow. When they finally came and told me Megan had been hit by a truck right out front of the apartment and was dead, I didn't even know what they were talking about at first. That's how far gone I was."

"She was playing outside in the street?"

"Yeah. Her and Mark. Kicking a ball around. The ball must have gone out on the street and the driver of the truck, he was pulling up to the curb but didn't have no chance at all to stop. She ran right out in front of him." She stared down at her Coke. "That's what they told me, anyhow. After, when I talked to the police. It wasn't the driver's fault."

"I'm sorry," Natalie said.

"It's okay." Cecile looked at her. "It's just really sad, that's all. She was only eight. She didn't have much of a life."

"Your son, Mark, must have been devastated."

Cecile blew out a stream of smoke and watched it drift toward the ceiling. "He was a funny kid. He was twelve when it happened. He didn't say a word about it to me, ever. Not when I yelled at him, not when I cried and asked him to forgive me for not being there, not ever. But he was always like that. Never said much of anything to anybody."

"Where is he now?" Tom asked.

"Who, Mark? Your guess is as good as mine. I haven't heard from him for a long time. Years."

"When did you last see him?"

She looked away, frowning. "I don't know. I guess it was about a year after Brenda died. He was in Grade Eleven, so I guess he was what, sixteen? Took off, just like his father."

"And you never heard from him again either?" Natalie asked.

Cecile shook her head. She dropped the rest of her cigarette into the Coke can and set it aside. "Story of my life, eh? Everybody leaves, sooner or later."

"What about James Bush? What became of him?"

"Another one, I guess. He went into a foster home after it happened, here in the city. I sent him Christmas cards, just trying to keep in touch, you know, so he'd feel like he still had family who cared about him. He sent me a couple back, but then I didn't get one, and I lost track of him after that."

She shook her head. "Another quiet one. He and Mark didn't get along so well."

"Oh? Why not?"

"I don't know. Mark was two years older. At that age, two years can make a big difference. They had a couple of fights. Greg had to pull them apart. Boy stuff, I guess."

Tom looked up as a stocky youth walked into the kitchen. He wore only a sweat-stained grey T-shirt and black boxers. He walked to the fridge, took out a plastic jug of orange juice, and chugged half of it without taking a breath.

"You should use a glass, Ben," Cecile said.

He put the orange juice back in the fridge, gave Cecile an unfriendly look, belched, and walked out.

"That's Ben," Cecile said. "Mack's youngest."

"A fine-looking young man," Tom said. "You were going to tell us how you met Joe Kohl."

Cecile tilted her head. "What? Oh, yeah. After Megan died, I swore off the alcohol completely and started going back to mass. A few times, anyway. I didn't want to take confession, though, and you know, you can't take the sacraments without first doing the confession, so when Brenda said she was going to this church in some guy's house in the village, I started asking her questions about it. It was Protestant, but she said the guy was real nice, you didn't have to do crazy stuff like the Jehovah's Witnesses or whatever, you just sang hymns, said prayers, and studied the Bible. It sounded okay, and I was really desperate for something, so I started going."

"Brenda already knew Kohl at that point?"

She nodded.

"How did he seem to you then?" Natalie asked.

"Good. Real nice. He was nice. He had this deep voice, but quiet, a soothing voice that I liked listening to. And the most amazing blue eyes. Kind eyes. He led all the prayers, said something about each hymn before we sang it, and he worked the tape recorder that the music was on. Organ music that somebody had taped for him, you know, for each hymn. Then he would make a little speech, the what-do-you-call-it—"

"The sermon, you mean?"

"Yeah." She lit another cigarette, her fourth since they'd been there, and studied the tip. "He wasn't a bad man. Not really. He just couldn't keep his hands off the girls."

"Did he pressure you to have an affair with him?"

Cecile shook her head. "It wasn't like that. He wasn't a rapist, nothing like that. He was divorced. He lived alone and just seemed kind of lonely. At first he was just real friendly to me. Because I was new, I guess."

She glanced at Natalie. "I'm like a lot of French girls, I guess, I like to touch the boys when I'm talking to them, on the arm or the knee. You know? Harmless stuff. But I guess it encouraged him. He invited me over one Saturday evening for a Bible lesson, just him and me. I said I couldn't, that I should stay with Mark because, you know, even though he was fourteen at that time, I still didn't want to leave him alone again. So Joe came over to see me that night after Mark went to sleep. It was just kissing and that, but it was the start of everything. After that he came around all the time whenever I wasn't working. When Mark was at school, in the afternoon. Like that. Sometimes he'd call on the phone at night and Mark would answer. Mark didn't like that much. He didn't like Joe."

"He didn't?"

"He knew what was going on, Mark. He didn't like it. He called him some pretty bad names one time, when he came home and found Joe and me together. After that, I stopped seeing him, but Mark still hated him."

"I see."

"He didn't like me seeing anybody, really. Even though his father was gone and not coming back, Mark thought I should be like a nun or something." She rolled her eyes. "Way too late for that. He was a handful, though."

"Mark was?"

She nodded. "Greg talked to him sometimes, gave him the sort of lectures he should've gotten from his own father, but Mark didn't listen."

"When did Brenda meet Joseph Kohl?" Natalie asked.

Cecile tapped her cigarette on the edge of the plate. "I don't remember. A few months before me, I guess. She was having a few problems at that time, and someone she knew in the group suggested she come to a Bible study meeting. This friend thought the religion and getting to know the others might help her. Brenda hit it off with them, and started going all the time. She told me she liked the religion part okay, better than the Catholic Church, you know, and the other people in the group seemed nice. That was how she convinced me to join, too. Her saying that Joe was really nice, and the other people were nice, too. Not stuck up or full of themselves."

"What kind of problems was Brenda having?"

Cecile shrugged. Tom could see she was getting tired of talking. Tired of the subject, tired of looking back at an unhappy, bleak past.

"Greg and Brenda weren't getting along, that's what you said, right?" he prompted.

She nodded. "Nothing major, though. He worked a lot of late shifts, she was at home all the time, and the kids were driving her nuts. She thought meeting new people would help, like I said."

"What was her reaction when you and Kohl started a relationship?" Natalie asked.

Cecile drew on her cigarette and blew smoke at the ceiling. "I'm not real proud of that, you know. Getting mixed up with him, especially knowing that Brenda had already, you know. But I couldn't let it sit between us. One night when Greg wasn't home and her kids were in bed she and I kind of got drunk together in her kitchen and I came out with it. She already knew. She said she was glad to get it out into the open. And she told me Greg had found out about her and Joe."

"And he wasn't too happy about it," Tom said.

"You got that right." Cecile looked at Natalie. "He went over to Joe's house. Punched him in the face and pushed him around. It was the only time I ever knew him to be that way. To actually hit another person."

Tom looked at Natalie. If she'd read the files closely,

she'd remember that this fight had caused the OPP investigative team to look at Joseph Kohl as a suspect to begin with, seventeen years ago. Detective Constable Hatton had used it to pressure Kohl, trying to get him to admit that he'd held a grudge against Greg Bush after they fought, that he'd eventually worked up enough courage to go over to the Bush house to retaliate, that he'd killed Greg in the kitchen, and then had panicked and killed the rest of the family in an irrational attempt to cover his tracks.

As investigative tactics went, though, it was weak. It fell apart when Kohl repeatedly denied everything and his alibi held up.

But Natalie was studying Cecile, and she surprised Tom by asking a different question. A question he couldn't remember anyone asking seventeen years ago.

"Cecile, how did Greg find out? That Brenda was having the affair with Kohl?"

Cecile slowly put out her cigarette. "I don't know for sure. It wasn't me. But I think it might have been James."

"James?" Tom repeated. "Why do you think it was him?"

Cecile made a face. "I think he found out. It's something I remember, from only a few days before Greg and Joe had that fight. One afternoon I was driving to work. At the far end of town, just before you get to the highway, there's this motel. I saw Brenda's car parked in front of one of the units, and Joe's car next to it. Across the road, there was a fruit and vegetable stand. It was closed, but I saw James kind of hiding on one side of it, like he was trying to stay out of sight while he watched the motel."

Tom frowned. "What would he be doing there? I don't understand. That would be miles from their house."

"No no no," she replied. "It was a school day, and the school's on the same road as the motel, remember? Just down a ways. He was probably outside during afternoon recess and saw her drive by. Followed her to see where she was going. Maybe he was like Mark. Maybe he'd already figured out that something was going on and wanted to see for himself."

"He never mentioned anything about it in any of his interviews."

"Boys don't like to talk about that kind of stuff."

"Did he seem upset afterwards?" Natalie asked.

"Well, like I said, he was a quiet kid anyways, like Mark. But I remember after that, he started getting in trouble at school. Fights in the school yard, flunking tests. I don't think he was very happy."

"What the hell's going on in here?" Mack Kiff walked into the kitchen with an aggressive swagger.

Tom pushed away from the stove. "Just a few questions for Mrs. Long. No big deal."

"You got a warrant to come in here asking questions?"

Tom held up a hand. "We're not police, Mr. Kiff, and Mrs. Long invited us in. We're just talking to her. Nothing to do with you."

"You're in my home," Kiff growled, "so it does have to do with me, and if you're not cops then get the hell out."

Tom took a step toward him, then caught himself. He didn't have a badge any more that could back a play like the one he'd been about to make. He settled for a staring contest, something he'd never lost in his life.

Natalie stood up. "We were just leaving." She smiled at Cecile. "Thanks for your time. If you think of anything else, please give me a call."

"She won't be calling anyone," Kiff said, breaking eye contact with Tom and moving around the table to hover over Cecile. "She's got nothing to say to pigs, real or fake. Do you?"

"No," Cecile said quietly.

Tom followed Natalie down the hallway and out the front door. Back in the Mercedes, she turned to look at him. "Are you all right?"

He chewed on the question while Charlie started the engine and pulled away from the curb, then spat it out. "I'd like to punch that son of a bitch on the snout. But other than that, I'm fine."

"It was a good interview. Like riding a bicycle, isn't it?"

It had been about two years since he'd last interviewed someone in connection with an actual investigation. All in all, he thought it had gone well.

"You handled most of it, Nat. You still have the touch. But I almost put my hands on that guy. It would have been a big mistake."

"Understandable, though. I didn't see any signs of physical abuse but there's plainly psychological abuse going on. I'm going to have a quiet word with someone I know in PPS about it, later."

"Good idea." Tom wondered if the Peterborough Police Service might already know where to find Mack Kiff's name in their database.

Natalie sighed, fastening her seat belt. "I think we should look at James Bush again. I think we should go over everything, from top to bottom, with him at the centre."

"I agree," Tom said.

"To the restaurant, please, Charlie."

Tom watched her close her eyes and rub her forehead. He suspected that she was battling a lot more stress than he'd realized.

Something else was going on in Natalie Stone's world that she wasn't sharing with him.

17

Charlie let them off at a restaurant downtown that featured Cajun cuisine. They found a table at the back, and Tom ordered a blackened catfish po'boy with sweet potato fries and baked beans. Natalie went a little deeper into the menu and ordered a Havana salad with blackened chicken. While they waited for their food to arrive, Natalie scanned her notes from the interview with Cecile.

"There's no point in re-examining her alibi on the night the family was murdered, is there?" she asked.

Tom shook his head. "She worked that night until two AM. She didn't leave during her shift. Her car wasn't working, so the night manager gave her a ride home. Dropped her off a little after two. There was no doubt the Bushes were already dead by then. Multiple witnesses verified her whereabouts."

"And Gavin and his team will be looking into where she was on Monday night," she added, "to rule her in or out on Joseph Kohl's murder."

"It wasn't her," Tom said flatly. "Not then, and not now.

She doesn't have the kind of anger or hatred it would take to kill someone. She's beaten-down, passive. On top of that, can you picture her hauling Kohl's dead body around and hoisting it up on a rope? Physically, she couldn't do it."

"Maybe she had help. Maybe the wonderful Mr. Kiff."

Tom shook his head. "Why would that son of a bitch do something that drastic for her sake? The dynamic runs the other way. She does what he says, not vice versa. It doesn't make sense."

Natalie said nothing.

Their food arrived, and Natalie put her notebook aside to concentrate on eating. After a while she asked, "Was her husband ever found?"

Tom nodded. "Long was tracked down in Ottawa a year later. He was in a rehab facility at the time of the murders. Meth."

"What about the son, Mark Long?"

"Disappeared at sixteen, as she said. The case was already a year old by that time. No one bothered to look for him because it wasn't considered a priority at the time, and resources had already been re-allocated."

"We should do that. Find him. I'll mention it to Jeremy."

Tom finished his po'boy, which had been delicious, and turned his attention to what was left of the sweet potato fries. An up-tempo blues number was playing on the overhead sound system, and although Tom didn't know nearly as much about blues music as he did progressive rock, he thought he recognized the vocals and guitar playing of Albert Collins.

"It bothers me," Natalie said, "that James Bush disappeared as well. I'll get Jeremy started on traces for both of them this afternoon."

Wiping his mouth, Tom reminded her that he had to go

home for about an hour.

"Yes. The phone company. Don't forget to pick up your cellphone from Jeremy before you leave." The restaurant was only two blocks from the office building, so they would walk back there together before he went home.

"All right." Tom dug into his pocket and pulled out his wallet.

"Don't be silly," Natalie said. "It's a business lunch. Sean Cage is paying for it."

He shoved his wallet back into his pocket. He might be able to get used to this consulting thing after all.

Outside the restaurant they turned south toward Simcoe Street. Natalie said, "You know someone I'd like to talk to? Just for the hell of it?"

"Who's that?"

"The woman who alibied Joe Kohl for that night. What was her name again? Blomquist?"

"Elina Blomquist. We could do that."

"I can't help but thinking, what if she recanted her story now, years later, and it turns out Kohl did kill the family after all? And what if James finally tracked him down and got his revenge?"

Tom sighed. "If we can find her, we can ask. I don't think it's very likely, though. I think it's pretty much a lock that Kohl didn't do it."

Natalie smiled. "You're probably right, but it's one of those things that gets stuck in your head. I'll add her to Jeremy's list and we'll see if we can find her."

Back at 200 Water Street, Tom walked into his office and found Jeremy sitting at his desk, feet up, reading a thick file from one of the banker's boxes. Other files were stacked in two piles, one already read and the other still to read.

"Can I get my cellphone back?" Tom asked, keeping

his voice polite. Where he came from, it was a breach of etiquette to sit at someone else's desk, reading files assigned to that person. Putting your feet up added insult to injury.

"Mmm?" Jeremy tore his eyes away from what he was reading. "What? Oh, yeah. Sure." He lowered his feet and set the open file aside.

Tom saw that it was the autopsy report, complete with photographs.

Jeremy held out Tom's cellphone. "It was clean. I installed an anti-virus app that'll help."

"Thanks." Tom slipped it into his pocket and took out the company phone.

Jeremy shook his head. "Natalie wants you to keep it."

"I don't need it."

Jeremy shrugged and went back to his reading.

Tom stood there for a moment, hand out, then returned the phone to his pocket and left.

Traffic in the city was a little heavy as people got an early start on the weekend. He took his time, relieved to be behind the wheel of the Town Car again. The afternoon was bright and warm. While waiting for a light to change he dug into the centre console and pulled out a CD. It was *Mirage*, by Camel. He put the disc into the player and turned up the volume.

Traffic was sticky all the way out of town, but eventually he turned off County Road 29 and drove up Sixth Line Road. As he approached Dalton Road, he saw a white van parked on the opposite shoulder up ahead. There were two extension ladders on the roof and a yellow bubble light, but no markings on the van. Tom pulled over and got out.

On the other side of the ditch was a small enclosure that contained metal cabinets belonging to the phone company. The little gate was open, and someone squatted in front of one of the cabinets, doing some kind of work.

Tom walked across the road. The ditch was dry so he went down and up, hoping there were no hornets' nests hidden in the tall grass.

The technician heard him coming. He stood up and turned around. In his early thirties, he was a few inches shorter than Tom, slender, and clean-shaven. He wore a yellow hard hat, an orange safety T-shirt with reflective stripes on it, jeans, and scuffed work boots. The tool belt around his waist was stuffed with pliers, snippers, screwdrivers, and a butt phone, a telephone test set that connects to a telephone line with alligator clips.

"Hi there," Tom said, leaning on the gate. "Are you with the phone company?"

"That's right. Are you the one who called in? Mr. Faust?"

"Yeah." Tom stared at the panels of circuits, wires, and LEDs inside the open cabinet. To a trained technician the layout and assembly would make perfect sense, but to someone like him it was nothing more than a confusing jumble. "How's it look?"

The technician holstered a small plastic hand-held meter and looked over Tom's shoulder down the road. "Well, I inspected the line from your house to here. This is your local distribution frame. Haven't found anything so far."

"There was a transmitter wired into the junction box in my carport," Tom said. "Come back to the house and I'll show it to you."

"Okay. Just let me finish up here. I'll be there in five minutes."

Tom went back to his car and drove down to the house. He used the washroom, found the bug where he'd left it on the kitchen counter, and went out into the carport just as the white van was turning into the driveway. The technician got out and looked around.

"Nice place. I love the country. The air's so fresh."

"Yeah." Tom gave the transmitter to him.

He gave it a quick once-over, front and back, then handed it back. "Where did you find it?"

Tom pointed at the junction box on the wall. "In there."

He squatted and opened the box. "Do you remember which wires?"

Tom showed him.

"Okay." The technician closed the box and stood up. "How does your phone seem now? All right?"

"Yeah. Come on in." Tom led the way upstairs into the kitchen and watched the technician pick up the receiver and listen. He punched in a number, listened, and hung up. Then he picked up the phone set and inspected it closely.

"Doesn't look like it's been tampered with," he said. "The case hasn't been opened." He removed the receiver and turned it around. "Receiver, neither."

Tom nodded. "That's what I thought."

"Okay, I'd say everything is fine now." He replaced the receiver, put down the phone, and walked around the room. "Nice kitchen." He looked through the sliding door. "Nice back yard."

"Yeah, thanks."

"Okay. If you have any other problems, let us know." Halfway down the stairs to the side door, he looked back over his shoulder. "Did you report this to the police?"

"I will."

"Not much they can do about it, but it might be good to have a report on file in case you find another one." He led the way into the carport and stopped short.

"Wow, that's nice." He was looking at the small stained

glass window Tom had saved for Pamela's garden, which was leaning against the back wall.

"Yeah. It's from a church I'm renovating. Up on Cedar Hill Road. This side of Bridgenorth."

"Sounds interesting." He showed Tom a friendly smile. "How far along are you?"

"Just about to get a quote for the rewiring."

"No kidding. How's that for synchronicity? I'm an LEC."

"A what?"

"Licensed electrical contractor. Did you know that only an LEC can legally do electrical work in Ontario?"

"I wasn't aware of that," Tom replied.

The man dug out his wallet, rooted around in it, and pulled out a dog-eared business card. "Here." He handed the card to Tom. "Sorry it's a little worn out from sitting in my wallet. It has my ESA licence number on it. I'd be happy to give you a quote on the job, if you like."

Tom looked the card over. Printed on it were the name Jim Woods, a Peterborough address, a local phone number, and an Electrical Safety Authority licence number.

"The phone company gig is just part time," Woods said. "I do contracting stuff on the side to help pay the bills. You know how it is. But I can give you references, if you want. And I charge less than the contractors in town, because I don't have their overhead. I can get you your permit, do the work, and arrange for the inspection so everything's on the up-and-up."

It occurred to Tom that it would save a lot of phone calls and related hassle lining up site visits with contracting companies in Peterborough.

"Okay," he said, putting the card in his shirt pocket. "When can you come out for a look?"

"Tomorrow's Saturday," Woods said. "I'm off. I could

come up then, if that'll work for you."

"Ten AM." Tom gave him the address and watched him write it down in a small spiral-bound notebook.

Woods put away the notebook and held out his hand. "Nice to have met you, Mr. Faust. I'll see you tomorrow morning."

As Woods backed out of the driveway and rolled off down the road, Tom thought, *Well, that was easy.*

18

It was dark when Tom drove up to the church. He sat for a while in the car to finish his can of Coke, thinking things over.

The interview with Cecile Long this morning had gone better than expected. He and Natalie worked well together, and they'd been able to keep Cecile talking long enough to unearth new information—that James Bush had likely known about his mother's affair with Joseph Kohl before the murders.

Tom's main regret was that he'd let Mack Kiff get under his skin. He'd bristled at the man's aggressiveness and dominance of Cecile, and he'd wanted to give the bastard's nose an interesting new curve. As a police officer Tom had been trained to stay focused and objective, but for a moment he'd felt his emotions slip. Not a good thing.

His thoughts moved from Kiff to Jade. Tom didn't particularly like her, and it was plain that she didn't like him, either. Which was fine; he wasn't expecting her to run for president of the Tom Faust fan club. He was beginning to feel sorry for her, though. She was fighting hard to put her life back together, and Tom could see it was a struggle.

He finished the Coke and put the can behind the passenger seat. Getting out, he opened the trunk and fished out his long-handled flashlight. He switched it on and walked along the front of the property, gathering up the crime scene tape. He broke the seal on the front door, walked inside, and turned on the lights.

The body was gone, along with the rope that had suspended it from the overhead beam. Several toolboxes were also missing, no doubt taken by Ident in order to process everything with a sharp edge. He made a mental note to ask for them back.

The place was covered with fingerprint powder, black on light-coloured surfaces and silver on dark-coloured surfaces. Work tables, step ladders, saw horses, scaffolding, lawn chairs, and Tom's table saw showed traces of it, as did all the door jambs, window frames, and any other surface that might have been touched at some point by a human being.

The floor beneath the spot where the corpse had hung was a bit of a mess. Body fluids had leaked down onto the battered pine floorboards, and Ident had scraped up healthy samples for laboratory processing. In addition, the boards around the spot had been scratched and scuffed by ladders, light stands, and other equipment used to process the scene.

In some instances it was necessary to call in a specialized cleaning service to restore a home or office to liveable conditions after the removal of a body. Blood and other various substances constituted a biohazard that needed to be cleaned up by trained professionals with the appropriate sanitation supplies and equipment. Fingerprint powder and various solutions used by forensic identification teams also needed the attention of a qualified service in some cases, as they could be very difficult to remove from upholstery and other surfaces. However, Tom wasn't particularly concerned. The interior of the church was still a shell. He would clean up a bit of the mess at a time. Since the floor would eventually be torn up and replaced, he didn't care about the stain. An application of bleach should disinfect it enough until then.

There was only the smell to deal with. He shoved his armful of crime scene tape into a garbage can and went around opening all the windows to the night air. Thank God the drywall hadn't gone up yet. The smell could seep into the very walls and ceilings of a home. He made another mental note to bring up a few cans of room deodorizer tomorrow in case the open windows didn't do the job tonight.

He hoped that Jim Woods wouldn't notice the odour and be discouraged from providing a good quote. If the numbers Tom received from him were at all reasonable and the references checked out, he'd probably go with the guy. He preferred to keep things simple and get the job done without undue hassle.

He grabbed a lawn chair, wiped it off with a handful of paper towel, and sat down. Tipping his head back, he stared up at the ceiling. The contractor had done a good job repairing and reinforcing the trusses and beams up there. Some of the wood had rotted and had needed to be replaced, but most was still solid and capable of bearing the load for another century or so, as long as the interior humidity was properly controlled and repairs were made as soon as they were necessary.

Unfortunately, the load had included Joe Kohl's lifeless corpse. Tom could see marks on the beam where the rope had borne the weight of the body, a combination of abrasions and shredding at the edges. A bit of stain might mask them, if he wanted to go up there and do something about it. Maybe he could get someone else to do it. If not, they would stay. They only bothered him because they were an annoying flaw, not because they were a reminder of Kohl's murder.

Not his first body, and not his first dance. Other people's deaths had never bothered him when he'd encountered them in professional circumstances. He included Kohl in this category. He'd discovered as a rookie provincial constable that he could deal with bodies unemotionally, objectively, with a strong stomach and a cool head.

Only the deaths of those close to him in his personal life had succeeded in reaching him. His parents' deaths, his sister's, and, of course, Linda's. There are no professional barriers to throw up when you lose someone close to you.

He listened to the vibrations of crickets outside the open windows. The sound was like a form of tinnitus, a constant pulsing in the ears, but he liked it. It was calming. Moths popped softly against the window screens, drawn by the light streaming out from inside the church. A plastic drop sheet tossed over a sawhorse crackled, stirred by air currents moving in through the windows.

He liked this place. It was his. It was the first place he'd ever actually owned. When he and Linda had moved to Orillia they'd rented a house, uncertain as to how long they might stay there, and after her death Tom had moved into an apartment close to the GHQ campus. This place, though, was all his, and he'd be damned if some son of a bitch was going to ruin it for him.

If the bastard thought that stringing up the corpse of someone connected to Tom's professional past would chase him out, then the guy had another think coming. This place was Tom's last stop on the road. Where he was going to make his final stand.

He laced his fingers behind his head and smiled, thinking of Gavin's question: *Why a church? Is there some kind of religious significance for you?*

When churches were consecrated, they were considered sacred ground. Tom wasn't sure if the Presbyterians who built this place shared that belief or not, but they probably did. It was a common Christian thing, wasn't it?

Then, of course, there was the additional question of whether the sacredness continued on after the building was decommissioned and sold. Did the Holy Spirit just drift out the front door as the pastor left the church for the last time, locking the door behind him? Or did It hang around, as a sort of gratuitous inclusion to the next owner?

Tom didn't really care. It hadn't affected the value of the property one way or the other when he'd negotiated to buy it. It would have been absurd, laughable: "including all appliances, two cords of firewood, and lingering holy benevolence."

As far as the secular worlds of real estate and banking were concerned, consecration was a non-issue.

He shouldn't make fun of it, though. Things like that were important to some people. Gavin, for example, was a practising Christian. An Anglican, if Tom remembered correctly. It was possible his question to Tom had had more than one level to it.

Tom's eye followed the grain on the beam above his head to a swirl that looked like a winking eye. Was the idea of holy consecration an issue as well for the killer?

Tom pursed his lips. It was an interesting thought that raised an obvious question. Was their quarry a religious fanatic of some kind who knew about church consecration and had chosen Tom's church as an appropriate place to display the punishment that comes to a sinner who masquerades as a religious man?

He mulled it over for a while, then rejected it. For one thing, the whole consecrated/non-consecrated thing was too confusing to pin a theory on. If the killer wanted consecrated ground but knew that decommissioning a church meant it was no longer sacred, then he wouldn't have brought Kohl's body here with that purpose in mind. He would have chosen some other church as a dump site, and certainly one much closer to Bancroft than Cedar Hill Road in Selwyn Township.

Besides which, the whole thing felt more cynical than that. Tom was certain the connection to him, personally, was the critical element. The killer clearly enjoyed the irony of leaving a murdered corpse in a formerly sacred building now owned by that most secular of human beings, a retired homicide detective.

Tom closed his eyes, nodding to himself. That line of thinking was a lot more solid. It had a ring to it. A delicious irony that the killer's twisted mind clearly couldn't pass up.

The Bushmaster. Tom knew in his gut that it was him. He'd known as soon as Armour had brought up the Apsley murders.

Without unlacing his fingers, he rubbed his ear with the palm of his hand to relieve an itch.

It fit. If anything, the Bushmaster seemed to enjoy his own wit. Wanted Tom to know how smart he was, how clever. Like his cards of condolence, a sneering dare to catch him.

Tom opened his eyes. A craving for bourbon gripped him. He could taste it. His throat worked, wanting a drink.

He fought with it until it passed.

He closed his eyes again and took a series of long, slow breaths.

Maintain an edge. Stay in the game.

Time passed.

He drifted for a while, then heard the crickets stop pulsing. In the silence, a katydid scratched. An insect tapped against a window screen.

The crickets started up again.

He fell asleep.

19

When Tom finally opened his eyes again and looked at his watch, it was nearly two o'clock in the morning. He struggled to his feet and stretched the stiffness out of his muscles, shut off the lights, and drove home to finish the night in bed, a much easier place to rest his joints than in a lawn chair.

He got back to the church shortly before ten o'clock and was surprised to see Paul Bliss's Honda Civic parked in the driveway. Inside, he found Jade upstairs in the loft, showing Bliss around.

"What are you doing here so early?" he called up, setting his bag down on a work table.

Bliss looked down. "Good morning. Jade's just giving me a little tour. I hope you don't mind. It was my idea. I wanted to see what she's been working on."

"No problem." Tom pulled a can of air freshener from the bag and walked around, spraying here and there. The windows were still open, but his sensitive nose could still detect a faint, lingering odour.

Jade thumped down the stairs with Bliss trailing after her. "What are you doing?"

"There's a guy coming at ten to give me a quote on the wiring. I don't want him turned off by the smell."

"What smell?" Jade headed for the nearest window. "Did you leave these open all night?"

Tom gave the air a last puff from the can. "Does it smell all right to you in here?"

Jade closed the window. "Why wouldn't it?"

Tom looked at Bliss, who shrugged diffidently. He tossed the can back into his bag. "Okay, well, that's good. This guy works for the phone company, but he's a certified electrician and does jobs like this on the side."

Jade said nothing, doing the rounds of the windows, closing each one. This morning she wore a pale green tank top, jeans, and white deck shoes. She looked even thinner than usual, her bare shoulders hunched and her head down.

"He's supposed to bring references," Tom added. "How about you check them out for me? Will you do that?"

Jade closed the last window. "Sure."

"This is a very cool place," Bliss said, looking up at a spot very close to where Joseph Kohl's body had been hanging four days ago. "Jade says you're fixing it up to live in."

"Yeah." Tom glanced at Jade, but her attention was elsewhere.

"What a great idea. It's a beautiful building. It'll be like something out of a magazine by the time you're finished." Bliss took a few steps toward the front door. "Is it possible to go up into the tower?"

"No." Tom heard tires crunching on the gravel road. He went outside just as Jim Woods pulled up in his white van. Tom thought it must be his personally-owned vehicle rather than one belonging to the phone company, since he was driving it on his day off. It would explain why there were no company markings on it.

They shook hands on the front lawn and Woods took a step back to admire the tower. "Wow, what a great structure. In such terrific shape, too. Nineteenth-century Scottish masonry."

He squinted at Tom, raising a hand to shield his eyes against the mid-morning sun. "Know how I can tell it's Scottish?"

"Nope."

Woods walked up to the tower and patted it. "The stones are square-cut. The Scottish preferred working with rectangular blocks. Germans, on the other hand, just split the fieldstones down to size and didn't bother reshaping them. Used more mortar that way, as you can imagine, to fill in around the irregularities." He smiled. "I've learned a lot about heritage buildings since becoming an electrician."

"I see. Interesting."

"Square blocks and a square Norman tower. Very solid." Woods raised the satchel in his left hand. "Can we go in? I'd like to get started."

Tom led the way. As Woods gawked around, Tom said to Jade, "This is Jim Woods, the electrician I mentioned."

"Hi," Woods said, walking over. "Nice to meet you."

Jade ignored his outstretched hand.

Unfazed, the electrician gazed up at the ceiling. "So this is where it happened, eh?"

"Maybe you'd like to get started on your estimate," Tom suggested.

Woods walked over to the stain on the floor and looked up. "Freaky. It must have shocked the hell out of you."

"It'll be a bigger shock if I don't get the wiring done right." Tom moved his bag from the work table. "You can use this to spread your stuff out."

"Oh, sure. Thanks. It won't take too long." Woods put his satchel on the table and pulled out a notebook, pen, and measuring tape.

Bliss moved up beside Tom. "Do you need Jade to stay?"

"Not if she doesn't want to." He thought of something and added, "Hang on. Let me get the references first. Jim, did you bring the references with you?"

"Sure did." Woods handed over a folded manila envelope.

Jade and Bliss had already started to move toward the door. Tom caught up to them and handed the envelope to Jade. "If you could call them this afternoon, that would be great."

Jade took the envelope.

Bliss said, "I don't understand. What happened?"

Tom frowned. "What do you mean, what happened?"

"What was he talking about, just then? Did something happen here?"

Tom stared at him. "You're kidding, right?"

"I *told* you, Paul," Jade said. "The hanging man. Faust found him here."

"Here? It was *here*?"

"Where the hell did you think it was?" Tom demanded.

"I thought it was in the other place."

"What other place? What the hell are you talking about, Bliss?"

"I thought you found it in your other place. The house where you live right now."

"I told him about the body," Jade said to Tom. "I never said where it was."

Tom shook his head at Bliss. "Don't you watch the

news? It was all over the TV, the radio, the newspapers."

"I avoid news programs. They're too upsetting."

"Jesus Christ." Tom turned away. Woods was standing in the little cubicle that had been framed off from the kitchen for a laundry room, shining a small flashlight into the old breaker box.

When Tom turned back, Jade and Bliss were gone.

Was the guy for real? How could he possibly not have known that Joseph Kohl's body had been found here, in the church?

Woods stuck his head out of the laundry room. "You're going to take this up to two-hundred-amp service, right?"

"Yes."

"I don't blame you, man. More power to you."

Tom sighed and went outside, leaving Woods to it.

20

After Jim Woods had driven off, promising to e-mail an estimate the next day, Tom was locking up when his company cellphone began to vibrate. He looked at the call display, saw that it was Natalie, and answered.

"I'm coming to pick you up in twenty minutes," she said without preamble. "Will you still be at the church?"

"I was just going home," Tom said.

"Okay, then I'll meet you there." The line went dead.

Tom drove back to the house, wondering how she'd known where he was. He hadn't mentioned to anyone other than Jade that he'd be up here this morning. Had she tried the landline at home, gotten no answer, and made a simple deduction that he was here at the church?

Naturally suspicious, he figured that Jeremy must have activated GPS tracking software on the company cellphone, something Tom normally didn't bother with himself. He could picture Jeremy stroking his hipster beard, chuckling at a little electronic blip on a map that represented Tom Faust's whereabouts.

He shrugged it off. The Cage Intelligence Group was paying him very well for his time, so he supposed it was a fair exchange that they should know where he was spending that time.

At home he changed out of his jeans and mostly-orange Hawaiian shirt and put on a white T-shirt, a navy jacket, and camel-coloured trousers. He was leaning against the back fender of the Town Car in the carport, polishing the lenses of his sunglasses with a tissue, when the Mercedes turned into the driveway. He slid into the back seat next to Natalie. "Who've we got?"

"Gerald Little, the next-door neighbour. Jeremy tracked him down in Lindsay."

"Okay." Tom looked out the window as they reached the end of Dalton Road and turned out onto the Sixth Line. "Is Jeremy tracking my whereabouts?"

"He's tracking all of our whereabouts. It's part of his job. Does it bother you?"

"Yes." He sighed. "No, it doesn't."

"We're not a mom-and-pop outfit, Tom. Cage Intelligence goes into places that carry a rather high level of risk. We follow strict security protocols even with contract staff such as yourself. Just a precaution."

She dug into her handbag and passed over a manila envelope. "Paperwork and some documentation for your private investigation certification test. There are fifty hours of online training to complete, then the test. We'll take care of the fees."

"Oh, for godsakes, Nat." He tossed the envelope onto the seat beside him.

"I know, I know, but it needs to be done. Put in the hours, pass the test, and then it's over with."

"I hate training."

"No, you don't. You're just trying to get under my

skin."

He looked at her. "How long was I under surveillance? Before we ran into each other last week?"

She shrugged. "A while, but it's not what you're thinking. Sean insists on seeing thorough background on all potential hires, right up to the morning of the day we make initial contact, but it wasn't anything you need to be paranoid about."

"Too late."

They sat in silence for a while, watching the countryside pass by on their respective sides of the road. Then, reluctantly, Tom picked up the envelope and took a look. It was all the basic forms required by the government of Ontario to complete the training, take the test, and apply for a private investigation licence.

The forms had already been filled out for him. They contained information he hadn't supplied to the Cage Intelligence Group when he'd signed his contract to work for them. Surprise, surprise. It was all complete and correct. He dug out his pen and began signing and initialling. When he'd finished with all the forms, he returned them to the manila envelope and dropped it on the seat.

"We'll have copies on your desk as soon as these are submitted," Natalie said, putting the envelope back into her handbag.

"Thanks."

"You're welcome."

Gerald Little lived in a small wartime bungalow on a side street near the edge of Lindsay, a town of about twenty thousand people in the municipality of Kawartha Lakes, about forty kilometres northwest of Peterborough. When Tom and Natalie got out of the car, Little walked out through the open garage door with an expectant look on his face. Someone, perhaps Kashi, had apparently made arrangements with him beforehand for the interview.

He was a tall, gawky redhead with a soul patch and wire frame glasses. He shook hands and invited them into the garage, where he'd set up lawn chairs. If he remembered Tom from seventeen years ago, he gave no sign. Natalie sat down, crossed her legs, and opened her notebook in her lap.

The garage was large, built for two cars. It had been converted into a workshop crammed with washers, dryers, ranges, and other small appliances. There was a small staircase on the left, made of two-by-fours, that led into the kitchen. Next to the staircase was a floor-to-ceiling shelving unit about twelve feet long that was filled with small kitchen appliances of all sizes and colours.

"Got a thing for blenders?" Tom asked.

"They're not blenders, they're food processors." Little's voice sounded nervous. "Well, a couple down at the end are blenders, hard-to-find models, but what I collect are food processors." He tried to smile. "I'm a small appliance repairman. I've got maintenance contracts for most of the big retailers in Kawartha Lakes and that's what pays the mortgage, but this is my hobby. Food processors. I buy and sell them online, I fix them up, and the best ones I keep for my collection."

"So what's the difference? Between a blender and a food processor?"

"Well, a couple of things, but most important are the blades. A blender has angled blades to create, like, a vortex," he twirled his finger around in the air, "to blend things and introduce air into the mixture. A food processor has straight blades to slice and cut food into pieces."

"They get pretty sharp, I guess. The blades."

"Yeah. You have to be careful handling them."

Tom looked at a tall red and white model. "Got much

money tied up in them?"

"A bit. It's a niche market, so for the most part it's very affordable." He pointed at the one in front of Tom. "That's the crown jewel of my collection. A 1947 Starmix, made by the German company Electrostar. I paid three hundred for it, and I know a guy who'd go six for one. It's in perfect working order."

He pointed at the one next to it. "This is an original Robot-Coupe, first invented by a company in France in 1960. It was for commercial use only. I paid only a hundred bucks for it at a flea market. A complete steal; I could sell it for five hundred, easy."

He tapped another one. "Parts for these early models are still available, but they're very expensive. A cutter bowl for this Robot-Coupe R2, for example, costs about a hundred dollars American."

"Interesting," Tom said. "Let's sit down, okay? We have a few questions to ask you."

"Oh. Sure."

"We appreciate your time this morning," Natalie said as Little eased into the chair across from her, his long legs splaying out. "We know it's getting close to lunch time and we won't keep you, but as Ms. Chopra explained on the phone, our company assists police departments by reviewing unsolved cases, hopefully generating new leads for them to follow up on."

"I'm not sure how I can help you with that."

Tom leaned against a work bench where he could watch Little in profile. Right away he felt annoyed by the man's obvious prevarication. Why would he pretend not to understand what they wanted to talk to him about?

"Well," Natalie continued, unperturbed, "we're currently assisting the OPP in a review of the Bush family murders that happened seventeen years ago. You were their next-door neighbour at the time, Mr. Little, and we'd be very appreciative if you could share with us anything you remember about it."

Little flicked a glance at Tom. "I remember you now. You were the head investigator or something."

"That's right." Tom folded his arms and looked down at him. "You were interviewed by Detective Constable Hatton. I had a few questions for you afterward."

Little nodded. "I didn't know what happened. I still don't, not really."

"You remember me, and you remember Detective Constable Hatton. Tell us what you remember about that night."

"Nothing, really." Little clasped his hands in his lap. Because Tom was standing off to one side, Little was forced to turn his head to look at him. The long vertical muscle on the side of his neck stood out like a rope, and his Adam's apple moved up and down as he swallowed.

"I was in Peterborough until late. That was the day our daughter Amy was born. I came home and went to bed. I didn't notice anything at all next door."

Tom glanced at Natalie, who was now watching Little's profile. The end of her pen rested on her chin in a pose he remembered well from years past.

"Are your wife and daughter home today, Gerald?" he asked.

"No, they're in Toronto for the weekend. My daughter wants to enrol at Sheridan College. They're doing a campus visit."

"An excellent college," Natalie said. "I live only three kilometres away, on the lakeshore. Oakville's a great community. What does she want to study?"

"Animation."

"What time did you get home that night, Gerald?" Tom

cut in. "The night of the murders?"

"I don't really remember. Around midnight, I guess."

"Were the lights on next door?"

"I don't know. I don't think so."

"The house was in darkness?"

Little clasped his hands more tightly together. "I just don't remember. It was too long ago."

"If lights were on, you would notice, right? It was the only house within sight of your place on that road, and it was only a couple hundred feet away."

"Yeah."

"So were any lights on over there?"

"Maybe. I just don't remember."

Tom shook his head. "At the time, you told Detective Constable Hatton you thought you saw a light on downstairs." He stared at Little, who swallowed nervously. "So, did you?"

"I guess. If that's what I said, I probably did. It was a long time ago."

Natalie leaned forward. "What was your relationship with the Bush family like, Mr. Little? Did you and your wife get along with them?"

"Sure, I guess. We didn't have much to do with them."

"Were there ever any disagreements? The kind of things neighbours get into now and again?"

"No."

"Were they noisy?"

"Not really."

"Did the kids trespass on your property or cause damage? Anything like that?"

"No."

"So, generally, how did you feel about them as neighbours?"

"They were okay."

"Very soon after the murders, you moved away. Why was that?"

"Donna Lee, my wife, is an elementary school teacher. She got a job offer here in Lindsay."

Natalie frowned. "So when did you move, exactly?"

"It was in February, I guess. The next year."

"I don't understand. The school year was already well underway. Don't they do their hiring in the summer?"

"She was doing supply teaching in Peterborough before Amy was born. A teacher at the school here in Lindsay had a heart attack and died in January, and Donna Lee had a good friend with the school board who pulled some strings and got her hired as the replacement."

"I see. Do you still have contact with anyone from the Apsley area?"

"No," Little replied, rather emphatically.

"No one at all?"

"We hated it there. We didn't know anyone and we didn't have any family there. It was like living in the Arctic, a thousand miles from civilization. We couldn't wait to get out of there."

Tom casually slid his hands into his pockets. "Do you know where I live, Gerald?"

"Huh? Pardon me?" Little turned his whole body toward him.

"I said, do you know where I live?"

"Where you live? No. Why would I?"

"Is there anything special to you about the first of November?"

Little frowned. "No. Why?"

"Do you buy a lot of greeting cards, Gerald? If I went up into your house, would I find a lot of them?"

"What?"

Tom pulled his hands back out of his pockets and

straightened. "Come on, Gerald. You know. Birthday cards, Christmas cards. Sympathy cards."

"Donna Lee takes care of all that stuff. I don't even know how much it costs to mail a letter any more."

Tom took a step forward. "Does Donna Lee know where I live, Gerald?"

"I don't think so. Why would she? She doesn't even know you."

"What's a Bushmaster, Gerald?"

"A Bushmaster? I don't know. A kind of chainsaw?"

Natalie put her notebook into her handbag and stood up. "Thanks for your time, Mr. Little."

Tom pulled out a business card and wrote the number of his company cellphone on the back. "If you remember anything that might help, call."

Little took the card and stared at it dubiously. "All right."

In the Mercedes, as Charlie backed out of the driveway and pulled away, Natalie's phone buzzed. She looked at the call display and answered.

"Yes, Derek."

She stared straight ahead, listening, her face a careful blank. Finally, she looked out the side window and said, "I understand."

Her husband evidently had more to say. As it went on, Tom watched her eyes go to Charlie, who seemed to feel their pressure on the back of his head. He turned around, nodded once, and went back to his driving.

"Not at this time," Natalie said. "Well, I think it's strictly need to know at this point, and he doesn't need to know."

Tom's ears started to burn.

"Jeremy's on it, but I'm convinced it's unrelated." She listened, then said, "Understood. I will." She ended the call and put away the phone.

"Gerald Little knows more than what he's saying," she said to Tom, "but we're obviously not going to get it just by asking him."

He said nothing. As much as he'd always been fond of Natalie Stone, Tom understood that he didn't really know her all that well. He didn't know whether her relationship with Derek was still good; he didn't know what kind of things Cage Intelligence had pulled her into; and he didn't know why she wanted him on board, now, after so much time had passed.

"I have something I need to do this afternoon," she said.

"Okay."

She tried a smile. It turned down a bit at the corners. "You're not being paid by the hour, Tom. Your time is your own."

He nodded. There was someone he should see, and today was as good a day as any.

21

In the afternoon, Tom gassed up the Town Car and drove to Port Hope, a town of sixteen thousand people south of Peterborough on the shore of Lake Ontario. It was an easy drive, straight down Highway 28, and it gave him time to build up a sense of dread toward what he was facing. He turned on the CD player and tried to listen to more of *Mirage* but found he wasn't in the mood and turned it off again.

Birchwoods Manor was a long-term care facility on Highway 2, just outside of the town. It was a single-storey building on a five-acre parcel of land bordering on a forest, hence the name. There were plenty of empty parking spots out front when he got there.

He'd been here once before, but that was more than a year ago and he wasn't sure what to expect. The facility was staffed by people from the community, many of whom had relatives among the residents, and he remembered it as a calm, friendly place. Still, his feet were dragging as he signed the guest book and passed through the central atrium toward the east wing.

Unsure of where to go, he stopped a passing personal support worker whose tag said that her name was Wendy.

"I'm looking for Will Eaton."

Wendy turned, pointing. "He's in his room right now, I think. Twenty-three. East wing."

"Thanks." Tom walked past a table where residents were playing a card game with a staff member who encouraged them in a loud, kind voice.

Eyes followed him from the table, from a nearby cluster of wheelchairs, and from a line of armchairs against the wall. He passed a central nursing station and started down the East Wing, tracking the room numbers.

As he approached Room 23, he heard a voice rising above the buzz of activity around him. It was a male voice, shrill and strident.

"I don't want to! Go away!"

Tom's feet felt like lead, and there was a sinking feeling in the pit of his stomach.

"Go away, goddamned Chinese bitch!"

He stopped outside the open door as a PSW walked out and smiled at him. Her black hair was pulled back in a short pigtail. According to the badge pinned to her smock, her name was Jane.

"Here to see Mr. Eaton?"

"Yes, but . . ."

"It's okay, he was just getting toileted and we're changing him right now. Little accident. You can wait; it won't be long." She marched off down the corridor, wiry and purposeful.

Tom leaned against the far wall, far enough away from the door that he couldn't see into the room. He could hear another woman's voice, presumably another PSW, coaxing Will to co-operate with her.

"Just lift your arms, Willie, that's a good boy."

"Let go!"

"That's it. Thanks, Willie. Now we'll just slip this on. That's right, put your hand through there."

Tom listened to low, throaty laughter that ran down and up the scale, ending in a wordless shriek. It was the voice of insanity. He felt sick at heart. He pushed away from the wall and was about to leave when the second PSW emerged from the room.

"Here to see Mr. Eaton?"

"Yeah, but . . ."

"He's all ready for you now." She waved an airy hand and went down the corridor into the next room.

Setting his jaw, Tom walked into Room 23.

The man sitting in the upholstered chair inside the door was long and thin. His white hair was neatly combed but needed a trim. He wore a blue plaid shirt, grey track pants, and corduroy slippers over white tube socks. He stared straight ahead, lip curled, jaw clenched, eyes narrowed. There was no other chair in the room, so Tom sat down on the edge of the bed.

"How are you doing, Will?"

The man muttered something, his eyes unfocused.

Will Eaton was originally from Brighton, a small farming community just down the road from here. He joined the OPP in 1968 and spent a number of years as a provincial constable in the Northwest Region with the Kenora detachment. After stints in bomb disposal and crisis negotiation, he transferred into Tactical and Rescue, shortly after the TRUs were first organized in 1975.

When Tom was assigned to Kenora as a fresh-faced rookie, he ran into Will from time to time. They became friends. When Tom left the region to work as a detective constable in Grey County, Will was already in his second year as regional director of support, but their friendship continued. When Tom finally arrived at GHQ as a staff sergeant assigned to manage the section in Behavioural Sciences responsible for ViCLAS, the Violent Crime Linkage Analysis System, Will was a superintendent, in command of field support. After briefly serving as deputy commissioner of Traffic Safety and Operational Support, Will retired shortly after his sixty-fifth birthday. Only five years ago.

Despite the difference in age and the fact that Will's passion was tactical response while Tom's had always been homicide investigation, they remained close friends throughout Tom's career. Will was his mentor, the one from whom he invariably sought advice and guidance, the one who listened while he rambled on about a case that was particularly baffling or especially horrific.

Will's even temper, his quiet smile, and his light sense of humour had never failed Tom whenever he needed to talk to someone. During the rough patches of Tom's career, Will was always there as his guardian angel, his rabbi. The one he felt closest to among all his colleagues.

Will looked into Tom's eyes suddenly and said, "I need to do something. When were you here?"

"I just got here a few minutes ago, Will."

"The dog. He's out."

"I think he's back in, now, Will. It's okay."

"Up and down the gullied night. Wax melts the trees. Goddamn it. I hate it all."

"I know, Will. I'm sorry."

Will closed his eyes and leaned his head back. His face was very pale and dotted with liver spots. He slowly raised his hand, as though to run his fingers through his white widow's peak in an old, familiar gesture, but lowered it again into his lap, palm up. As Tom sat there, watching him, his thin, purple lips parted. He began to breathe through his mouth.

Shortly after his sixty-fourth birthday, Will began to show the signs of early-onset Alzheimer's disease, but at first no one understood what was happening. He became indecisive and failed to understand the various options staff presented to him to solve the everyday problems which invariably crop up in a bureaucratic environment. He lost track of dates and times of meetings, could no longer do arithmetic in his head, and experienced surprising spikes of anger. His staff thought he was distracted by something, perhaps connected to his ex-wife in Oshawa or his two sons in British Columbia.

After he got lost driving home one day, however, it became apparent what was going on. He lived only fifteen minutes away from the GHQ campus, but somehow lost his way. Three hours after leaving work, he called Tom from a restaurant in Gravenhurst, half an hour from Orillia, asking for help. He had no idea where he was or how to get home.

As Tom stared at Will now, watching his eyeballs flutter beneath paper-thin lids, he fervently wished he hadn't come. He'd thought, idiotically, that maybe he could talk to him one more time about a case.

As a matter of fact, he'd bent Will's ear several times on the Bush murders. Will had seen the merit in pursuing Joseph Kohl as a suspect and agreed that they should press Elina Blomquist particularly hard. If Kohl's alibi cracked, they'd definitely have him where they wanted him. But it had held up, and the case fell apart. Will had felt particularly bad that he'd supported an approach which hadn't panned out, but he'd had plenty of company and Tom didn't hold it against him.

"What did we miss, Will?" Tom stared down at his fists

now, clenched tightly between his knees. "We overlooked something. Or someone. Who the hell was it?"

Will began to snore.

"Sorry, Will," he whispered. "Sorry."

It was stupid to have come. Stupid to have expected Will to be there for him one more time. Stupid to have thought that time had stood still for Will Eaton while he was in here, that the damage to his brain would have stopped happening once he'd arrived at a safe place with nice people and daily care.

Stupid, Tom, and selfish.

Once, when Tom had returned to a crime scene on a different case and was frustrated to have found it all changed around, things gone and new things added, Will had smiled at him and said that he had unrealistic expectations of the universe.

"It's like this, Tommy," he'd said. "You walk up to the bank of a river and you look at the water flowing by, on its way to the ocean far away. You notice sticks floating on the surface, a leaf, little eddies and whirlpools. Then you turn around and walk away, but you change your mind and go back for another look. You have to understand you're not looking at the same water. The water you looked at before is gone. This is different water. Different sticks, different leaves, different eddies and whirlpools. That's life, Tommy. As soon as you turn your back, it moves on without you."

As cops went, Will could be unusually Zen about things when he wanted to be. "And the point is, Will?"

"Stay in the moment. Experience it as fully as you can. Get as much out of each single moment as you can, because as soon as you blink, it's gone, man. It's gone."

Tom glanced at his watch and decided to give it ten more minutes. As a favour to an old friend. In case he woke up and wanted someone there with him.

The time crawled. Jane paused in the doorway, saw that Will was asleep, and gave Tom a quick smile and a thumbs-up.

Will stirred, his hand flopping once on the arm of the chair. Then he grew still again, snoring quietly. Tom reached out, hesitated, and gripped Will's hand. It was dry, papery, but warm. He held it for a moment, feeling the bones and the thick knuckles under his palm. He squeezed, squeezed again, and then let go.

A resident passed the doorway in her wheelchair, shuffling her feet on the floor to move herself along the corridor. She looked in and smiled.

Tom checked his watch again. Only three and a half minutes had passed. It had felt like an eternity. He couldn't take any more.

"Later, Will," He whispered, easing up off the edge of the bed. He touched his friend on the knee and left the room.

In the corridor he passed a nurse who said, "He's having one of his better days today. Are you his brother?"

"Brother in arms, I guess you could say. We worked together."

"He talks all the time about his brother, that's why I asked."

As far as Tom knew, Will Eaton didn't have a brother. He had a sister who was three years older and lived in Australia, if she was still alive.

"Does he get any visitors?"

She shook her head. "You're the first I've seen."

"He started getting the anger spikes just before he retired," Tom said, "but he was always an extremely good man. A really nice guy."

She nodded. "It's part of the dementia. Along with the loss of body control, the aphasia, and all the rest of it."

"Aphasia?"

"Progressive damage to the speech centre. First they have difficulty thinking of a word, then they constantly use the wrong words so that nothing makes sense, then they yell a lot, then they eventually go quiet altogether."

Tom stepped back. "Thanks for taking care of him."

"It's what we do. Have a good day."

Out in the parking lot, he got into the Town Car and sat behind the wheel for several minutes with the keys still in his hand. He was surprised to find his eyesight blurring. He wanted a drink, very badly.

Even more, though, he wanted his friend back.

Unfortunately, the Will Eaton he'd known was no longer there. Tom had turned his back, and Will had gone.

Cursing softly, he wiped at his tears and drove away.

22

On the way back to Peterborough, Tom received a text message on his personal cellphone. He pulled over onto the shoulder of the highway to read it. It was from Rick Thompson, an old contact in regional intelligence. The text said that he was in the city and wanted to meet with Tom at a location they'd used before. Tom texted back that he'd be there.

He picked up coffee at a drive-through and continued east along Lansdowne Street to the Memorial Centre, the large arena that was home to the local major junior hockey team, the Peterborough Petes. He turned onto Lock Street and pulled into the parking area behind the building. Since it was summer, there wasn't much going on in the arena, and the only other vehicle in the lot was a dirty grey pickup truck. Tom parked next to it, grabbed the coffee, and slid into the passenger side of the truck.

"Tommy," Rick Thompson said, extending his hand, "how the hell are you?"

Tom shook his hand, smiling. "Not bad, Rick. Long

time, no see. You're looking great."

"Fuck you." Now that he'd reached his mid-forties, Thompson had put on quite a bit of weight. His straw-coloured hair was rapidly thinning, his face was lined, and his eyes looked tired.

Accepting one of the coffees, he flashed a quick grin. "Don't bullshit an old bullshitter. I hear you've had a bit of excitement lately."

"You could say that." Tom sipped his coffee. Passable.

Thompson shifted behind the steering wheel. "I can't stay. A mutual friend of ours said you'd reached out for info on these guys you're working for."

"The Cage Intelligence Group." Tom understood Thompson was referring to Tracy Drummond. Trace must have gone out to his network for more information after Tom had called him on Wednesday night.

"The very same." Thompson's eyes roved around the parking lot over the rim of his coffee cup. "They're a spooky crew, Tommy. I assume you know what you're doing, but our friend thought there might be information you didn't have that you could use."

"Such as?"

"As I understand it, the Canadian half of the company concentrates on investigations, headed by your friend Natalie Stone. The UK half is intelligence, run over there by a guy named Nicholas West. As president, Derek Winter, Natalie's husband, oversees both halves for Sean Cage. Okay so far?"

Tom nodded.

"Word is that one of West's ops in eastern Europe spilled over onto Stone's turf here in Canada. Some major stuff went down a month ago that left a trail of wreckage from Pearson International Airport all the way down to Niagara Falls. Winter had to pull some major strings to contain it. I don't know what exactly happened, but we ended up having to clean up a few messes for Cage down there."

Tom understood him to mean that "we" referred to the OPP. "I didn't hear anything."

Thompson glanced over. "Exactly. But Tommy, what I'm being told is that it isn't over. Some kind of network got rolled up when Winter IDed somebody important coming into the country through PIA, but your people only exposed the western half, the one running down through the Golden Horseshoe. Word is, there's also an eastern half running up the St. Lawrence to Montreal, with a hub in Ottawa, that's still dark."

"Are we talking Islamic terrorists?"

"I don't know for sure, but my understanding is that it's Russian."

Tom studied the deserted parking lot for a moment, drinking coffee. "Just so I'm clear on this. There's no connection to the case I'm currently working?"

"No, man. The connection is, you're now working for people who just stirred up a fucking shitstorm. Your old friends, myself included, don't want to see you caught in it, that's all. Savvy?"

Tom nodded. Now he thought he understood the presence of Charlie Danko as a driver *cum* bodyguard and Jeremy's assignment to keep track of everyone's whereabouts. The organization must be on high alert, ready for anything.

Thompson started the engine. "Gotta run, man."

"Thanks, Rick. I appreciate the heads-up."

"What the hell are friends for?" Thompson grinned. "Stay safe."

"You too." Tom opened the door.

"Thanks for the coffee, Tommy."

"Any time." He got back into the Town Car and waited until Thompson had been gone for five minutes before starting the engine.

What the hell had he gotten himself into?

23

The next morning Tom found an e-mail in his Inbox from Jim Woods. Taking a bite of toast, he put on his reading glasses and opened the message.

> *As promised, here's an estimate for the work on your church. I think you'll find it very reasonable. Hope we can do business together.*

Tom clicked on the attached document and scanned through it. The estimate included replacing the existing electrical panel to accommodate an upgrade to 200-amp service and installing new wiring, baseboard heaters, outlets, switches, several large ceiling fans Tom had bought at the Home Depot, and two outdoor outlets, one at the side to plug in his car in winter and another at the back. It also included outdoor spotlights, front and back, and everything else they'd discussed. The amount quoted was well within what he'd budgeted, so he figured he'd probably go with this guy and get it done quickly.

He took out his company cellphone. Last night he'd decided it was rather annoying to be carrying two phones around, so he'd texted Pamela the company number, copied his contacts from his personal phone into the new one, and made the switch. Paranoid or not, he preferred to keep things simple.

He called Jade, and was once again surprised when she answered.

"Hello?" She sounded groggy.

"Did I wake you up?"

"Yes."

"Did you check out the references on the electrician, Woods?"

"I left messages. They haven't called back."

"Okay, well, call them again, Jade. His quote looks good and I may go ahead and get him to do it."

"Jesus. When I get up."

"All right, Jade. Look, I've got Pamela's Lexus down here again, okay? I have to gas it up. I'll bring it up later."

"Whatever."

"This is a company phone I'm using right now. You can reach me at this number for the next while."

"What*ever*."

Tom ended the call. Immediately the phone began to vibrate. He looked at the call display and answered. "This is Faust."

"Jeremy's located Elina Blomquist," Natalie said. "She runs a trailer park on Pigeon Lake."

He still needed to shower and get dressed, but he said, "Great. I'll be ready in fifteen."

"We'll send you the co-ordinates. Can you get there yourself? I have a few errands to run."

"Sure, no problem. Anything I can help you with?"

"No. I'll talk to you later."

The Sunny Daze Resort turned out to be a seasonal campground and cottage rental business on Fire Route 71, just south of where the channel known as Gannons Narrows connected Buckhorn Lake to Pigeon Lake. The trailer park had thirty sites for campers with metered hydro, septic, and boat launch access. There were also six two-bedroom waterfront cottages available to rent. A seventh structure, first in line as Tom drove through the gate and down the lane to the lake, had a sign on the front identifying it as the office.

Tom got out of the Lexus and looked around. The grounds were tidy and well kept. The trailer park looked full, and all the cottages within sight down the lane appeared to have cars parked beside them. The neon "Open" sign above the office door was illuminated.

The office was a typical set-up with a desk and chair, computer, and filing cabinets, but the décor had been deliberately chosen to appeal to the kind of customer from which Sunny Daze made their money. The wood-panelled walls were covered with fish mounted on plaques and displays of vintage lures and fishing rods. Stuffed birds lined the tops of the filing cabinets. A large set of deer antlers hung above a doorway leading into the main part of the building.

A woman appeared in the doorway. In her mid-fifties, she wore a short-sleeved white blouse and green pants that gave her a summery look. Her skin was deeply tanned and her shoulder-length hair was tinted back to a close approximation of its original auburn colour.

"You're in luck, I just had a cancellation if you're looking for a cottage."

"Are you Ms. Blomquist?"

"Who's asking?"

Tom handed her a business card. "My company is

consulting with the OPP on a review of the Bush family murders. Are you Elina Blomquist, formerly of Apsley?"

"That's me." She glanced at the card and sat down on the corner of her desk. "Do I know you?"

"We met seventeen years ago."

"I don't remember you. Good-looking guy like you, you'd think I would."

"I was with the OPP, investigating the murders of the Bush family near Apsley."

"A cop. That explains it."

"Sorry?"

"Why I didn't bother remembering you."

"I work for the Cage Intelligence Group now. I need to ask you a few questions about your connection to Joseph Kohl."

"Mmm-hmm." Looking him up and down, she eased off the desk and sat down in the chair. "I hear he finally got what was coming to him. Too bad."

"When was the last time you saw him?"

"Joe? Not since the day my husband beat me up and walked out. Thanks in no small part to you and your Gestapo buddies."

"When was that?"

"Let's see." She touched her chin with the tip of her middle finger and frowned at the ceiling. "That would be about an hour after the cops forced their way into my house and pushed me around until I told them Joe was with me the night those people got their throats cut."

She looked at Tom and tapped the finger against her chin to make sure he was getting the message.

Tom pulled over a folding chair and sat down. "You're saying you haven't seen Joseph Kohl in seventeen years?"

"That's right."

"Were you telling the truth when you said Kohl was

with you that night?"

Blomquist gave him a long stare, then shrugged. "Sure."

"How long were you having an affair with him?"

"Let me explain something to you." Blomquist crossed her legs. "Joe was a creep. He picked out a girl, went after her, and didn't give up until she gave him what he wanted. He played this act of being a nice guy, very religious, sympathetic and willing to listen. He picked out girls who were having trouble at home. Know what I mean? Then he was always around, always available when she needed to talk, just needed to get out of the house for a break. He worked on her and worked on her until she gave in and went to bed with him."

"Is that what happened to you?"

"Sure. The guy I was living with at the time was an asshole. He knocked me around, spent all his time with his fishing and hunting pals, and spent all our money on booze and blow. I was thinking about leaving, but the place was mine, right? I inherited it from my grandfather. So why should I leave? But I couldn't get rid of him, the frigging leech. I was stuck."

"How'd you meet Joseph Kohl?"

"Through a friend." Blomquist laughed at the expression on his face. "No no, she was probably the only one he *wasn't* balling. Patsy Walters, her name was. She was a tiny, mousy thing who worshipped her husband. She bought into Joe's line of religious crap and thought I might feel better if I started coming out to some of their Bible classes."

Tom looked at a stuffed mallard duck sitting on top of the filing cabinet. The green feathers on its head were iridescent, beautiful. Unlike most of his former colleagues, Tom didn't like hunting or fishing. He preferred to look at wildlife when it was still living and moving around.

"Have the police questioned you about where you were on Monday? When Kohl was killed?"

"Sure. I was here. Working. I can prove it."

"Oh?"

She pointed at a large walleye mounted on the wall behind her.

Tom had given it only a cursory glance before, but now that he took a longer, second look he noticed its left eye, the one facing the room, was not the usual glass orb used by a taxidermist. "A pinhole camera."

"My security system for the office." She laughed. "I gave your cop buddies a dupe of the recording to shut them up and get rid of them. Last Monday was a busy day. Any other stupid questions?"

"Just one. Tell me again, was Kohl with you the night the Bush family was murdered?"

"Yes. Yes. Yes. He was. It makes my skin crawl, just thinking about it. I'd rather just forget about it. I've put all that stuff behind me."

She waved a hand around the room. "I own a hundred per cent of this place, free and clear. No mortgage. No partners. Just me. I'm making money hand over fist, and it feels great. So maybe you can understand why I just want to be left alone about all that bullshit from the past."

Tom stood up. "Thanks very much for your time."

Outside, Tom's phone began to vibrate. He didn't recognize the number, but answered. "This is Faust."

"He called, Faust. He called me. I think he's coming here."

"Who is this?"

"It's me, it's me. Christ, Faust. He called. He said I opened my big mouth and I'd have to pay for it."

"Little? Is that you?"

"I didn't say anything, man. I didn't tell you any fucking *thing.*"

"Who called you, Little?"

"I can't talk right now. I have to get out of here. I'll call you later, okay?"

"Little—"

The line went dead.

24

It was a thirty-minute drive from Gannons Narrows to Lindsay, and Tom made it in just under twenty. When he turned down the side street on which Little lived, he saw no activity at all. There was a car parked along the curb several doors up from Little's house, but it was unoccupied. Curtains were drawn in the front windows on both sides of the street. It was still an hour before noon on a Sunday morning. Perhaps people were at church, or sleeping in.

As Tom approached Little's house, he could see that the garage door was closed. Unlike yesterday, when he and Natalie had been here to interview him.

The front door, however, was standing wide open. There was something on the front lawn. Tom's adrenaline spiked. He knew what he was going to find.

He got out of the car and crossed the sidewalk onto the lawn. He crept forward, keeping a practised eye on where he was stepping, until he could see everything.

Gerald Little was sprawled on the grass with his arms out and his legs spread, in the same angel-like pose Tom had seen seventeen years ago. His golf shirt and jeans were soaked in blood that still looked fresh. He'd been stabbed in the stomach and his throat had been cut. His eyes were open, staring up at the sky above him.

Something had been shoved into his mouth. Tom's stomach thumped as he realized that Little's zipper was down and his belt was undone. His jeans rode low on his hips, showing blood-soaked boxer shorts.

Tom looked at the open front door of the house. A broad smear of blood led from inside, across the porch, down the stairs, and across the lawn to where Little had been posed.

Tom wanted badly to go inside. He knew that Little must have been killed in the kitchen. It made the most sense. The Bushmaster would have forced him there, wanting to maintain the pattern of his killings. He took a step in that direction but stopped himself.

The timing of the thing suddenly struck home. Little had been killed less than twenty minutes ago. The scene was still very fresh. Was it possible the Bushmaster was still inside?

He looked up the street at the parked car he'd passed, and saw a young woman getting in behind the wheel. He trotted to the sidewalk as the engine started. The car made a quick U-turn and drove away.

"Hey! Hey!" He ran down the sidewalk, waving his arms.

The car reached the corner and swung right, disappearing out of sight.

But Tom remembered the licence plate number, having memorized it out of habit as he'd driven past.

He looked at the house again. What was in the back yard? He and Natalie had not gone inside. They'd remained in the garage while interviewing Little, and so he had no idea what might be out back. Maybe a deck off the dining room, a fenced-in lawn, a swimming pool? Beyond it was probably the back yard of a house on the next street over.

If the Bushmaster was already gone and the house was empty, it was possible he'd left through the rear, avoiding the front altogether. It would be necessary to canvass the houses back there, as well as the ones on this street.

He stopped at the edge of the lawn, catching himself.

Not his job.

Not his crime scene.

He took out his cellphone and made the call.

25

"Tell me again what you did this morning."

Tom ran a hand through his hair, willing himself to remain patient. He'd been a guest of the City of Kawartha Lakes Police Service for about three hours now, all of it spent in this tiny interview room, most of it sitting by himself, waiting for someone to come in and question him.

Detective Shane Benson was a short, stocky cop with a brush cut and narrow, dark eyes. He sat on the edge of the metal desk with his arms folded. "From the beginning again, Mr. Faust."

Tom walked through his whereabouts and activities this morning for the third time. When he was finished, he saw Benson involuntarily glance up at the camera in the corner of the ceiling. Tom understood that the gesture meant Benson was about to shift gears.

"Let's cut the bullshit. You and I both know the truth, Faust. If you'll just explain what it's all about, why you keep doing this, you'll feel a hell of a lot better. I've seen it happen so many times."

Tom leaned back, forcing a smile. "You've seen what happen, Detective?"

Benson smiled back with equal insincerity. "Confession's good for the soul. Why'd you have to kill Little? Was he going to pop on you?"

"Were there any eyewitnesses? Did anyone see the guy, either coming or going?"

"It's part of the profile, isn't it? You serial killers like to insert yourselves into the investigation, keep tabs on everything, steer us in the wrong direction. Like you did with that hanging, right? Pretending you just happened to find the guy and calling it in, like any other innocent witness."

"You've run my background. You know who I am."

"Yeah." Benson shrugged. "You had thirty-five years in when you pulled the pin. Pretty good cover for all your sicko activities, I'd say."

"You fucking bastard."

"Pardon me?"

"You heard me."

"Sure I did. And you know what? I don't take it personally. We've both been around the block a few times; we know how this works. You string me a bunch of bullshit, I pretend to take it seriously, we do the dance, and sooner or later I show you a file with all the physical evidence in it and you get to decide whether you want to confess or fight it out in court. Either way, you lose and I win. But it's up to you."

"I'm not your guy, Benson. You're wasting time."

"It's all pensionable service."

The door opened and a female uniformed officer stuck her head inside. "Detective Benson, Inspector Lynch wants you to bring him down to the boardroom."

"We're in the middle of something."

"Uh, I think the inspector and the chief are waiting for you now."

"Shit." Benson got up off the desk and followed her out of the room.

Tom waited. Less than five minutes later, the detective came back and put a hand on Tom's elbow. "Let's go."

They went down the hall and into another, much larger room. A tall, gaunt forty-something in a baggy brown suit came around the long boardroom table and stuck out his hand. "I'm Inspector Jack Lynch, Criminal Investigation Branch. This is Chief Fredericks."

Tom shook hands with a small, white-haired man in a neat charcoal suit.

"Gavin and I were just talking about the connection between this homicide of ours and the one he's in charge of," Fredericks said.

Gavin Elliott nodded from the other side of the table. He looked tired and stressed. Tom sat down. Lynch took the chair across from him, next to Gavin. Benson left, closing the door behind him.

"I've explained to our friends here the contract the OPP has with Cage Intelligence," Gavin said, "and why you and Natalie interviewed Gerald Little yesterday. What happened this morning, Tom? Why did you come back up here again?"

"Have you talked to Natalie?"

Gavin shook his head. "I couldn't reach her."

"I see." Tom took a moment to think it through. He trusted Gavin Elliott with his life. It bothered him, though, that Natalie was suddenly incommunicado. Signing a contract with Cage Intelligence apparently didn't guarantee that they would have his back whenever he needed them. An interesting factoid to be filed away for future reference.

It left him uncertain about how much he was able to discuss openly in front of the Kawartha Lakes police at this point in the investigation. However, he trusted Gavin. And he trusted his own ability to handle other law enforcement agencies.

"Nat called me up this morning," he said, "to tell me that Elina Blomquist had been located. She runs a campground at Gannons Narrows. Nat said she had some errands to run and asked me to do the interview myself. So I did."

The door opened behind Tom. Benson rounded the end of the table and dropped into the seat next to Lynch.

"Who?" Chief Fredericks frowned. "Who's this Blomquist person?"

"An important witness in the Bush mass murder cold case," Gavin said. "Cage Intelligence is doing a review, as I said, and re-interviewing people."

His eyes moved back to Tom. "And?"

"When I was leaving the campground Little called. I'd given him my card yesterday. He said, 'He called, Faust. He called me. I think he's coming here.'"

"That was it?"

"And something about payback for opening his big mouth. Which he didn't really do. The guy pretty much stonewalled us. Again."

"And you're sure it was Gerald Little?"

"Reasonably sure. I'd given him my card. You've got my phone; check the call log."

Detective Benson leaned forward. "Did he identify himself as Gerald Little?"

Tom thought about it. "No. He said, 'It's me, Faust,' and I said, "Is this you, Little?' or words to that effect. He just kept on talking."

"Did you recognize the voice as Gerald Little's?"

"I thought I did."

"What about the incoming number? Did you recognize it?"

"No, but I don't know Little's number. The interview was set up by Cage Intelligence beforehand."

Benson looked down the table at Lynch and Chief Fredericks. "We found the call on his phone, all right. The number's unregistered, which means it was likely made from a burner. We'll know more when we get the warrant."

Gavin frowned. "A burner?"

"Maybe your friend here is stringing all of us along. Maybe he's got a partner. Sometimes these guys work in pairs—"

Gavin slapped his hand on the table. "That's absurd, and you know it. Tom, is it possible it wasn't Little? Think, man."

"I'm thinking, goddamn it. Yes. Yes, it's possible it wasn't Little. The voice was familiar, though. I thought it was him."

"What if it wasn't?"

Tom stared at his friend as the possibility sank in.

"Christ, Gavin. It was him. It was *him*. The Bushmaster."

26

"I'm getting a little tired of having my cars impounded," Tom said.

Gavin glanced over. "Actually, it's Pamela's car."

"Yeah, true enough." Tom tried to smile, but it came out a little flat. "Thanks for being there."

"It's my job to be there." His eyes on the highway in front of them, Gavin scratched his cheek. Tom recognized the gesture as an indicator that he was choosing his words carefully.

"Before they brought you in, Chief Fredericks and I agreed this needs to be treated as a multi-jurisdictional major case. Which means major additional headaches for me on the administrative side. It'll also mean we bring in Benson as part of the team."

Tom laughed shortly. "Great. He can't stand me."

"Neither can Armour. They'll get along well."

"Thank God Bell cuts me some slack."

"Don't take anything for granted, Tom." Gavin let a few moments pass, concentrating on his driving, before he shrugged a shoulder. "We've pretty much wrapped up the early stages of the Kohl investigation. Ident has processed all the physical evidence from both scenes, Armour and Bell have interviewed everyone worth talking to, and now we've got a second one. It's time to bring in the cold case, because I think you and I both know the Bushmaster is active again."

"Whoever the hell he is."

"Yeah."

"Tomorrow," Gavin said, "I want you and Natalie to sit down with us and go through what you've done so far. Where is she, by the way?"

"I haven't a damned clue." Without a cellphone once again, Tom would have to wait until he got home and retrieved his personal phone from the charger on the kitchen counter before he could try to re-establish contact with her. "Tell me something."

"If I can."

"It's my understanding from what you said before that bringing Cage Intelligence in for this case review was your idea. That you reached out to Natalie and not the other way around."

Gavin said nothing, watching the road.

"Why'd you do that?"

Gavin shrugged. "It was a way to bring you in."

"Okay." Tom hesitated. "How much do you know about Cage? Do you trust them, Gav?"

"It's a good question. I'm not sure how to answer it."

Tom waited.

"Natalie's a friend. She's intelligent, experienced. She's a friend of yours. The company's record on cold case review is pretty good."

"McGraw. Elliott Lake."

Gavin nodded. "Kate still talks about it. Their profiler,

Baker, really helped her out. Natalie made it happen."

"Okay. They're fucking weird, though, Gav. There's something about that company, those people, that gives me the creeps. Don't you feel it?"

"Sure. But for the most part, it's not my concern. We contracted for their services, we expect them to deliver something in return. The rest I just have to compartmentalize." He glanced over. "While you were cooling your heels in the interview room, they brought in Little's wife and daughter. They were en route from Oakville when Benson reached them."

"What did they have to say?"

"Lynch got her to admit there was something going on with Little, all these years, that he wouldn't talk about. For quite a while she thought he was having an affair."

Tom snorted.

"It happens. We've both seen it, many times. But after a while she realized it wasn't that sort of thing. He was scared about something. Afraid, all the time. He had a security system installed in the house. Changed phone numbers. Stuff like that."

Tom thought about it for a moment before turning to look at Gavin. "Why now? If it's the Bushmaster, why has he suddenly started killing again, after seventeen years? What the hell's happened to set him off again?"

"That's the five-dollar question." Gavin huffed out a breath. "If I follow my nose, I'd say he went after Kohl because the guy started up his church bullshit again, and the Bushmaster really, really hated that stuff. As for Little, I'd guess he saw the Bushmaster that night, kept his mouth shut, but when you and Nat went to interview him the Bushmaster knew he'd probably end up talking, sooner or later. Hence the dick in his mouth."

"The simplest solution that fits the known facts."

"Yeah. Occam's Razor."

"He's had Little under surveillance. Probably for a long time. Maybe the whole time."

"Makes sense."

"Why not kill him right away, get it over with?"

"I don't know, Tom. I'm not there yet."

"I'm not sure I mentioned to you that I found a bug on my landline Thursday night."

Gavin looked over. "I wasn't aware."

"It was very clumsy. Open, like giving me the finger. Nat swears it wasn't Cage, so I'm thinking it was him."

After a moment, Gavin said, "He's kept tabs on you. That's a given."

Tom nodded. Gavin was aware of the taunting condolence cards the Bushmaster had sent every year on the anniversary of Linda's death. At first they'd been addressed to his home in Orillia. When he sold the house and moved into an apartment, the cards had followed him there. Each year he'd dutifully sent them to the lab for processing, which of course had turned up nothing. Afterward they were entered as evidence into the Bush case file. Last November, after his retirement, he'd received another card at his current address here in Peterborough County. He'd sent it on to Gavin to add to the pile.

"Unfinished business."

"Yeah."

"Man," Tom said, "I *hate* unfinished business."

27

That evening Tom took the Town Car to Bridgenorth to pick up a few things. He bought a lottery ticket and a couple bags of salty snacks for the evening, and then he returned home. Pulling into the carport, he thought he might break down and have a quick drink before bedtime.

When the current president of the United States had embarked on his quixotic trade war against Canada, despite ongoing negotiations to modernize the North American Free Trade Agreement, Tom sat up and took notice when the Canadian government announced that retaliatory measures would include a tariff on Kentucky bourbon. The next time he was in the liquor store, he splurged on a bottle of 1792, a product of the Barton distillery in Bardstown, Kentucky, named for the year in which the state joined the union. It was his favourite sipping bourbon, and at the time he'd thought it might be his last chance to stash some away at an affordable price.

He got out of the Town Car and leaned against the fender, hesitating. Although it had been a very stressful day, he didn't really need a drink. He could taste the liquorice and cream tones over the rye kick, though, and thought it would help him relax. Just a couple of fingers in a glass. Then off to bed.

He pushed away from the car and abruptly stopped moving.

Something was wrong.

The door looked all right. Undisturbed. Nothing in the carport seemed out of place. But there was something in the air. A vibration, almost, or a lingering presence.

He listened intently, but heard nothing other than the sound of crickets. Everything was still.

He breathed deeply.

Something in the air.

Did he smell . . . disinfectant? Bleach?

Something.

He moved slowly toward the door. He owned a personal firearm, a SIG Sauer P226 for which he had a licence and a registration certificate. It was currently stored in a gun safe in his bedroom, where it was supposed to be. Wishing it was in his hand right now, he tried the doorknob.

It turned, and the door opened.

He crept up the stairs into the kitchen. It was after eight o'clock in the evening and getting close to sundown, but he could clearly see that someone was sitting on a high stool at his kitchen island.

"Hi, Tom."

"Christ." He hit the switch inside the doorway, turning on the wagon wheel lights.

Natalie smiled weakly at him. Her handbag lay on its side on the island in front of her. She slowly drew her hand out of it. The hand was empty.

"Jesus, Nat, you scared the shit out of me."

"Sorry. We're still on a security window that has about

twelve hours left. I need to sort of stay under the radar until then."

"I don't understand. There's no car outside. How the hell'd you get here?"

"Charlie brought me. He'll be back," she glanced at her wristwatch, "in ten minutes."

Tom looked at a dark spot on the arm of her light blue blazer. "You're bleeding, Nat."

"Shit." Her hand moved toward the spot but didn't touch it. "It's all right; don't worry about it."

Tom understood now why he'd smelled disinfectant out in the carport. "What happened?"

"I zigged when I should have zagged, and it nicked the skin over my bicep. Charlie's a very good field surgeon, although I think he'll need to take another look at it."

"Christ, you've been shot?"

She tried the smile again. It was still weak. "Need to know, Tom. And you don't need to know, believe me."

"Are you sure?" He sat down on a stool across from her. "It looks serious. Maybe I should help."

"No. Definitely not. This is *not* the sort of thing you can help with. Sorry. I should have stayed back, myself, and let the experts handle it, but since it was about me—" She broke off. "No. Leave it at that. Look, I'm sorry I wasn't there for you today."

"Well, it looks like you were otherwise occupied."

"Tell me about Little."

Tom ran through it all for her, from the phone call he'd received at Gannons Narrows to the discovery of Little's body, the arrival of Kawartha Lakes police and his rather unfriendly interrogation by Detective Benson.

"I don't like being treated as a suspect," he ended.

"Thank goodness Gavin was there to set them straight. Do you think it was the Bushmaster who called you, and not Little?"

"Yeah. I left Little a card, remember? I wrote that phone number on the back of it. He must have found the card and called me, pretending to be Little."

"Why?"

"I don't know, so that I'd be the one to find the guy and call it in, I guess. Like Kohl, in my church. He wants me front and centre in this whole thing. For whatever reason."

"What does Gavin think?"

"He wants us to sit down with his team tomorrow and go through what we've covered so far in the case review. Wait." He frowned. "Is it possible he wants to pull us off and terminate the contract?"

"I don't know. Probably not. It would cost him. There's a penalty clause. He may want to redistribute assignments, though." She sighed, fatigued. "We'll find out tomorrow."

They looked at the kitchen door as the sound of a vehicle pulling into the driveway reached them from outside.

Natalie got to her feet, a little unsteadily. As she gathered up her handbag, Tom hurried around the table and took her arm.

"I'm okay," she said, gently disengaging from his grip. "Come in to the office for lunch tomorrow. We'll see where we stand."

"All right, Nat." He stepped back. "Are you sure you're okay?"

"Nothing a good shot of vodka won't settle," she said, walking carefully. She shifted the weight of her handbag and stopped. "Look, I'm sure this . . . other thing won't touch you, but it wouldn't hurt to stay frosty tonight. Know what I mean?"

He nodded as Charlie opened the door and came upstairs. Knowing what he now knew about Cage, he figured that a quiet review of his credit card purchases would have been included in their background check before offering him the contract. If so, they would have seen the frequent, regular purchases at the liquor store and put two and two together.

"All right," he said.

At the top of the stairs, Charlie reached out his hand. Natalie shook her head and edged past him. Charlie looked at Tom. His face held no expression, but his eyes were angry.

After they had gone, Tom looked at the cupboard door where the bottle of 1792 hid behind a box of corn flakes.

So much for that, he thought.

28

The following afternoon Gavin Elliott paid a visit to the Water Street offices of the Cage Intelligence Group. With him were Detective Constables Armour and Bell of the county crime unit, and Detective Shane Benson of the City of Kawartha Lakes Police Service. They sat down with Natalie and Tom to hash out where they were with the cold case review.

First, Bell put Tom through the wringer, questioning him extensively about his discovery of Gerald Little's body. Benson listened with a skeptical expression on his face but didn't interrupt.

Bell then took Tom and Natalie through their previous interview with Little. Natalie confirmed Tom's belief that Little was being evasive in his answers to their questions and that he was clearly nervous about something.

Armour then took over and walked them through their interview last Friday with Cecile Long. Tom answered questions about Cecile's connection to the original Bush family massacre, and Natalie covered the interview itself,

Cecile's answers, and their impressions of whether or not she was telling the truth.

Benson wanted to know more about Tom's whereabouts yesterday morning before receiving the call that he thought was coming from Gerald Little, so Gavin waved him on. Tom had already answered questions about his interview of Elina Blomquist, but where Benson hadn't bothered to hide his disbelief yesterday, he took a different tack this afternoon and went into greater detail. When Tom explained that Blomquist had confirmed Joseph Kohl's alibi for the Bush murders, and that he believed her, Gavin nodded.

Bell jumped back in, wanting to know more about the Bushmaster and why Tom believed he'd surveilled Gerald Little and was stalking Tom. He walked her through the conversation he'd had with Gavin yesterday in general terms, mentioning the condolence cards, the clumsy listening device on his landline, and the obvious attempt with both murders to bring Tom back into the forefront of the case.

"There's some kind of unfinished business," he concluded, as he'd done yesterday with Gavin. "I don't know what it is."

"Let's go back to Cecile Long," Gavin suggested.

Tom glanced at Natalie. She looked tired but gave no hint that she'd suffered a gunshot wound the day before. "All right," he said.

"Jim and Pat talked to her this morning," Gavin said. "She was home all day yesterday, and she took a while to remember who Gerald Little was. She lived in the basement of the Bush house for a while, and Little was the next-door neighbour, but she really didn't have a clue."

"That's right," Armour said. "There's no connection between her and what's going on right now. But she confirms what you just told us, that you had questions for her about James Bush and her son, Mark Long. Both individuals have been unaccounted for since the mass murder, so we'd like to know if you've done anything to follow up on either of them."

"Yes," Natalie said. "One of my staff members here on site is an experienced skip tracer. We're working on finding both of them as we speak."

"Would you be willing," Gavin said, "to continue with that over the next twenty-four to forty-eight hours? We're going to have our hands full for the short term."

Tom looked at Natalie. He understood that Gavin was telling them his team would be working with CKLPS in Lindsay to process the Little crime scene, analyze the physical evidence, and conduct ongoing interviews of witnesses, including the young woman who'd driven away from the scene. They'd tracked her down through the licence plate number Tom had memorized.

"Of course," Natalie said.

"The way we see it, Long and Bush are still part of the cold case, and if you could carry on with that, it'd help."

"Our pleasure."

Tom nodded at Natalie.

They were still on the case.

29

It was after dark when Tom finally got away from the office and left the city. The rush hour traffic heading north up Water Street had thinned out somewhat, but he still found himself following a trail of red taillights as the highway wound past the zoo and beyond the city limits. Ahead on the right, the lights of the Trent University campus glowed in the sky. He drove slowly, trying to reduce the stress that was giving him a slight headache.

He and Natalie had spent more than an hour with Jeremy, going over his efforts to date to track Mark Long and James Bush. So far, he'd come up with absolutely nothing.

As Cecile Long had said, her son had disappeared the year after the Bush massacre at the age of sixteen. Where he'd gone was a complete mystery. He'd vanished, leaving no trace whatsoever that Jeremy could pick up through his usual database sources. He'd tracked down Chris Long, the boy's father, in Ottawa and sent a local Cage operative to interview him on Saturday. The man hadn't seen his son in years and had no interest in his whereabouts or welfare.

Jeremy was beginning to wonder if Mark Long was dead.

Tom watched the red taillights of the cars ahead of him. He was much more interested in James Bush, and so far Jeremy was drawing another blank. After running away from foster care, the boy had also dropped completely off the grid. How old would he be now? Thirty years old?

He could be anyone.

Tom slowed at the turnoff onto Sixth Line Road and waited for a break in the southbound traffic. He made the turn and flicked on his high beams.

The road was narrow, with no shoulders to speak of, and the brush crowded in quite close on both sides for long stretches. More than once while driving along this stretch after dark he'd been forced to brake abruptly to avoid raccoons, skunks, and deer that appeared in his headlights without warning.

His rear-view mirror glowed as someone appeared behind him and switched on their high beams. The mirror dimmed automatically to reduce the glare. He reached a relatively clear part of the road, with rolling fields on either side, and accelerated until he was doing seventy kilometres an hour.

Passing the lights of a farm on the left, he topped a small rise. The vehicle behind him was close. Too close. Some asshole tailgating him after dark on a narrow road. Tom glanced again in the rear-view mirror and shook his head in aggravation.

It suddenly occurred to him that James Bush was close. He'd assumed a new identity, built a new life somewhere, and he'd returned to this area to resume his vendetta against everyone connected to the murder of his family. If—

The headlights behind him suddenly charged his back bumper and swung around. The vehicle began to pass.

Dickhead. You'll get us both killed.

He caught a glimpse of white or grey beside him, then the car shook as he was broadsided.

"What the *hell*—"

He was struck again. He fought to stay in control of the Town Car as it began to fishtail. His foot found the brake but he was struck once more and knocked violently sideways, the wheel flying out of his hand.

He was aware of a snake fence as he plunged through it, shards flying in the headlights, then there was a brief feeling of weightlessness as the car spun sideways and dropped into an irrigation ditch, striking the bottom with a finality that pounded him into the darkness of oblivion.

30

He awoke in a room with small electronic noises and a strange odour he couldn't place. His eyes opened enough to see that there was light. Sunlight, through a window.

He'd been aware of pain while approaching consciousness, and now it filled his head, forcing his eyes closed again. More pain seared in his left shoulder and shot down his arm into his hand. He groaned through dry lips.

"You're awake," someone said. It was a female voice, low-pitched and gentle.

He heard someone move to the side of his bed. A hand touched his right arm.

There was nothing in his mind except the pain. No names, no idea where he was or what had happened, no sense of time or place. His mind was an emptiness into which pain had been poured like hot molten steel.

It forced him back down into unconsciousness.

31

When he awoke again and opened his eyes, the blinds had been lowered and the light came from the ceiling. There were soft electronic noises, and he could smell an odour he recognized as institutional.

A woman sat in a chair next to him. She was young and beautiful. When she saw that he was awake and looking at her out of the corner of his eye, she came to the side of the bed and gently touched his forehead.

"Oh, Daddy, you're awake. I'm here, Daddy."

He knew her. He didn't know her name, or why he knew her. He knew he was glad to see her.

"Thirsty," he managed through dry lips.

"There's water right here, Daddy." She turned away and came back with a plastic tumbler. A straw poked at his lips. He opened his mouth and sucked. Water hit the back of his throat and went down. It felt good.

He tried to move his right hand to take the tumbler, so that he could drink on his own, but he didn't have the strength to lift it from the covers. He tried with his left hand and instantly regretted it, as pain shot through the hand and up his arm into his shoulder.

The straw went away. He managed to swallow the water left in his mouth without choking.

"Get some more rest, Daddy. I'll be right here the whole time."

As the pain modulated down to a dull ache, sleep seemed like an excellent idea.

"Okay," he mumbled.

As he drifted away, he thought, *Who the hell is she?*

32

He awoke in a darkened room. He heard the soft electronic noises made by monitoring equipment, and smelled the unmistakable odour of a hospital.

"Jesus," he murmured through dry lips.

Someone stirred in the darkness, and a hand touched his right arm. "Daddy? Are you awake?"

"Pam? What . . ."

"Oh, thank God." The hand squeezed his arm.

"Thirsty."

"I'll turn on the light, okay?" The sound of movement, and then an overhead panel illuminated the room. Pamela smiled at him, coming over to the bed with a plastic tumbler in her hand.

He sucked on the straw, grateful for the water splashing down his throat. Then dizziness hit him, and a wave of nausea. He forced the straw out of his mouth with his tongue. "Sick. Gonna."

"Oh. Here."

A bedpan materialized under his chin. He retched up

the water. When the spasms faded, he nodded and sank back onto the pillow.

"Sorry."

"Don't be silly, Daddy. You've thrown up a bunch of times already."

"I have?"

She stroked his forehead. "Don't worry about it. Don't worry about anything. You're all right. That's what matters."

It took him what seemed like forever to process her words. What matters? All right?

"Why are you here?"

"You had an accident, Daddy. Someone ran you off the road. Do you remember?"

"No." He tried to recall, but nothing connected to an accident came to mind. "Driving home. Dark. The university. Nothing." He closed his eyes, exhausted.

"Thank God for that much, anyway." She sat down on the edge of the bed. "You had temporary amnesia, but it seems to be going away. You didn't know me, or even who you were."

"I didn't?" He sighed. "I don't remember that."

She laughed, dabbing at tears with the cuff of her long-sleeved T-shirt. "Well, you wouldn't, would you?"

"How long?"

"Since last night. You went off the road near a farm on the Sixth Line. They heard the crash and found you. You've been awake a few times today and we've talked, but you were totally disoriented. You didn't have a clue."

"I don't—" He stopped, trying to recall talking to her, trying to force his mind to remember everything. He shook his head. "Damn."

"Never mind, Daddy." She stroked his cheek. "The doctor said everything will probably return to normal, but you may never remember the accident. Which is just as well, as far as I'm concerned."

He noticed that his left arm was immobilized in a sling. "Did I . . . break it?"

"Just a bad bruise on your shoulder. Your little finger's broken, though."

"How'd you get here?"

She rolled her eyes. "Well, I flew, obviously." She smiled teasingly. "Stephen let me use his jet. It's incredible. I want one for Christmas, okay?"

"Sure. I'll look into it."

"Ms. Stone called me. I met her when I got here. She's very nice. You two knew each other, back in the day?"

Who? Oh, right. Natalie.

"Yeah." He was feeling very drowsy again.

"I thought she was nice. And *very* worried about you."

"Trying to get back into the game."

She laughed. " 'Once a cop, always a cop.' Isn't that what you always say?"

Movement in the doorway caught his eye as a nurse walked into the room.

"We're awake now, are we?"

Pamela stood up and backed away. "He remembers me now."

"Does he!" The nurse picked up Tom's right wrist to take his pulse. "Good looking, and smart, too."

Tom looked at Pamela, who gave him her best stage wink.

"I'll let the doctor know you're back among us," the nurse said, releasing his wrist. "I'm sure you have a few questions for her."

"When?"

"See? There's one already." She reached over and brushed away a lock of hair that had fallen over his eyes.

"Darn. Your daughter told me you comb it straight back. Now I know for sure a part on the side doesn't work at all, does it?"

He looked up at her brown, shoulder-length hair. It had been curled on each side, and the curls were streaked blond. Although she was in her middle forties, judging from the crow's feet at the corners of her eyes and the lines on her forehead, it was a look that he could appreciate, despite his semi-conscious state. It set off her blue eyes and her smile.

She gave him a pretty good copy of Pamela's stage wink and left the room.

Embarrassed, he closed his eyes.

"She asked me if you were married," Pamela whispered, leaning down. "When I said no, she said, 'Oh, good.' I think she really likes you."

"Bourbon," he said, and fell asleep.

He awoke sometime later to the sound of two women's voices. One was Pamela's and the other one he didn't recognize. He opened his eyes and saw a young Asian woman standing next to the bed. She wore a white lab coat, had a stethoscope around her neck, and was carrying a tablet in her hand. The detective in him surmised that this was the doctor.

"Ah, there you are," she chirped. "I'm Dr. Pham. I was here last night when they brought you in, and here I am again!" She dimpled her cheeks at him. "Do you remember what happened? The accident you were in?"

"Not really."

Dr. Pham nodded. "Not surprising." She glanced at Pamela. "You remember who this is?"

"My daughter. Pamela."

"What's your full name? First, middle, and last."

"Thomas Troy Faust."

"Date of birth?"

"November 5, 1960."

"What month are we in now?"

"Month? Uh, August."

"Are you sure?"

"Somebody told me it happened last night. Last night was August."

Dr. Pham grinned. "How does your head feel?"

"A dull ache."

"Is the light bothering you?"

"It's a little bright, but otherwise I guess it's okay."

Dr. Pham consulted her tablet. "You may have noticed your arm's in a sling. You suffered a contusion to your shoulder. We'll keep it immobilized for the rest of the night, then if you don't want to wear the sling in the morning, you don't have to. You also suffered a fracture of the middle phalanx of your little finger. It was a simple fracture, so no big deal. It should stay in the splint for as long as you can stand it, basically. If you want to take it off after a week or so, you could buddy tape the finger after that. Use surgical tape from your first aid kit. I'm assuming you have one at home. Just tape the broken finger to your ring finger. It'll take four to six weeks to heal, so use that as a guide for how long to keep it immobilized, okay?"

"Okay. How long will I stay here?"

"Well, you suffered a mild traumatic brain injury, an MTBI. A concussion, in other words. You were unconscious for about ninety minutes, then you were in and out of consciousness after that with temporary retrograde amnesia. I'd say you're making a nice recovery now, but we're going to keep you overnight for observation and see how you are in the morning. Any other questions?"

"No."

She grinned. "Okay! See you tomorrow!"

He watched her leave and said to Pamela, "You don't need to stay."

"I'm not going anywhere." She folded her arms and tried to look tough.

"They shouldn't have called you. It was practically nothing."

"Right. Your car totalled, a concussion, amnesia. Nothing."

He winced. "Oh, *shit*. The Town Car."

"Sorry, Daddy. It's a write-off. I know you love that car."

"Damn. Damn!"

She sat on the side of the bed. "They told me you fishtailed and went into the ditch on your side. The driver's side, I mean. You hit your head on the window; that's how you got the concussion. And you hurt your arm and your finger when you tried to brace yourself for the impact. That's what they said."

"Damn."

"Please don't be upset, Daddy. You can always get a new car. There's only one of you, though."

"They don't make them any more," he groused. "Ford discontinued them. Now what the hell will I drive?"

"Just use the Lexus until you find something else, Daddy. It's no big deal."

"Man. I loved that damned car."

"I know, Daddy. It's the car Raylan Givens drives in *Justified*."

"Never saw that show."

"Liar." She smiled. "We'll find you another one; you'll see."

He didn't say anything for a while, his mind drifting. Pamela patted his arm and sat down. He thought of something and turned his head in the direction of her chair. "Didn't catch her name."

"Who, Daddy?"

"The nurse. The nice one."

"Ohhh, now you're interested, are you? Her name badge said 'Reed,' if I remember correctly. Nurse Reed, to you."

"Slender as a reed."

"You should probably get some rest now, Daddy. You're getting maudlin."

"No, I'm not." He closed his eyes. "Did she ask for your autograph?"

"No, she didn't."

"Good."

The sound of a magazine page turning. "Practically everyone else did, though."

"Sorry."

Another page turning. "It's okay. It's part of the job. Like John says, I'll be more upset when they stop asking. It sometimes gets a little weird, though."

"Oh?"

"Some doctor guy got me to sign one of those masks they get people to put on when they come in with a cold. The cheap cotton things that cover your mouth and nose? Then he said he could put it on and always have my name on his lips."

"I can run a background on him. Wants and warrants."

"No you can't, Daddy, but thanks for offering. He was fine. People just get a little weird when they meet someone famous. They say stuff, and you can see in their eyes they feel stupid and wish they'd hadn't said it. It's human nature. Whatever."

Later, when she'd turned off the light and was dozing in the chair, he discovered that his mind was working against the painkiller they'd given him after the doctor's visit. There was something he should be remembering. About the case.

He plodded through it doggedly, item by item. A body in the church. Joe Kohl. Cecile Something. The woman at the fishing camp. Natalie had particularly wanted to talk to her. That skinny guy. What was his name again? Little. Christ! He'd been butchered, just like the others. There was someone he'd been thinking about, though. Right at the end, after leaving the office. Right before—

Damn. Whatever it was, it was just inside the black hole in his head.

Will Eaton. God, yes. He'd gone down to visit Will on the weekend. Shocking to see how far he'd regressed. In the car afterward, he'd cried. Thinking about poor Will.

Afraid. Afraid of it happening to him, too.

Now it had, hadn't it? He'd suffered a loss of memory. He was struggling to bring things back and some of them just weren't there, no matter how hard he tried.

Come on. What was I thinking about just before everything blacked out?

He struggled but couldn't remember. Exhausted, he finally gave up.

Tears slid down his cheeks again. This time, though, they were all for himself.

33

In the morning he was tucking in his shirt when Gavin Elliott and Detective Constable Patricia Bell appeared in the doorway.

"Going somewhere, mister?" Gavin asked, smiling.

"I'm out on parole." Tom tightened his belt. "I finally passed all their tests this morning. Plus, they apparently want the damned bed."

Gavin laughed. "We saw Pamela downstairs as we were coming in." He glanced at Bell, who blushed. "Pat got her autograph. In her notebook. Not sure how that'll look in court, but anyway."

Tom sat down on the edge of the bed to tie his shoes. "She's on her way back to work. It was great to see her."

"She looks well," Gavin said. "Worried about you, of course. So's Natalie. Saw her downstairs, too. With her driver, the military guy."

Tom nodded. "Apparently he gets stuck with me for today. I'm not allowed to drive for another twenty-four hours." He stood up. "Not that I have a car of my own to drive any more."

"On that subject," Gavin said, "we have a couple of things to go over with you. Do you mind if we do it now?"

Tom shrugged. "Why not?" He'd already spoken to two provincial constables from Traffic to give a statement on what little he could remember about the mishap. He'd awakened with a headache, but the Tylenol they'd given him had eased it. He still had a small lump on the side of his head, and his little finger was buddy-taped to his ring finger, but he'd been able to get rid of the sling and his shoulder, although sore, was fully operational. Another interview wouldn't do him any harm at this point.

"Did you want to go down to the cafeteria for a coffee?" Gavin asked.

"Have you actually had the coffee in this place before?"

"Yeah. Sorry." Gavin leaned against the doorframe and folded his arms. "Do you remember anything else from the night before last that might help find who ran you off the road?"

"No. There's still a gap in my memory, and according to the doctor, it may stay that way. Something about my brain being interrupted in the process of converting short-term memory into long-term memory when the concussion happened. So everything still in short term was erased when my brain crashed. Something like that. I just remember driving past the university, turning onto the Sixth Line, and headlights in my rear-view mirror. That's it."

"Well, we know a little bit about the vehicle," Gavin said. "There was all kinds of paint transfer on your car, and it was white. The lab might be able to give us an idea of a make and model. We'll have to wait and see."

Someone had a white vehicle, Tom thought. *Someone*

I knew, someone I'd talked to recently who drove a white vehicle. Who the hell was it?

"Is there any doubt in your mind at all, Tom, that this was a deliberate attack and not just carelessness by some drunken idiot?"

"I don't believe in coincidences, Gav. Never did."

"If we're going to connect this to the Bush family killer, and the Kohl and Little cases, I need to understand the change in MO. Why run you off the road instead of catching you at home and cutting your throat like all the others?"

Tom shrugged. "I've been giving that one a lot of thought, believe me. I don't think he was trying to kill me. I think it was just another message. Like the condolence cards and the clumsy phone tap. 'I've got your number, and there's nothing you can do about it.' Boo-yah."

"It's a big step up from planting a bug to running someone off the road in the dark," Gavin said. "Are you sure it's not connected to something else? Some other Cage business?"

"Pretty sure." At least he fervently hoped it was unconnected.

"Okay." Gavin glanced at Bell. "We have something else to go over with you. I know it's not the best time, but Pat's on her way to Lindsay and we need to run this by you now."

Tom sat down again on the edge of the bed. His energy level still wasn't high enough to stay on his feet through an entire conversation.

"Go ahead."

Bell said, "Armour and I interviewed Donna Lee Little and her daughter yesterday. They came back from Oakville and immediately went into protective custody."

"Who?" He frowned, annoyed at not being able to place the people she was talking about.

"Gerald Little's wife and daughter," Bell said, taken aback.

"Gerald Little?" He thought hard for a moment. Little? Bush? Apsley?

Right: the next-door neighbour. Tall, gawky redhead with a soul patch. Oh, shit. Throat cut and spread-eagled on the front lawn. In Lindsay. The daughter visiting a college in what's-its-name. Where Natalie lives. Her name's Amy.

"Okay," he nodded. "Go on."

"The daughter was completely clueless about why it happened. She was hysterical most of the time. Very close to her father."

Tom felt an upwelling of sympathy for the girl, an only child now stripped of a loving parent in an act of cruel violence.

"You okay, Tom?" Gavin pushed away from the doorframe and took a step toward him. "Should we maybe do this later?"

Tom caught himself in the middle of an emotional tidal wave. He remembered such episodes were a post-concussion symptom mentioned by Dr. Pham. Apparently it was something he had to look forward to for a while until he fully recovered, along with fatigue, irritability, slower than normal thought processes, and other delightful stuff.

He pulled himself together and forced a smile. "I'm good. What about the wife? What did she say?"

"She confirmed what we've been suspecting," Bell said. "Little saw something that night and kept it to himself."

"Oh? What?"

"She didn't know or wouldn't say. Armour thought she was holding back the same way her husband had and really pressed her on it, but I think she honestly doesn't know, that he never told her what it was. What she *did* know was that he was being threatened."

"Threatened?"

"Yeah. Turns out he admitted to her, several years after they moved, that someone had contacted him. The threats were mostly directed toward their daughter. 'Keep your mouth shut or your little girl will suffer, like the Bush punks did.' That kind of thing."

"Seventeen years," Gavin said. "A long time to live with that kind of fear."

There was a noise in the doorway, and Natalie appeared. "How are we doing up here? Ready to go?"

"Yeah," Tom said, standing up. "Seventeen years is a long time to withhold vital information in a homicide investigation. Little should have trusted us."

"We can go over all that later," Natalie said. Behind her, in the doorway, Nurse Reed waited with a wheelchair.

As they fussed, Pat Bell touched Tom on the arm. "I hope I didn't do the wrong thing. Asking your daughter for an autograph, I mean."

"Don't worry about it." He couldn't help but grin, wondering if she'd said something foolish to Pamela in the process.

Downstairs, after his ride in the wheelchair, Nurse Reed helped him to his feet.

"Thanks," he said, embarrassed.

Just inside the main entrance, Natalie was talking to Doreen Lacey, the only reporter in sight. Her videographer, Les Hume, spotted Tom and raised his camera, but Charlie Danko stepped in front of him. Hume quickly gave up on the idea and lowered it again.

Reed patted Tom's good shoulder and tucked a folded piece of paper into his shirt pocket. "Don't be a stranger."

"You're kidding, right?"

"I never kid about salt-and-pepper hair combed straight back."

"What's your first name? I should at least know what to call you. When I call you."

"It's Kelly. Kelly Reed."

"All right, Kelly. Thanks for all your help."

In the car, Natalie gave him a look. "You're going to call her, aren't you? Nurse Reed?"

"Why are we going this way? I thought we were going to the office."

"We're taking you home, Tom. Doctor's orders."

"Oh, for chrissakes. I need to get back up to speed."

Natalie put her hand on his arm. "Here's the plan. Go home, get settled back in. Maybe have a nap. I have a few things to do. After lunch, we'll have a team meeting to decide where we go from here."

"Now you're talking. I'll get Jade to give me a lift into town."

Natalie shook her head. "We'll bring the meeting to you, Tom. Your place. Okay? Play nice."

He nodded, grouchy and irritable. He sat back and stared out the window. He hated not being in control, having others tell him what to do. The old rebel blood stirred in his veins once again. To hell with . . .

He dozed off and didn't wake up again until Charlie pulled into the carport and Natalie nudged him.

"Home, Tom," she said.

34

After lunch Tom sat out back in the lawn chair with his feet up on the chunk of wood, listening to *The Yes Album* blare out through the open sliding door.

He'd changed into khaki shorts, a Hawaiian shirt that was mostly green, and sandals. Behind his sunglasses his eyes were focused on the house on top of the hill, but his mind was elsewhere. He was playing a trivia game with himself, to exercise his memory and his cognitive functions.

This was Yes's third studio album, released in 1971. Correct? Correct. Steve Howe replaced Tony Banks for this one, and Tony Kaye was on keyboards, to be replaced by Rick Wakeman at the end of the year. Okay, good.

He sang along with Jon Anderson through "Starship Trooper" and felt pleased to be able to remember the words. Most of them, at any rate. The ones that were understandable. Anderson had a tendency to slur things a bit, now and then. Or perhaps it was because of his accent. Where was he from, again? Tom knew that he knew this, being a big Yes fan. Somewhere in northwest England, wasn't it? Lancashire?

In the silence between tracks he heard a noise behind him. "Listening to old man music, are you?"

He jumped and swung around in the chair, his right hand closing on the gun in his lap. Jeremy stepped out, shielding his eyes against the glare.

"Jesus, you scared the shit out of me," Tom said.

"Sorry." Jeremy lost the grin as he saw the gun in Tom's hand. "Whoa. Very sorry."

Tom put the gun on the table as Natalie appeared in the doorway.

"How do I turn this off?" she called out over the noise of the next track on the album.

"Touch the top of the player."

The music suddenly stopped. Kashi Chopra came out and looked around, her eyes wide.

"This is lovely, Tom. Look at that house! Who lives up there?"

"My daughter." He got to his feet as Natalie and Charlie came out to join them.

"We'll have our meeting inside," Natalie said. She looked at the gun on the table, the bottle of bourbon, the shot glass next to it, and the can of Coke. "You shouldn't be drinking alcohol with the medication you're taking."

"I'm not. I tried, but it tastes like gasoline, so I'm sticking to the Coke. It tastes like root beer." He waved at the door. "Shall we?"

Inside, he locked the gun away in the safe in his bedroom and came out to find Natalie sitting at the kitchen table, notebook open, file folders arranged in neat piles. Kashi was pouring coffee from a twelve-cup Tim Hortons take-out container. The toilet flushed and Charlie emerged from the washroom. Jeremy was studying the liner notes inside the Yes CD case on the kitchen island.

"Pretty psychedelic stuff."

"Not exactly," Tom replied. "Progressive rock. Big difference between it and psychedelic rock."

Jeremy smiled. "Yeah, I know, man. I'm just dicking with you." He waved at the shelving unit next to the refrigerator. "You've got a lot of progressive, looks like. I couldn't see anything later than 1979. Emerson, Lake and Palmer? King Crimson? Tai Phong? You're stuck in a groove."

"Yeah, it's a groove, all right."

"We don't want to push you too hard," Natalie said as Tom sat down next to her, "but if you're up to it, we need to go over where we are right now and what our next steps need to be."

"Sounds good." In addition to the trivia game he'd been playing in his head, Tom had also been mulling over the case. He'd discovered, to his relief, that most of the details seemed to be right where he'd left them before the concussion. The only thing he still couldn't remember was what he'd been thinking about just before being forced off the road. It was very important, but try as he might, he couldn't bring it back.

Natalie said something he missed, and now she was looking at Jeremy. "What about James Bush? Any progress finding him?"

The name triggered something in Tom's brain. He remembered the unpleasant glare of high beams in his rear-view mirror, and then it came to him: *James Bush is close.* It meant something, but he wasn't sure what. Close, in what way?

Jeremy leaned against the kitchen counter, a tablet in his hand. "No, not so far. Here's the sum of what we have on him right now. After the murders he went into foster care and lived in two foster homes in Peterborough until he was sixteen, when he was moved to Oshawa. A year later, he disappeared from that home and there's been no other trace of him whatsoever."

"What about the foster parents?" Natalie asked. "Were they any help?"

"Not really. Kashi and I interviewed both pairs. The Peterborough couple agreed he was quiet, withdrawn, and largely unresponsive to positive reinforcement. In Oshawa it was a little different."

"Adolescence would be hitting him full force by that time," Natalie said.

"Yes," agreed Kashi, "and in the usual negative way. He grew more sullen, angry, bitter, and resistant to guidance. What was interesting, though, is that he found a girlfriend."

"Oh?"

"A girl named Allie Whetung. She was at the foster home when James arrived. She was a year younger than James. According to Mrs. McCoy, the foster parent we talked to, they argued a lot at first but eventually became friends. There were four foster children in the home, which is the legal limit, and apparently the youngest was a real handful. Once Allie and James became friends and settled down, Mrs. McCoy spent less time on them and more with the young one. Allie and James were gone for ten hours before she realized something was wrong."

"It was a school day," Jeremy put in, shifting his weight against the counter. "They never showed up."

"So they ran off together," Tom said, sipping his coffee, which was already cold. "Any leads on the girl?"

"Not so far," Jeremy replied. "They both must have assumed aliases. There's nothing on file in the provincial databases for either of them, so they didn't file for legal name changes." He shrugged. "Needle in a haystack, at this point."

"I thought you were a skip-tracing phenom," Charlie suddenly said. "Giving up so soon?"

"No," Jeremy replied, irritated at being needled. "Look, the name is *the* key datum in any skip trace. Without a correct name the usual sources of information just aren't going to help, Charlie. You know that. Driver's licence, EI claims, credit cards, phone accounts, all the stuff you'd hack out of the system, they all depend on having the correct name."

He sighed. "There's absolutely zero connected to Allie Whetung after her disappearance. As far as James Bush is concerned, there are fifty-eight James Bushes that turn up in Ontario alone. Of those fifty-eight, eleven are within the ages of twenty-five and thirty-five, our James now being thirty years old. Of those eleven, all of them completely check out as *not* being the James Bush we're looking for. I spent a lot of time running them all down and ruling them out, plus all the other James Bushes in other provinces. He stopped using the name James Bush and started using another name, period. Get me that name and I'll trace him."

Charlie shrugged. "Maybe the guy's dead."

"Not according to any database I have access to."

"Probably at the bottom of a hole that's not in any of your databases."

Tom got up and put his coffee in the microwave to warm it up. Nettled by Charlie's barbs, Jeremy moved out of his way, settling against the end of the kitchen island. Natalie poured more for the others.

Tom completely understood Jeremy's frustration, although he had to smile inwardly at Charlie for putting the needle into him. Jeremy liked to flash a hipster know-it-all condescension that rubbed people the wrong way. Still, the guy was working very hard and getting nowhere. He had a right to feel frustrated.

Tom fished his coffee out of the microwave and burned his lips on it. Better. He stared out the window over the sink at the bourbon that was still sitting out there on the plastic table.

What if my taste for it never comes back?

Wouldn't hurt, he decided. Renovating the church was supposed to have been the answer to the lack of focus in his new life. It was supposed to have been the thing that took off the edge, instead of the booze, when night fell and his mind started gnawing on itself. He needed to give the renovation project another chance, throw himself into it, get busy so that he could move into the place before the snow began to fall.

It suddenly occurred to him that he hadn't responded to the guy's quote for the rewiring. "Shit."

"Problem?" Natalie asked.

Tom went back to the kitchen table and sat down. "No, I just forgot to follow up with Jade on a reference check on the guy who's giving me a quote for rewiring the church. Jim, uh, Woods. Jim Woods. She was supposed to let me know if he checked out okay."

Charlie snorted. "Get Jeremy to do it. He's good at that sort of thing."

"Piss off," Jeremy replied.

"It was the guy from the phone company," Tom said. "The one who came around to check out the phone line for me after I found the bug. Turns out he's a certified electrician who does extra work on the side."

"Wait a minute," Jeremy said. "Say that name again."

Tom burned his lips on another sip. "Shit. What name?"

"The name you just said. The electrician."

"Jim Woods."

Jeremy snapped his fingers. "Jim Woods. James Woods. Jim. Where did I see that name before?" He began swiping furiously at his tablet.

"We need to focus on James Bush," Tom said to Natalie. "He's either in danger or he's the cause of all this. Either way, we need to track him down."

"Easier said than done, obviously," Kashi said.

"Here it is," Jeremy walked over and leaned down between Natalie and Kashi. "I saw that name, Jim Woods, several times on the Facebook page Joseph Kohl was using for his religious group, The Fellowship. See? He left a number of comments on posts three to five months ago. Like this one."

He pointed at the screen. Kashi and Natalie leaned over. Tom got up and walked around the table to look over Jeremy's shoulder. Only Charlie remained where he was, completely uninterested.

" 'I agree,' " Kashi read aloud, " 'forgiveness is a divine luxury many of us cannot afford. But we must try our best anyway.' "

"Pithy," Tom said.

"Look at this exchange, in May." Jeremy swiped to another page.

Tom leaned down for a closer look:

Brother Joseph Kohl
May 12 at 8:04am Bancroft, Ontario
It's important to remember that the idea of original sin was invented by a bishop almost 200 years after Christ died. It was embellished by Augustine, who thought it was based on the writings of Paul. Never

was Our Lord and Saviour actually quoted on this idea. This negative belief takes away the power of our own free will as individuals to approach God and serve him through Jesus Christ on our own terms as his servants.

5 people like this.

Sister Mary Richardson A blessing for sure! We come to God freely, like innocent lambs!!!

Like Reply May 12 at 8:09am

Jim Woods Are you certain you've read Augustine correctly, Brother Joseph? He taught that Adam's sin was transferred down the generations by moral con-cupiscence, complicated by sexual con-cupiscence, which we see all around us today. Or am I off track here?

Like Reply May 13 at 7:46pm

"He made several comments like that," Jeremy said, "all in the same tone, challenging Kohl on stuff that was either directly or indirectly connected to sex. I remembered his entries because he was the only one belonging to this group who seemed interested in theological discussion. The others, like this Richardson woman, just posted stuff that stroked Kohl's ego. I can show you more, if you want."

"Let's look at his profile," Tom suggested. "You can't tell anything from that little thumbnail picture."

Jeremy tapped his way to the Facebook profile page for Jim Woods. The profile photo was a beagle dog's head, cute but not human. The cover photo in the background showed a meadow filled with daisies, obviously clipart.

According to the profile, he worked as an electrician, got his education from a community college Tom didn't recognize, lived in Peterborough, Ontario, was single, and was born on April 10, 1989.

"That's James Bush's DOB," Tom pointed out.

"Yes, it is," Jeremy agreed, "but you'd think he'd know enough about maintaining a new identity not to use his own date of birth."

"He's probably waving it under our noses, daring us to find it." Tom straightened. "I can't believe it. This guy was in my house. In my church. James Bush, pretending to be a guy named Woods. And I didn't recognize him."

"Maybe." Jeremy scrolled down the page. "There's not much here. He made very few posts, mostly cutesy pictures and jokes copied from various Internet sites. Enough to build up a believable page."

Tom pulled out his cellphone and called Jade. It went to voicemail. "Jade, this is Faust. Bring that sheet with the Woods references on it down to the house, will you? Right away? Thanks." He ended the call and said, "She told me she called the numbers and left messages, but never heard back from any of them."

"Probably phoney," Natalie said. "Jeremy, let's run a full background on James Woods. We've got an employer, the phone company, and Tom can give us a physical description. Assume for the moment that the DOB is accurate and work with that."

"Right away," Jeremy said.

Mention of the phone company suddenly re-established another connection in Tom's mind. "A white vehicle. Woods drove a white van. It didn't have any logos on it, but it was white. Maybe he was the one who ran me off the road."

"It didn't have a company logo on it?" Jeremy asked.

"No. A couple of ladders on the roof, but no signage at

all. Probably his personally-owned vehicle."

"Maybe he's a ringer. I don't suppose you got the licence number."

"Oh, shit." He squeezed his eyes shut, trying to visualize the van. He'd seen it three times—on the shoulder of the road at the corner of Sixth Line and Dalton, in his carport, and at the church.

"Damn. I can't remember. I would have memorized the plate number. I always do. Damn it."

"You'll remember," Natalie reassured him. "Everything's coming back to you, piece by piece. Don't force it, and it'll come back."

35

By the time everyone cleared out it was getting late in the afternoon. Charlie stayed behind, temporarily assigned to keep an eye on Tom and provide a ride if he needed to go somewhere. Feeling a little tired but encouraged by the connection they'd made between Jim Woods and Joseph Kohl, and possibly between Woods and James Bush, Tom made a fresh pot of coffee. Charlie accepted a cup with a polite nod.

"I'm sorry you're stuck with babysitting duty." Tom leaned back against the kitchen counter, flexing his left arm. His little finger ached. It would soon be time for the ice pack and another dose of Tylenol.

"No problem." Charlie lifted his left leg and rested it on the kitchen chair beside him. He took a cigar from his shirt pocket, peeled off the cellophane, and stuck it in his mouth.

Tom had seen him chewing on a cigar before but never actually smoking one. Charlie left the band on, and Tom could see it was a Cohiba. An expensive cigar.

"You can light that if you want."

"You sure? Won't give you a headache?"

"If it does, I'll let you know." Tom brushed the crumbs from a sandwich plate he'd used at lunch and put it on the table. "Ash tray."

"Thanks." Charlie lit the cigar and blew out smoke.

Tom opened the kitchen window behind him. "Ventilation."

"Good idea." Charlie picked up the paperback he'd brought in from the car and opened it. It was a dog-eared copy of a book called *American Cipher.*

Up to now, Tom had mostly seen the back of Charlie's head in the Mercedes, or his face in profile as he listened to Natalie's instructions. While at the office or even here earlier this afternoon, despite his sparring with Jeremy, he tended to blend into the background. Now, however, Tom had a chance to study him more closely.

Somewhere in his mid-forties, Charlie wore a pale green short-sleeved shirt that was untucked and open at the neck to show thick black chest hair. His jeans were faded but clean. His shoes, however, were definitely less than casual—black high-top Reeboks with thick soles and zippers on the side. They looked expensive and durable, the kind of footwear off-duty military personnel would favour.

"What happened to Natalie, Charlie? How'd she get hurt?"

"Need to know," he replied, eyes on his book.

His arms were muscular and hairy. He was almost completely bald, except for very short, dark hair at his temples and around the base of his skull. A four-inch scar ran diagonally across the top of his head. His jaw was strong and stubbled. His cheeks sucked in as he drew on the cigar, then relaxed almost casually as the smoke leaked from his mouth. His eyes, focused on the book, were narrow and dark. The hand that rubbed his left thigh was like a farmer's, hard and short-fingered, the knuckles prominent, the nails trimmed short, the back covered with dark hair.

"Where are you from?"

"A ways from here," Charlie replied, still reading.

"Where's that?"

Charlie lowered the book and studied Tom for a moment. It was much the same look as he'd given him in the rear-view mirror when they'd first met, when Tom was getting out of the Mercedes to have a talk with Natalie on that first day. The look of a soldier assessing a civilian, deciding whether he was a threat, an annoyance, a possible ally, or nothing at all.

"Timmins," he finally replied.

"No kidding." Tom sipped his coffee. "Lots of famous people come from Timmins. Shania Twain. A lot of hockey players from back in the day."

"Yep. Not much else to do up there."

"What did you do before you signed on with Cage?"

Charlie exhaled a long stream of cigar smoke and squinted sideways at him. "You want the full bio?"

"I'm just trying to make conversation, Charlie."

"Should I call a lawyer?" A smile wormed around the cigar.

"Only if you're thinking of buying a house or getting a divorce."

"Not married."

"See? Now we're rolling."

Charlie removed the cigar from his mouth. He examined the ash and tapped it onto the sandwich plate. "Army."

"Overseas?"

"Spent some time in JTF2."

"No kidding. Special forces. Joint Task Force Two. Afghanistan?"

Charlie nodded. Not everyone had heard of this elite special operations force that carried out counter-terrorism missions for the Canadian Armed Forces. The fact that Tom recognized the name was an ice breaker of sorts, and Charlie seemed to relax a fraction.

"Ever hear of Task Force K-Bar?"

Tom smiled. "You're giving a memory test to a guy just coming off temporary amnesia. Give me a sec. Sure. A joint forces op that ran for a year after 9/11, led by the Americans. Hell, I actually remember it. I was following the news pretty closely then. You were in that?"

"Can't talk about it. Classified."

"Sure."

Charlie drank some coffee, rubbed his thigh, and said, "I was a master corporal when I made the unit. Some kinda badass. Sergeant after a few years. Join the army, see the world."

"Scary times, back then."

"Scary now, comes to that." Charlie examined the tip of his cigar, checking to make sure it was burning evenly. "We ran a lot of missions in southern Afghanistan, rooting out Taliban and Al Qaeda from their caves and holes. A lot of them we turned over to the Americans, knowing full well they were going to end up in Gitmo. The way it was. War's war." He frowned. "The worst part was the chopper rides."

"Oh?"

"We did our work on the ground, my friend. Up in the air, riding in those choppers, well, you're just a passenger. Helpless. We got shot up a few times passing over their units on the ground. No worse feeling in the world, believe me. You sit there and damned well have to take it. These days

I don't fly if I can possibly help it. Ground transportation only, unless I have to travel overseas. Then I just sit there and suffer."

Tom had his own misgivings about flying and airplanes that tended to crash, so he nodded. "Sounds like you should have better ways to spend your time than hanging around here with me."

"Natalie's my current assignment. Up to now, I've been working with her husband, on Nick West's side of the business."

Tom looked puzzled, not immediately recognizing the name.

"Nicholas West. Vice-president of Cage's intelligence division. Works out of London. Anyway, as I say, Natalie's my current assignment, but Kashi's covering her while they see if they can figure out who's taken a sudden dislike to you."

"More likely a long-standing dislike."

"Could be," Charlie agreed. "If it's connected to this case only, then I can relax."

"Hey!" Tom pretended to be offended.

Charlie winked. "Don't sweat it. Relax is a relative term in my line of work." He rolled his cigar between his thumb and index finger. "If it's something else, though, then there might be a bit of mission creep going on. Nick and Derek won't be happy with that."

Tom thought of his meeting with Rick Thompson behind the arena. The OPP regional intelligence co-ordinator had talked about Cage business spilling over into southern Ontario. Rick believed there might be more of it up in eastern Ontario. He'd given Tom a head's up on it, just in case. Is that what Charlie was driving at now when he talked about mission creep? That Tom was becoming a target for someone connected to the intelligence side of

Cage's operations?

Tom's cellphone vibrated. He looked at the call display, saw that it was Jade, and answered. "Are you okay?"

"Yes. Your concern's touching. Got your message. You must be a little confused, Faust. I already told you I gave up on the Woods guy. I've got somebody else coming up to the church. Right now, as a matter of fact. Do you want to be here or not?"

"You called someone else? Another electrician?"

"No, I called a rocket scientist, Sherlock. Apparently you don't remember the conversation. In the hospital? I actually came up to visit you? You wanted to get the rewiring done ASAP? Ring any bells?"

Tom shook his head. "None, Jade."

"Well, look. None of those references for Wood got back to me. I'm not even sure they exist."

Tom suddenly thought of something. "There was an ESA licence number on his business card. Did you check with them to see if it matched up with Jim Woods?"

"What am I, a private detective? You gave me a sheet of paper with names and numbers on it. I never saw a business card."

"Wait one." Tom shifted off his haunch and pulled out his wallet. He put down the phone and dug around. There it was. His shoulders dropped. He should have given this to Jeremy before they left. He grabbed the phone. Jade was talking.

"—got this guy, Peter Cadmon. He should be here any minute."

"You're at the church?"

"Are you coming up, Faust, or should I handle it?"

Tom closed his eyes. He felt like crap, but he wanted to be there. "I'll be there."

The line went dead.

Charlie was looking at him expectantly. Tom said, "You haven't seen the church yet, have you?"

Charlie lowered his leg and dog-eared the page in his book. "Let's go."

Tom sat in the front passenger seat. Charlie slid behind the wheel and transferred a holstered handgun from under his shirt to a compartment in the centre console. He saw Tom looking at the gun and said, "It's legal."

Tom's gun, the SIG Sauer P226, was licensed and registered only for possession at his place of residence. Carrying it around in concealment, the way Charlie was doing, was against the law in Canada except under specific circumstances. Exceptions were rare, including on-duty peace officers, guards riding in armoured cars, trappers, or people living in remote wilderness areas. Short of asking to see Charlie's ATC—his authorization to carry—Tom would have to take his word for it that he was legally carrying the gun.

He had recognized it as a Browning Hi-Power MK1 9mm pistol. The MK1 was standard issue for the Canadian Armed Forces. As Charlie started the engine and backed out of the carport, Tom wondered if his ad hoc bodyguard was in fact still on active duty status. Charlie had never actually come out and said that he'd retired from the military to join the private sector.

Peter Cadmon had just arrived at the church when they got there. Tom walked him through what he wanted, pointed out spots where he'd like the outlets to be located, showed him the large ceiling fans he wanted installed, and then left him to it with Jade as a guide. Charlie wandered around, giving the place the once-over with the practised eye of someone who focuses on ingress, egress, and security rather than interior decoration or architectural aesthetics. When Tom caught up to him he was outside, walking a perimeter around the building, casually checking out sight lines and avenues of approach.

"You're a cautious man."

Charlie smiled neutrally. "It's a pretty spot."

"Bullshit. You were scoping it out, like any seasoned combat veteran would."

"Just enjoying the air."

When Cadmon finished up his assessment and left, promising to provide a quote within twenty-four hours, Jade didn't bother to stick around. Tom tried to talk to her, concerned about her state of mind, but she brushed him off. As he watched her car disappear down the road in a cloud of dust, Tom heard Charlie's footsteps in the grass behind him.

"I'd like to stick around for a while," Tom said. "Is that a problem for you?"

"Be my guest. When do we eat?"

Tom glanced at his watch and was surprised to see that it was getting close to dinnertime. "I'm not too hungry. I could order a couple of pizzas. There's a good place in Bridgenorth; they've delivered out here before."

"Sounds good. Extra-large Canadian for me, and whatever you want for yourself."

Tom dug out his cellphone and called it in, adding an assortment of soft drinks to the order.

"Thirty minutes," he told Charlie as he put the phone away.

"I'll try to survive that long."

The sun was now behind the tower, so Tom grabbed a couple of lawn chairs and they sat down in its shadow, facing the road. A cool breeze moved across his face and stirred the hair on his bare forearms. Clouds moved overhead, like front-runners of an incoming storm front. He thought it might rain overnight.

"How long were you a cop?" Charlie asked.

"Thirty-five years."

"All with the OPP?"

"Yep."

"Did you like it?"

"It was my life," Tom said.

"I hear you."

Tom laced his hands together behind his head. "What about you? You're still on active duty, aren't you?"

Charlie grunted, staring out at the road. After a moment he said, "Guys like us, we wouldn't know what else to do with our time. I don't know how you found the courage to pull the pin."

"Second-hardest thing I ever did," Tom said.

"What was the hardest?"

"Burying my wife."

They spent a few moments listening to a robin singing for rain in a tree behind the church.

"This is the greatest country in the goddamned world," Charlie muttered, tilting his head back to look at the sky.

"I agree."

Charlie rubbed his scalp. "When you go on a mission, you have to have a reason. There has to be something you can tell yourself you're doing it for. When you're sitting in a fucking chopper waiting for a round to come up through the floorboards and make a mess of your insides, you better be able to put it into words. What you're doing it for."

Tom said nothing.

"Maybe you had the same experience, being a cop. I mean, you do the job because you love it. You love the job. But what do you do it *for*? To catch bad guys and keep people safe, right? For me, I went overseas to kill bad guys and keep people safe here at home."

Tom nodded.

"I talk too much," Charlie said. "I take after my old man. He was a motor mouth, too. Typical salesman. Loved to tell stories." He chuckled. "Mine are all classified, though."

They heard the faint bass notes of a car engine on the road in the distance. As they listened, it grew louder. It was too soon and coming from the wrong direction to be the pizza delivery guy.

Charlie sat straighter in his chair.

The sound gradually rose up the scale and increased in volume, accompanied by the steady crackling of gravel under tires.

Charlie stood up. He took two steps forward and another to his right, placing himself at Tom's ten o'clock.

A brown SUV appeared on their left. It was pulling a boat on a trailer. As it passed, the driver looked at them and raised a hand in greeting.

"It's okay," Tom said, watching it disappear into the trees on the right. "I've seen him before. He lives around here somewhere."

Charlie nodded. He stood there, listening, until the sound of the tires had completely faded away. Then he sat down again.

"They always this slow delivering their pizza?" he asked.

36

The following morning, Charlie drove him into the city. Their first stop was a car rental place on George Street, where Tom leased a Chevrolet Malibu that was a premium option but felt like a long step down from his lost Town Car. From there they went to the office, where Natalie was waiting for them behind her desk.

"How are you feeling?" Tom asked, sitting down.

She smiled. "That was my question. How's your head, Tom?"

"Better. The black spots in my long-term memory are getting smaller." He looked around as Charlie left the office, closing the door behind him. "Interesting guy."

"He certainly is. He's moving on to other duties today. I thought perhaps Kashi could stay with you for a while."

Tom shook his head. "It's not necessary. I don't need a babysitter. Unless you know something I don't."

"I know a great deal that you don't," she said, "which goes without saying, but as far as external, ah, difficulties are concerned, we're certain that you're under no risk at this point."

"So the bastard who ran me off the road . . ."

"Is connected to something else."

"The Bushmaster."

"It's a strong possibility."

"Okay. So moving right along, what's happening with the Gerald Little case?"

"We're on the outside looking in," Natalie replied. "Gavin wants us to stay that way."

"I see. So what do you want me to do now, Nat?"

"Take today as a training day. Work on your PI course. How many hours have you put in so far?"

Tom thought for a moment. "I'm not sure. Five or six. I'd have to look."

"It requires fifty altogether," she reminded him, "so you really should get moving. Spend today on it. Tomorrow we'll meet for an update on James Bush-slash-James Woods. How's that sound?"

"I hate training."

"No, you don't. You just like to bitch about it."

Tom stood up. "Yes, boss." He paused, realizing that she hadn't moved in her chair the entire time he'd been in her office. "How's your arm?"

"Fine, thanks."

"Bullshit." He took a step toward her. "Let me see it."

"Tom, no. It hurts. I think it's infected."

"You need to have it looked at, Nat."

"Someone's coming over." She glanced at a clock on the wall. "In about an hour."

"Really? A doctor who makes house calls?"

She sighed. "Don't ask questions you don't need to ask, Tom. This is a different world from the one you were used to. Hell, different from what *I* was used to."

"Yeah. I hear you." He started for the door.

"Thanks," she said.

He stopped. "For what?"

"For coming on board." Her eyes left her hands and found his. "For being here. It means a lot to me. You have no idea."

"Me too, Nat. Me too."

He spent the rest of the morning in his office, working on his online training material. One of the support clerks brought him a sandwich and coffee for lunch, and he kept on going. He was just beginning the module on provincial and federal statutes, thinking there was no way he could put in fifty hours on material he already knew backwards and forwards, when his cellphone began to vibrate. He looked at the call display and didn't recognize the number or the caller ID: KREED.

"Tom Faust."

"Hi, Tom," a feminine voice said, "this is Kelly Reed. How are you feeling?"

It took him a moment. Reed? Kelly Reed? Then it hit him: *slender as a reed.*

"Fine," he said. "I'm feeling fine, thanks. How are you?"

"I'm well. You hadn't called, so I thought I'd take the initiative. What are you doing?"

"Uh, you mean right now?"

"Yes. I'm in the park across the street. Any chance you could take a break and come down?"

Tom looked at his watch and was surprised to see that it was three o'clock. "Sure, I guess so."

"You can buy me ice cream."

"Okay. I'll be right there."

Millennium Park was a strip of green space that ran for several blocks between Water Street and the river. He found Kelly Reed sitting on a bench not far from the boathouse.

She wore a white crocheted top over a sleeveless T-shirt, a long khaki skirt, sandals, and Chanel sunglasses.

"Hi," he said, sitting down beside her. "It's nice to see you again."

"You remember me now, do you?" She smiled, curved dimples appearing at the corners of her mouth.

"Oh, yeah. How could I not? Are you off today?"

She shook her head, removing her sunglasses. "Four to midnight. I was downtown running a few errands and thought I'd check up on you. Seriously, how are you feeling?"

"Tired, but okay."

"Headaches? Dizziness?"

"The occasional headache, I guess."

"What about memory and cognitive processes?"

He didn't respond for a moment, looking at her. He wasn't the sort of person who felt comfortable talking about himself, particularly when it came to his health. Her dark brown eyes, though, were concerned, and the smile was gone. He felt an odd tickling sensation in the pit of his stomach.

"I still can't remember the accident, but apparently I may never. There's a bit of disorientation now and again, when something comes up that I can't remember, but I seem to be able to work through it. More stuff is coming back all the time."

She reached out and touched his left wrist. "How's your finger?"

He hadn't bothered buddy-taping it this morning, conscious of Charlie waiting for him in the living room, and wished he had. It was still swollen and purple, and it ached. "It's coming."

"Liar."

"It only hurts when I play cards and shoot dice."

"A man of many vices."

"Not really. Speaking of which, where do you get ice cream around here?"

She stood up and offered her arm. He took it, self-consciously, and she led him along the walkway to the boathouse, which featured a café offering ice cream cones and sundaes with a variety of unusual toppings.

"My secret vice," she said, releasing his arm and moving up to the café window. She ordered a double-scoop sundae featuring kiwis and lime cordial. Tom thought it looked dreadful but smiled at the childlike pleasure on her face as she dug right into it.

He studied the menu for a moment and couldn't resist ordering something called Southern Charm, a sundae with chopped pecans and bourbon-flavoured syrup.

They walked back to the bench and sat down, concentrating for a while on their ice cream. Tom thought the bourbon syrup was a little too sweet, but otherwise the whole thing was delicious. After a few mouthfuls he felt a headache coming on from the coldness, so he put the dish down on the bench beside him and leaned forward, hands clasped between his knees.

"So this isn't a random just-happened-to-bump-into-you kind of thing, is it?"

She shook her head, the plastic spoon in her mouth.

"How'd you know I was here?" He glanced across the street at the office building.

"Kashi," she said, swallowing. "I called."

"What, you're on a first-name basis already with the people I work with?"

"Don't be like that."

"Like what?"

"Suspicious."

He laughed. "My dear, they paid me very good money

for thirty-five years to be suspicious of everyone and everything all the time, and I kind of got used to it."

"Well, you don't have to be suspicious of me."

"I don't?"

"No. My motives are pure." She grinned suddenly, the dimples bracketing her mouth. "Well, maybe that's not the most accurate word I could use, but you know what I mean."

"I'm afraid I may."

"Don't be afraid. I won't hurt you."

He picked up his ice cream and took a small spoonful.

"May I ask you a question, Tom?"

He nodded.

"Are you in danger?"

He shook his head. "You sound like my daughter. Some guy coming out of the past to play head games with me, who doesn't really know who he's up against." He raised a hand. It was his sore one, and the movement hurt. "Ouch. Not to sound all macho. But I've been threatened before. It goes with the job. It doesn't bother me."

"I can see where Pamela gets her acting skills. Do you rehearse lines like that in front of the bathroom mirror in the morning, or are you a natural?"

He smiled, swallowing more ice cream. He watched her stand up and walk over to the garbage bin to toss away her dish and spoon, then he watched her walk back to him. The odd tickling sensation started up again in the pit of his stomach.

"I'm not shy," she said, taking her sunglasses out of her handbag. "Never have been. I'd like to see you again."

"Okay."

"I married a hockey bum when I was twenty," she said, "and we divorced two years later. No kids. I haven't had much luck with men, although God knows I've tried. I always manage to say the wrong thing at the wrong time, it seems, and end up scaring them off. Like I said, I'm not shy. Anyway, I'll try not to do that this time."

He said nothing, thinking that the smile on his face was probably a little more nervous than he wished it would be.

"Come over for dinner tomorrow night. I'm off for the next two days. You can meet Aunt Alice and Aunt Nancy."

"Who?"

"My aunts. I live with them. I sort of look after them. You'll love them."

He hesitated.

"If you'd rather not, I completely understand."

"It's not that. God, no. It's just . . ."

"I'm a helluva cook. Pamela said you like to eat. What's not to like about the whole thing?"

He nodded. "I'll be there. Text me your address and what time."

"I will." She slipped on her sunglasses and walked away without looking back at him. Not even once.

37

As he pulled up to the curb on Homewood Avenue across from the house where Kelly Reed lived, Tom discovered that his throat was tight and his breath was short. Although this didn't qualify as a date, per se, he was a little surprised to find himself suffering from an acute case of nerves.

He stood on the curb and looked across the street. It was a nice-looking brown brick house with stucco on the upper levels. There was ivy growing on the sunroom extension on this side. A Volkswagen Jetta was parked in front of the garage. Next door, someone was washing a car with a brush on the end of a garden hose. The man glanced over at Tom, yanked at the hose, and moved around to the other side of his car.

Although it wasn't far from downtown, it was a quiet street. The houses along here spoke of old money and a comfortable lifestyle. The city hospital and a medical centre were only a few blocks away, and many of the houses on this street belonged to doctors or hospital administrators. As he crossed the street Tom noticed a tag hanging from the rear-view mirror inside the Jetta. It looked like a parking permit for the hospital, suggesting the car probably belonged to Kelly.

He knocked on the front door and it opened almost immediately.

"You made it," Kelly said.

"I did." Hearing the nervousness in her voice helped smooth out his nerves a little. He stepped into the entry and sniffed. "Oh lord, that smells good."

She shut the door. "Pot roast, baked potatoes, gravy, snow peas."

"My favourites."

"I know."

"You do?"

She smiled. "My informant."

He frowned in mock concern. "My daughter?"

"No comment."

He followed Kelly into the living room, admiring the antique furniture and the Persian rug on the floor. Someone in the next room was playing the piano. Kelly led the way through a pair of bevelled glass doors. An elderly woman turned her head, still playing.

"Aunt Alice," Kelly said, "this is Tom Faust."

She stopped playing and stood up. She was tall and slender, like her niece. She smoothed her black, knee-length dress, patted her white hair, and held out her hand. "I'm Alice Gillespie. It's a pleasure to meet you."

Tom smiled at the firmness of her grip. "The pleasure's mine. I didn't mean to interrupt your playing."

"Oh, you didn't interrupt." She tapped her temple with a long index finger. "It's still playing up here."

"I'll just give Tom a quick tour of the house," Kelly said, "if that's all right with you. Then we'll come down and I'll serve dinner."

Aunt Alice winked. "Nancy's in her study."

"We'll give her a wide berth," Kelly promised.

Tom followed Kelly out into the hallway. She showed him the dining room, where sunlight streamed through a bay window across a large table set for four, and the kitchen, equipped with a combination of vintage and modern appliances. They went upstairs, pausing on the second-floor landing.

"Aunt Alice and Aunt Nancy are up here," Kelly said. "Two bedrooms, each with an ensuite bathroom. There's also a guest room and Aunt Nancy's study. My rooms are on the third floor." Hand on the banister, she started up the next flight of stairs.

"Jesus fucking Christ!" a voice snapped from a room down the hallway.

Kelly looked down at Tom and motioned with her head for him to follow. When he caught up with her, halfway up to the third floor, she whispered over her shoulder, "Aunt Nancy. She's blogging."

They reached the landing at the top of the stairs. Kelly led the way through a narrow door. "This is where I live. This is my sitting room."

He looked at a flatscreen television, a bookshelf filled with books, two comfortable armchairs, and a large coffee table. The ceilings were sloped. Sunlight streamed through a skylight, stamping a warm yellow rectangle on the carpet. He didn't see many personal possessions. Diplomas and a few photographs of family members hung in frames on the walls.

"It's nice," he said.

"It's small." She took him back out into the hallway and pointed to another door, which was closed. "Bedroom. Bathroom at the end. My world, and welcome to it."

"It's nice," he repeated.

"You're kind." She patted his arm. "I like that. But it *is* small. I moved in nine years ago when Aunt Nancy was diagnosed with colitis. I'm comfortable, though. It's home."

"It's quite a house."

"Yes, it is. Let's go downstairs. I've got a meal to pull together, and you should spend some time with Aunt Alice." She smiled. "She's the nice one."

"Okay."

Aunt Alice was waiting for him in the living room. She was standing at a liquor caddy on wheels, pouring something from a bottle into a crystal wineglass. "Would you like an apéritif?"

"No thanks," he said, watching Kelly sweep off toward the kitchen.

Aunt Alice nodded. "It's a wise man who's careful with his alcohol. How about tonic water with a slice of lime?"

"That would be fine, thank you."

"Ice?"

"Thank you."

She used tongs to add two ice cubes to a tumbler, poured tonic water over them, slipped a slice of lime over the rim of the glass and handed it to him. "To new friends," she said, raising her own glass.

Tom smiled, touched glasses with her, and drank. The back of her hand was cabled with purple veins, but the fingers were long and supple. "That was nice music," he said. "What was it?"

She sat down in an armchair and gestured him to another. "It was an aria from one of the *Goldberg Variations.* Johann Sebastian Bach."

"I don't know much about classical music," he said.

She sipped and smiled. "That's quite all right. My excuse is that I've taught music since I was eighteen."

Tom nodded politely, thinking of his high school music teacher, a nasty piece of business hated and feared by every student in the school.

"But that's only for fun, and a little pocket change. My profession is, or rather was, mathematics. I'm retired now. Kelly tells me you're a retired police officer."

"Yes, that's right. Thirty-five years with the OPP."

"Really. You don't look a day over fifty."

He wasn't sure how to respond, but she saved him the trouble by plowing ahead on her own. "A dangerous profession. Kelly says you've joined a consulting company that works with police organizations. Is it the adrenaline rush, the thrill of the chase, that keeps you at it even after retirement?"

"Something like that."

She nodded over her glass. "I can understand it. I pursue a different kind of quarry, you see."

She waited for him to take up his cue, so he asked, "What kind is that?"

"The mind of a genius." She grinned, revealing large, slightly crooked teeth. "The mathematical mind of Bach. You see, he wrote his music with God as his intended audience, not us human mortals. Furthermore, he understood that the language of the universe created by God is mathematics. Therefore, his music contains such mathematical precision while achieving such exquisite aesthetic beauty that it leaves one breathless."

"Aunt Alice has published books on the subject," Kelly said from the doorway.

"Only two, and they're far too dry for the average lay person to enjoy, I'm afraid. But I used to force my third-year students to read them, mostly because I had the power to do so."

"Aunt Alice taught math at Trent," Kelly explained.

"Well," Tom said, inwardly embarrassed at having thought she'd been a high school teacher.

"I'm going to risk my life and call Aunt Nancy to dinner," Kelly went on. "You two finish up your drinks now."

"Yes, dear." Aunt Alice waited until Kelly was gone, then bolted her drink and went to the liquor caddy to mix another. "How's yours? Want a refresher?"

Tom stood up. "No thank you. It's fine."

He watched her mix another drink in a clean, tall glass. It was a Manhattan—whiskey, red vermouth, and a dash of bitters. She sipped, nodded to herself, and chugged it like an undergrad.

Another followed that one in quick succession, then Tom trailed after her out into the hallway just as the second aunt reached the bottom of the stairs. She wore jeans, a green sweatshirt with Trent University printed across the front, and sneakers. Her hair was dyed jet black and chopped off in a bowl cut. She glared at him before turning to Aunt Alice.

"Who's this?"

"This is Kelly's friend, Nancy. Tom Faust."

Aunt Nancy made a face. "Oh, Christ, yes. I forgot. The cop." She stomped off toward the dining room.

Aunt Alice gave Tom a friendly grin. "Charmed, I'm sure."

Kelly was carving a large roast of beef on a platter. Aunt Nancy had already assumed her place at the head of the table and was spooning gravy onto her baked potatoes. Aunt Alice settled down at the foot of the table.

Kelly pointed at the chair directly in front of Tom. "You can sit there."

"Thank you." He sat down. His nerves were now pretty much settled. He thought he was going to enjoy this dinner after all.

Aunt Nancy stuffed food into her mouth, chewed noisily, and said, "You pronounce your name Fahhhhst, like an American, instead of Fowwwst, the way it's supposed to be pronounced."

"Yes, that's right."

"What's the matter, no appreciation of the classics?"

He leaned back as Kelly set a loaded plate in front of him. "It was my dad's fault, I guess."

"Don't tell me. He drove a gravel truck for a living."

"Actually, he taught biology at Queen's."

Aunt Nancy's eyebrows shot up. "An academic? I'm shocked."

Aunt Alice broke a roll in half and buttered it. "So we don't have to worry about you having made some kind of dark bargain with Mephistopheles, then?"

Tom shook his head. It was a conversation he'd occasionally endured, and he no longer found it annoying. "Nope. I'm strictly a self-made man."

Aunt Alice set down her butter knife and lifted the roll to her mouth. "Although some might argue that it might be necessary to make a pact with the devil in order to survive fifteen years of homicide investigation."

Tom glanced at her. She obviously knew more about him than she'd let on. "There were days when I was tempted."

"I can imagine."

Aunt Nancy burped and pointed her fork at him. "I don't like cops. Never have."

"Aunt Nancy was a Marxist in her younger days," Kelly said, passing Tom the gravy boat.

"You don't say." He drizzled gravy across his food.

Aunt Nancy shrugged, stabbing at snow peas with her fork. "It was the sixties. Political sentiments ran pretty high on campus back then. We had to take a stand against the establishment." She shoved the peas into her mouth and chewed at him defiantly.

"Nancy's an urban geographer," Aunt Alice said. "You may be too young to remember, but at that time it was all about getting back to the land, finding a new harmony with nature, respecting the environment. It was a purer time than what we have today. Much more idealistic."

"The Woodstock generation," Kelly said.

"Nancy's convictions were so strong," Aunt Alice said, "that she got herself arrested a couple of times for participating in demonstrations in public places. Here in town, if you can imagine."

"I don't want to talk about it," Aunt Nancy snapped around a mouthful of beef. "Talk about something else."

"I read in the paper," Aunt Alice said to Tom, "that you're renovating an old church."

"That's right," he replied cautiously, not sure if she intended to bring up the homicide investigation. It was the last thing he wanted to discuss at table.

"How nice." Aunt Alice looked down the table at Aunt Nancy. "It's the old St. Mark's Presbyterian, in Selwyn township."

Aunt Nancy grunted and swallowed. "Does it have a heritage designation?"

Tom shook his head.

"Then I suppose you're just going to go ahead and do whatever the fuck you want with it."

"Something like that." He smiled.

"Go ahead, laugh, but nobody gives a shit about preserving the past any more. Nobody."

"Well, certainly the Presbyterians didn't in this case," Aunt Alice said, "or else they wouldn't have let their fine old church fall into such disrepair that this gentleman has to spend his own hard-earned money to make it useful again."

Tom glanced over at Kelly and caught her hiding a grin.

"Alice," Aunt Nancy said, rapping the table with the edge of her fork, "you hit the nail right on the head. If there's anything worse than jackbooted cops it's True Believers who don't realize their spaceship took off for home a long time ago."

"I understand you write a blog," Tom said.

Aunt Nancy nodded. "I'll send you the link and you can read it yourself. That way I don't have to talk about it. I hate chewing my cud twice."

"It's about urban planning, land use, that sort of thing," Aunt Alice said. "Nancy's professor emeritus of geography at Trent. She still teaches classes. She's an expert in RUF, the rural-urban fringe. You'd probably find her books much more interesting to read than mine."

"Bullshit." Aunt Nancy tore a dinner roll in half and used it to mop up her gravy. "Nobody gives a shit about any of that stuff any more. Nobody can focus on a serious subject for more than five fucking minutes. If it weren't for the students, I'd be lucky to get a hundred views per post. It's a very distracted society out there, my friend." She pointed her dripping bun at Tom. "Distracted to the point of being in a complete haze. And not a purple haze, either. An information haze. Pumped out by social media."

When the meal was finished, Aunt Alice disappeared into the sunroom to have a little doze in her recliner. Tom began to gather up the plates and silverware, intending to help Kelly feed the dishwasher and tidy up, but Aunt Nancy stepped in front of him and held up two cigars.

"She's all right. Come with me for a post-prandial smoke, Fahhst."

Kelly took the plates from his hand. "Don't be too long."

"As long as it takes to smoke this," Aunt Nancy replied, handing him one of the cigars. "Come on, we'll light up outside."

He followed her out into the back yard. It was overgrown with tall, mature trees with low-hanging limbs that needed to be trimmed back and lilac bushes that begged to be pruned. Nancy used a clipper to remove the cap from her cigar and produced a small box of wooden matches from the pocket of her jeans. "Gas lighters transfer an odour to the tobacco, I don't care what you say. A wooden match is the only way to go."

He accepted the tool from her and clipped the end of his cigar. He looked at the band: Upmann. Expensive. He watched her light her cigar, then exchanged the clipper for the matchbox. He wasn't much of a cigar smoker, but he figured he should be able to match an old lady puff for puff. He stripped off the band and lit the cigar.

"You don't leave the band on," Aunt Nancy observed.

"Can't stand the taste of paper on my lips." He gave the matches back to her.

"It's pretentious to leave the band on. Like you want the whole world to know what fine taste in cigars you have."

Noticing that she'd left the band on hers, he said nothing.

She gestured at a nearby picnic table. He sat down. She parked herself on the opposite corner, exhaling smoke at the early evening sky. "Nice house, isn't it?"

He agreed that it was.

"Built in 1914. This street started out as a nine-acre park, did you know that?"

"I'm from Kingston," he said.

"No excuse for ignorance." Aunt Nancy studied the tip of her cigar, found it burning to her satisfaction, and took another long pull. "Settle in for the lecture."

"I'm all ears."

She studied him for a moment. "Nice-looking ears, at that. In fact, you're a damned fine-looking man. I can see why Kelly's attracted to you."

He raised his eyebrows at her.

"She's a good girl. Loyalty's her gift and her curse. Do her wrong, and I'll hunt you down like a sick dog and put you out of your misery."

"Understood."

She turned her attention back to the sky, puffed for a moment, then waved the cigar. "When Sandford Fleming surveyed this city in 1846 he set the western boundary at Park Street, which puts us one block outside the city limits as they were then. The land we're sitting on right now was one of eight nine-acre park lots created by the Crown as a buffer between the city, which was growing along the Otonabee River, and farmland to the west of us." She pointed her cigar behind her. "The farmland started right there, where Monaghan Road is now, at the end of this block."

Tom drew on his cigar and released the smoke slowly, enjoying the taste.

"This parcel of parkland was owned by a couple of different people, but mostly it was controlled by a man named George Cox through his company, the Toronto Savings and Loan. The park lot was subdivided a bunch of times and people started building houses. This particular lot was sold to a woman named Julia Trebilcock, who hired William Blackwell to design the house and Thomas Ephgrave to build it."

She looked at Tom and grunted when she saw that the names meant nothing to him. "Blackwell was a very well-known architect around here at the time. He designed the YMCA, Queen Mary School just up there on

Monaghan Road, and a lot of other important buildings." She examined the ash on the end of her cigar, decided it was long enough, and tapped it off. "The thing that makes all this stuff interesting is that when Trebilcock bought this lot to build her house, there were a lot of restrictions placed on the sale. Only one house could be built, it had to be constructed of brick, stone, or a combination of the two, outbuildings like a barn or shed were forbidden, and Toronto Savings and Loan got to approve any design before she could construct."

"Why was that?" Tom asked.

"Because," she drawled, looking at him out of the corner of her eye, "these were prestige lots. The park lots were bought up by rich community leaders as country estates. Today we're only a few blocks from the downtown core, but at that time this was out in the country. Wealthy businessmen built huge estate homes and were very fussy about what other houses were built around them. It was such bullshit.

"Having grown up in this house, on this street, with such an intense interest in the use of land and responsible urban growth and all the rest, I can't help but get pissed about it. They were so pompous. Now they have buildings and streets and shit named after them and local historians fall all over themselves praising our ancestral community fathers and their wonderful fucking money. Well, it was greed and not altruism that motivated them. It always is."

Tom waited, drawing on the cigar, watching her profile.

"The city annexed the lots in 1872," she went on, "moving the town limits west from Park Street to Monaghan Road. So the rich boys could get out of Monaghan township and enjoy all the benefits of living the urban life, such as it was back then, as Peterborough's new west end. That's when they started subdividing like crazy, to capitalize on their investments. It all went downhill from there.”

“You don't believe in progress?” Tom asked. “In people taking advantage of opportunities to generate wealth for their families?”

“You're a shit disturber, aren't you?” She wagged her cigar at him. “That's all right. I'll let you in on a little secret. In the nine years Kelly's been here, she's brought home two other guys. One was a doctor she met at the hospital, and the other was some kind of a businessman. Insurance broker or some damned thing. Ask her about them if you want the nitty-gritty. Don't ask me. None of my damned business. Bottom line—neither of them came back again after they met me.”

Tom puffed on his cigar.

“For an ex-cop,” she said, “you're all right. I hope you come back again.”

They smoked for a while in silence, enjoying the quiet sounds of the city around them, then dropped what remained of their cigars into a flowerpot with an inch of rainwater at the bottom. They went inside to find Kelly in the kitchen, putting the last of the leftovers into the refrigerator.

“I'll leave you two alone now,” Aunt Nancy said. “I have to go upstairs and kick some ass.”

Kelly closed the fridge door. “You look as though you survived Aunt Nancy.”

“I like her.”

“It must be the lingering effects of that concussion. You should see your doctor right away.”

“No, really. I like her. I like both of them. Anyway, I don't have a regular doctor.”

“You should. Did you like Dr. Pham?”

“Yeah. I guess.”

"She's taking new patients. Call her and make an appointment for a follow-up. Seriously."

"I'm okay."

"Seriously."

His cellphone pinged faintly in his pocket. He took it out and saw that he'd received a text message. "I'd better look at this."

"Feel free."

It was a text from a contact he didn't recognize and didn't remember having on his personal phone:

> *Hello, Tom. Be outside in yr car in 5 mins.*
> *You'll want to take this call in private.*

He slowly thumbed a reply:

> *Who is this?*

He waited for a moment, and then another message pinged:

> *LMFAO. Who do you think, Tom?*

He looked at Kelly, who was watching him. "I think I'd better leave."

"Oh, dear. That's a shame. Is everything all right?"

"I'm not sure. I don't know who this is." He put the phone in his pocket. "Thanks so much for dinner. This has been really nice. I've really enjoyed myself."

"I'm glad. We should do it again sometime."

"I'd love to. Soon."

She leaned forward and kissed him on the cheek. "Call me when you can."

"I will," he said, meaning it.

38

He got into the Malibu and started the engine so that the air conditioning could run while he sat there. He put his phone on the centre console to wait for the call to come through. He hadn't bothered pairing it to the car's audio system, since he didn't expect to be driving it for more than a few days, so he left the radio off.

After a few minutes a cellphone began to vibrate. He picked it up and looked at the display. It showed the same contact name and number as the text he'd received.

"This is Tom Faust."

"*Mr. Faust, how very good to speak to you again.*" The voice was distorted, deep and blurred, as though coming through a voice changer of some kind.

"Who is this?"

"*You know who it is. I'm sorry to cut your dinner date short. How did it go?*"

"Never mind that. It's time for you to give yourself up. Just call 911 and explain who you are, and they'll send someone to pick you up."

The voice laughed ominously. *"Oh, I don't think so, Tom. Listen to me. Nurse Reed seems like a very sweet little thing. Looking after those two old biddies like that. Just play along with me and I won't have to pay her a visit. Know what I mean?"*

"Listen, you—" Tom stopped short. He knew better than to argue with a suspect and let his own emotions enter into the situation. He took a deep breath and slowly let it out.

"That's better, Tom. Much better. By the way, how do you like this voice-changing gadget? Effective? Does it give you the creeps just listening to it?"

"It's very effective," Tom said, forcing his tone to remain neutral.

"Yeah. It's a toy. Just a second." There was a crackling sound, a bit of fumbling, and a clatter as something made of hard plastic was tossed aside.

"There," the voice returned, sounding normal, "so much for that. Can you believe these things cost six hundred bucks new? That model? I got it a lot cheaper than that, of course, but it's expensive because it has a lot of features. I could have talked to you as a girl with a southern accent, or any one of fifty other weird and strange voices. Great, huh?"

"Why are you calling me?"

"Very direct, as always. You recognize my voice, don't you?"

Tom hesitated. "Of course."

"Oh, shit. You're still having problems. It must be the after-effects of the concussion. Look, I'm really sorry about that."

"I'll bet you are." Logically Tom knew it was the Bushmaster and that he was listening to the man who'd called himself James Woods while posing as a phone technician and electrician, but the sound of the voice wasn't immediately familiar to him, and unfortunately Woods had picked up on it.

"No, really, I am. I was just putting a scare into you. I thought you'd just go through the fence and into the field. I didn't realize there was a big-assed ditch there and that you'd hit it so hard. I'm sorry, man."

"You'll be sorry when we put you behind bars. Is this James Bush? Did you kill your family seventeen years ago? Why did you come back to get Kohl so many years later?"

The voice laughed. "I like you, Tom. I always have. You're kind of my role model, know that? Strong. Decisive. Smart. I've always wanted to be like you. Anyway, that's enough for now. I just wanted to ask you a question."

"What's your question, James?"

He laughed again. "You're a dog with a bone, aren't you? Anyway, I just wanted to know how it feels."

"How it feels?"

"Yeah. To be the one who's being stalked, chased, instead of the one doing the stalking and chasing. Must make you feel very uncomfortable. Very vulnerable."

"Oh, I'm coming after you, James. Make no mistake about that."

"Sure, that's the spirit. Anyway, I just want to remind you that the shoe's on the other foot now. And by the way. Maybe you shouldn't share our conversation with anyone else. Nurse Reed might not like it. Know what I mean?"

"Keep her out of it. This is between you and me, James. Just you and me."

"I'll be in touch."

The line went dead.

39

"Our story actually begins with Allie Whetung," Jeremy said, sitting on the corner of Natalie's desk. "Although I didn't realize it until I was part way through chasing down James Woods and saw that I should backtrack on her as well."

Tom sipped his third cup of coffee of the morning. He remembered that Allie was the girl in the foster home in Oshawa with whom James Bush had disappeared at the age of seventeen, four years after his family was murdered. "You said you hadn't been able to pick up any trace of her whatsoever after they took off."

"I did say that, didn't I?" Jeremy pointed at the monitor on Natalie's desk, which he'd turned around to face his audience after connecting his tablet to it. "Here's what she looked like seven years ago, at the age of twenty-two."

They leaned forward to stare at a photograph of a young woman with indigenous features and a sour expression. Her straight black hair was pulled back away from her face, and her dark eyes were hooded. It looked like a mug shot.

"Meet Allie Woods, a.k.a. Allie Whetung." Jeremy pushed his glasses back up onto the bridge of his nose.

"This pic's taken from an Ontario health card she applied for under her new name. But I'm getting a little ahead of myself. What you say, Tom, is quite true. She doesn't appear as Allie Whetung in any of the usual places. But once I had the James Woods name to work with, the doors started to open. I went back and found her as Allie Whetung in one place, and one only." He paused for dramatic effect.

"Today would be good, Jeremy," Natalie prompted.

"In the human resources database of a hospital in Toronto. She'd applied for several jobs there in 2009, but didn't get hired. Finally, in December of that year, they accepted her into their volunteer program and she was assigned to Emergency. Which is where the fun begins."

He swiped to a map of the northern portion of the Greater Toronto Area. He zoomed in on the neighbourhood known as Downsview. "So here's where she was working that month," he moved the cursor in a circle around the hospital, "and here's the address she listed on her application forms." He slid the cursor to the left. "As you can see, it's only eight blocks away from the hospital. Walking distance."

"Phoney address?" Tom asked.

"No, actually, because the address is a key link in the chain. But hold that thought for a minute. She began working in Emergency as a volunteer on December 8. As I understand it, volunteers serve as greeters, gofers, messengers, mess cleaner-uppers, and whatever else the regular paid staff don't have the time to do. On the surface, it looks like she was very determined to start her career in health care, whether paid or unpaid. But it didn't last."

He brought up a news item dated December 15, 2009. "There was a big snowstorm that buried the entire GTA on this particular day. It was a Sunday, and that night there was a huge pileup on the freeway. Six fatalities, dozens injured. This was the closest hospital, so they got an influx of casualties in a rush. They were already overloaded and understaffed as it was. According to this article, the corridors were filled with patients on gurneys waiting to be processed. EMS staff were dumping them and going back for more, and those that stayed with patients until they were admitted said it was chaos."

"Understandable," Natalie said.

"Quite." Jeremy removed his glasses and polished them with a tissue. "Allie Whetung was there that night. It was the last time she reported for work. She never showed up again."

"What happened?" asked Kashi.

"Not so fast." Jeremy grinned, slipping his glasses back on. "Let's talk about James Woods for a minute. I told Charlie the other day that I needed a viable name in order to be able to do what a skip tracer does. Well, if he were here right now I'd rub his nose in it a little bit. The name James Woods has done the trick."

"Jeremy, *please* get to the point," Natalie said.

"Oh, sure. Sorry. Suffice it to say that a shit-load of James Woodses cropped up, but this is the one I zeroed in on." He showed them a credit report on a James Woods who was born on June 15, 1986, in Niagara Falls, Ontario. His residence was listed as an address in Brampton. "You can see that the DOB and POB don't match our guy, James Bush, but bear with me. His credit card, health card, and driver's licence information all show a change of address request filed on Monday, December 16, 2009."

"The day after Allie Whetung stopped showing up at the hospital," Tom said.

"Exactly. Plus, employment records tell us that up to this point James Woods worked as a graphic designer at an advertising agency in Brampton. I did some checking and talked to a senior partner there who still remembers Woods. He said he was a very talented young man who loved his job and was popular with his co-workers. Then one day he didn't show up for work, and they never heard from him again."

"Interesting," Kashi said.

Jeremy nodded. "There were two John Does who died at that hospital on the night of the fifteenth during the storm. The staff took the usual steps to try to identify them, but none of the paramedics could remember bringing either one in, they had no identification on them, and a check of fingerprints went nowhere. It happens, right? Big city, bad storm, a lot of chaos. People get separated from their vehicles, IDs get missed at the scene because everything's in panic mode. What I think happened is that Allie Whetung searched our guy's pockets, found a wallet, and stole it."

"A wallet belonging to James Woods," Tom said. "You're talking about identity theft."

"Yes, indeed. Now, here's where it gets interesting." Jeremy showed them a photograph of a rough-looking four-storey brick building. "This is the address Allie Whetung listed on her application forms when she was applying for positions at the hospital. It's the same address James Woods used when he sent in his change-of-address requests. It's a crappy apartment building in a so-so neighbourhood, owned by a numbered company. From what I could learn, almost a third of the apartments in the building were reported as vacant on an ongoing basis, which was ridiculously far above the vacancy rate in Toronto for that year. I figure they were dealing in cash for those so-called vacant apartments and not reporting the income."

"I see," Kashi said.

"Yeah, and even more interesting is the fact that this

numbered company owns a lot of other things besides apartment buildings in bad neighbourhoods. Among their holdings is the Buckaroo chain of pawn shops. A search of municipal records turned up a few police reports for vagrancy and causing a disturbance at one of the shops, located on a pretty rough side street not far from the hospital. This shop was managed by a person by the name of James Woods."

Tom sat back, folding his arms. "So you're saying that James Bush, under the identity of James Woods, lived in this apartment building and worked at a nearby pawn shop owned by the same people?"

"Yes. And this numbered company has known connections to organized crime."

"Oh? How so?"

"It comes from our intelligence side," Jeremy shrugged, "so I won't go into any details. But a chain of pawn shops is a natural medium for money laundering, so you can see the connection."

"I don't know much about that kind of business," Kashi said.

"That's right," Jeremy said, "you do all your shopping at the Eaton Centre."

Kashi rolled her eyes.

"The main focus of a pawn shop's daily operations," Jeremy went on, anxious to show off his knowledge, "is pawn loans. Someone brings in an item as collateral, they receive cash for a fraction of what the item is worth, and they're charged about 25 per cent interest per month on the outstanding loan. Buckaroo, for example, reported last year that they operated forty-seven stores across the province. They loaned out twenty-eight million dollars and received back fifteen million in repayments. They made another eleven million in interest, six million from scrapping jewellery, and another eighteen from selling forfeited merchandise. The grand total, in case you're not bothering with the mental math, is a profit of twenty-two million. That's what they reported.

"Now with this many transactions happening, there are plenty of places to conceal the flow of unreported cash. Or, on the other hand, transactions could be grossly inflated. For example, the average loan transaction in a pawn shop runs about one hundred and twenty bucks. These guys could use a lot of these small transactions to cover larger movements of cash.

"The other thing about Buckaroo is that their stores tend to be located on side streets, away from normal foot traffic, and their hours are weird. They're closed more often than they're open."

Kashi nodded, writing in her notebook.

"So what you're telling us," Tom put in, "is that James Bush ran away from his foster home in Oshawa and resurfaced on the grid three years later in Downsview as James Woods, working for some organized crime group. Anything in between?"

Jeremy shook his head. "He and Allie were probably on the street for a while, but there are no arrest records, nothing at all during that time. They must have made some connections in the early going and found a safe way to stay under the surface."

"Okay. Then Allie steals a wallet belonging to the deceased James Woods of Brampton, brings it home, and James decides to assume the guy's identity and come back out onto the grid. Why bother? He seemed to be doing okay staying under the radar."

"I think it was a mental health issue." Jeremy folded his arms. "I'd say it was a health card Allie was originally looking for, first and foremost."

"Why would she want that?" Kashi asked.

"I think James Bush was suffering from severe depression that was going untreated. It may be why Allie tried to get a job in the hospital, to find a way to get him medication. That's just speculation, though. What I know for sure is that the credit card in the name of James Woods at the new address soon began showing purchases at a drug store down the street from the pawn shop where he worked. Two different medications, an anti-depressant and another prescription to treat insomnia. Refilled on a regular basis. I think that as soon as he got his hands on James Woods's health card he got himself in to see a doctor, obtained legitimate prescriptions, and has stayed on them ever since."

"He may have been getting by on street drugs before that," Kashi said.

"Not the best idea in the world," Tom said.

"By that time," Jeremy continued, "he'd decided it was safe to move around in his new identity. He got a cellphone and an online bank account. He came out as James Woods and started living in the open."

"But what about this electrician Jim Woods that I met? I don't see a connection here."

Jeremy nodded. "That's the tricky part, but would it help if we could place James Woods here in Peterborough right now?"

"Can you?"

Jeremy tugged at his beard. "The others may be forgiven, but you've been around Peterborough for a while now, Tom. Doesn't the name Buckaroo Pawn Shop mean anything to you?"

"There's one over on Charlotte Street." Tom stared at Jeremy's grin. "Are you saying he's working there now?"

"He's not only the manager of said store," Jeremy

gloated, "but he lives in the apartment above it."

Tom ran a hand through his hair, aware of a growing headache. "Are you telling me we've been looking for James Bush all this time, and he's been living only four blocks from this office?"

"That's exactly what I'm telling you."

"Jesus H. Christ on a stick." Tom sat back, folding his arms. "So how does Jim Woods-slash-Bush go from managing a pawn shop to being an expert with electrical wiring, phone circuits, and surveillance equipment?"

"Why don't you go over to Buckaroo's and ask him?" Natalie said.

"Now there's a damned good idea." Tom got to his feet.

"Take Kashi with you."

Kashi began to gather up her things. "It might help clear up some of the confusion I'm having right now about who's who."

Leaving the room, Tom didn't miss the look of frustration on Jeremy's face as he turned his attention back to his tablet.

40

Although the Buckaroo Pawn Shop was only four blocks away, Kashi insisted on driving them over. The rain that had been falling earlier this morning had lessened to a light drizzle, but Kashi said she didn't want him to catch cold.

He grumbled but she insisted, so he gave up and rode with her in the elevator down to the parking level. She unlocked a leased Lincoln Navigator and opened the passenger door for him.

He climbed in, a little annoyed that she was treating him like a fragile old man.

A few minutes later, she found a parking spot on Charlotte Street several doors down from the pawn shop. As she turned off the engine and unlatched her seat belt, Tom held up a hand.

"Hang on a minute."

She looked at him, puzzled.

"Before we go any further," he said, "I want to know a little more about you."

"What, now? Why? What do you need to know?"

"Humour me." Tom unfastened his seat belt and turned sideways to look at her.

She wore no rings or bracelets, no jewellery of any kind. Her makeup was applied with professional care, and her long, black hair was pinned up in a neat bun at the base of her neck. She wore a light rain jacket over her navy pantsuit. She displayed the same care and attention to detail with her appearance that Tom had watched Pamela develop as a young model and refine as a film actor and Hollywood celebrity.

"How old are you?"

"I thought gentlemen your age were taught not to ask that question."

"Humour me," he repeated.

"I'm twenty-nine. I'll be thirty in November."

"Do you have any law enforcement experience?"

"No." She gave him a direct look. "I have a doctorate in forensic psychiatry."

"Do you, now."

"Yes. I'm a behavioural profiler. My mentor is Dr. Baker. But I've also published two articles on interviewing techniques, so I understand the principles behind what you're about to do, and I've been well coached to appreciate the considerable difference between theory and practice. I'm looking forward to watching you work."

"Dr. Ryan Baker, you're referring to?"

"Yes."

Baker was the behavioural analyst and profiler on the payroll of Cage Intelligence, the one Tracy Drummond said Kate Greene had brought in on the McGraw case in Elliott Lake.

Tom was himself an agnostic when it came to the subject. He'd seen profiling produce results, and he'd also seen it fall flat. He considered it a useful tool when available. If Kashi had mentored under Dr. Baker, then she must be very good. A guy like Baker didn't waste his time on the mediocre.

He remembered Jeremy expressing disdain for behavioural analysis. He'd compared it to casting someone's horoscope. Now Tom thought he understood why Jeremy didn't seem to like Kashi very much, and why he'd been upset when Natalie had chosen her instead of him to accompany Tom. He probably thought he should be the one assisting with field work.

"Tell me about your parents."

"My parents?" Kashi looked a little confused. "My father's a dentist, and my mother's a pediatrician. They're both still living. In Toronto."

"You're not married, or you just don't bother wearing a ring?"

"I'm single. I have a boyfriend, but we're not really serious at this point."

"What do you think about Natalie Stone? Do you like working for her?"

"Oh, yes. Very much."

"How much does she pay you?"

"Not as much as you're making right now."

Tom smiled faintly. He could see that she wanted to ask why he was firing these questions at her at such an odd time but was holding it back. She maintained eye contact with him, and her breathing was slow and regular. She didn't seem overly upset or stressed. He could see her figuring it out, that he was assessing her ability to stay calm and professional.

"Okay," he said, opening the car door," "I'll take the lead."

"Of course."

"And don't use that judo stuff unless I give you the signal."

"I don't—" She saw that he was smiling and shook her head.

The Buckaroo Pawn Shop was located on the north side of the street in the middle of a short block. It occupied the ground floor of a two-storey standalone building that was a hundred years old and looked as though it should have been torn down a long time ago. They walked down to it, the drizzle dampening their faces and hair.

As they passed the front window of the shop, Tom saw a customer inside, browsing in the centre aisle. On the sidewalk at the curb, almost directly across from the front entrance, were two empty metal newspaper boxes. Between the shop and the building next to it was a narrow space filled with trash and weeds. It was almost impossible to get through. If they flushed James Woods/Bush and he ran outside, Tom was confident he'd catch him if he tried to duck between the buildings. If he tried to run across the street, he'd have to dodge the newspaper boxes, costing him precious seconds. Even if he stayed on this side and went either left or right, Tom thought he could probably run him down.

A bell chimed as Tom opened the door. He walked in ahead of Kashi, paying no attention to what she might expect from a "gentleman of his age." In his world, when approaching an unknown situation with a civilian in tow, a police officer went through the door first. Simple as that. Some other time he'd hold the door open for her.

Straight ahead was a centre aisle that led all the way to the back. On the left was the cash area. Beyond that were glass counters holding jewellery, watches, and electronic equipment, shelves of video games and movie DVDs, and a rack of music CDs. On the right was another aisle with shelves displaying power tools, hardware, and sporting goods. A quick look around told him that there was only one customer in the store at the moment, the one he'd seen from outside.

A young woman watched them from a high stool behind the cash register. Her sand-coloured hair had purple streaks in it, matching the plastic frames of her glasses, and her jaw moved as she chewed gum. She was not Allie Whetung.

There was no sign of James Woods/Bush.

"Hi," Tom said, putting a hand on the glass top of the display case and looking down at the wrist watches, "is Jim around?"

The woman popped air out of the gum between her molars. "Sorry, who?"

"Jim Woods." He looked up at her. "He's the manager here, right?"

"Who's asking?"

"My name's Faust. My colleague and I are working with the OPP on a couple of things. Jim might have some information that would be helpful to us. Is he around?"

"Just a minute." The woman slid off the stool as the customer approached the cash register with a handful of DVDs.

Tom looked at Kashi and nodded. She gave him a brief, neutral smile and moved down the counter a few steps to look at the rings while the cashier rang through the customer's purchases. They were all well-known horror films, including *The Evil Dead, Evil Dead II,* and *Army of Darkness.* Someone had apparently dumped their Bruce Campbell collection, and this lucky fellow was the benefactor.

When the customer left the shop, the woman returned to her stool. "You're wasting your time. Jim hasn't been here for about a week."

"Oh? Where is he?"

"I don't know. Haven't seen him."

"Is that usual? To take off like that and not let people know?"

She shook her head. "He left a note saying he was taking a few days off and would be back. That was it."

Something in her tone of voice suggested that she was genuinely disappointed. Tom put a sympathetic look on his face and said, "What's your name?"

She hesitated. "Lisa."

"What about Allie, Lisa? Is she around?"

Her expression flattened. "No."

"She's not in the picture any more?"

"Not as far as *I* know."

"Since when?"

"Since a while ago. Look, what's this got to do with the OPP stuff you're talking about?"

"We think Jim may be able to help us with a few things. How long have you two been seeing each other, Lisa?"

She shook her head. "None of your business."

"On again, off again, huh?"

"Something like that. Maybe if you come back next week, he'll be here and you can ask him your questions instead of me."

Tom eased away from the counter and slowly walked down the aisle toward the back.

"He lives upstairs, right?"

Lisa slid off the stool. "You can't go back there."

He passed two racks of books and stood in front of a doorway with stairs leading up to the next floor.

"His apartment's up here, right? Do you live here, too?"

"No. Look, you can't go up there without a warrant."

"We're not cops, Lisa. We don't need a warrant to do stuff. Is it locked?"

"Yes."

"Do you have the key?"

"He left his keys with the note. I'm supposed to cover for him until he gets back."

"His keys. Does he drive, Lisa?"

"He doesn't have a car."

"May I see the note?" Kashi asked.

Lisa frowned. "Why?"

"I'm a bit of an expert at handwriting. I might be able to tell something from it."

"It was printed. From his computer."

"I still might be able to tell something from what it says."

Lisa reached into the back pocket of her jeans, pulled out a folded piece of paper, and passed it over.

Kashi took it by one corner and shook it open. She studied it for a moment, then gave it to Tom. He held it by the opposite corner. It said, simply: "Will be out of town for a week. Personal stuff. Cover for me. Jim."

"May I keep this?" he asked.

"No. Oh, hell. Whatever."

"Could I have a plastic bag?"

Sighing, Lisa handed him a plastic bag with the shop logo on it. Kashi took it from her and opened it so that Tom could drop the note inside.

"Does he often leave notes for you like this?" Tom asked.

Lisa shook her head.

"Where did you find it?"

"On the front counter when I came in, last week. Next to the cash register. I have my own key for the front door because I'm usually the one who opens in the morning."

"What day was that?"

"Last Wednesday."

"So he's been gone for more than a week."

"Yeah."

"Are you sure this note is from Jim Woods?" Kashi asked.

"Who else would it be from?"

"It just seems a little impersonal," Kashi replied, glancing at Tom, "coming from someone you've been romantically involved with. Did you fight?"

Lisa's mouth formed a tight line.

Tom stepped through the doorway and looked up the stairs. "Do you have any idea what he meant by 'personal stuff'?"

"No. You shouldn't go up there."

He put his foot on the bottom step. "Maybe he went back to Allie."

"I doubt it."

He turned around to look at her. "You sound pretty definite about that."

"I talked to her yesterday." Lisa put her hands on her hips. "Allie walked out on him four months ago and moved in with someone twice her age. Some woman who runs a pet store on Hunter Street. Across the bridge in East City. She hasn't seen him for more than a month and really doesn't give a shit."

Tom started up the stairs.

"You shouldn't go up there," Lisa repeated, following.

"You've been in his apartment before," he said over his shoulder, "and he left you his keys. We'll help you look around, see if there's anything that can tell us where he went."

"It's important that we find him," Kashi said, following Lisa up the stairs. "You must be worried."

"I just don't know what's going on," Lisa complained, her voice rising. "I thought everything was fine between us, then this. I was going to suggest we move in together next month. My roommate's bringing her boyfriend in. I have to get out."

They stood together at the top of the stairs. A wall had been thrown up to seal off the upper floor. The drywall had been poorly taped along the seams, and many of the screws were visible beneath the thin coat of paint. Tom held out his hand for the keys.

"Let me," Lisa said. She edged past him and unlocked the door. Opening it, she moved inside and called out, "Jim? Are you here?"

Tom followed her into the apartment. The floorboards were wide pine planks that probably dated back to the original construction of the building. At some point they'd been sanded and refinished. The walls were covered with tongue-in-groove wallboard painted white, and the high ceilings showed off well-preserved pressed tin. The air smelled stale, with undercurrents of dirty clothing and old wallpaper. Lisa walked directly to the bedroom on the far side. He followed.

"Jim?" She stopped in the doorway.

He moved her gently out of the way and went in. He looked at an unmade queen-sized bed, mismatched dressers, an end table beside the bed, and a cedar wardrobe serving as a closet. Discarded clothing littered the floor and the bed. The dressers and end table were covered with empty beer bottles, balled-up fast food wrappers, and other assorted garbage. He picked up an empty plastic bag and used it to open the drawer of the end table. It was crammed with empty candy bar wrappers, cough lozenges, loose change, pens and pencils, and similar junk.

The wardrobe door was open. Several long-sleeved

dress shirts were hung up inside, along with two pairs of black trousers, a green cardigan sweater, a couple of plaid shirts, and a cheap black sports jacket. The dresser drawers held balled-up pairs of socks, boxer shorts, rolled up T-shirts, several pairs of jeans, a grey track suit, and other items of clothing.

There were no photographs anywhere. No albums, no framed pictures, no personal images at all.

He left the room as Kashi was coming out of the kitchen. She shrugged. They walked through the large living room together, looking at a beat-up leather couch, two recliners, and a rocking chair, none of which matched. A TV stand held a widescreen television, a Playstation, and an assortment of games.

The place could have used the services of a competent housekeeper.

Tom sighed. There were no work tables, tools, electronic instruments, or anything else that would connect the apartment to the electrician he'd met. Tom wondered if perhaps Woods/Bush kept that stuff somewhere downstairs.

As Kashi walked over to the high, arched windows to look down at the street below, Tom wandered back through the living room into the kitchen. He stepped over garbage bags and half-filled recycling bins. The sink and tiny table were covered with dirty dishes and empty food containers. The cupboards held an assortment of dishes, packaged pasta, a half-empty bag of white sugar, canned vegetables, and other odds and ends. The refrigerator was almost empty. The freezer compartment held a few frozen dinners, ice cube trays with a few cubes missing, and a package of pork chops.

"What's through here?" he asked Lisa, pointing at a door at the rear of the kitchen.

"It goes into the back room."

"Back room?"

"Yeah, a back room. You know? It's pretty much empty, as far as I know. I never go out there. There's a fire escape on the back of it."

He picked his way through the trash and tried the knob. The door opened. He flicked a switch on the wall. A light came on inside. He swung the door wide open.

It had served at one time as a pantry, from the looks of it. The shelves on the walls were empty except for a few stray cans of soup, vegetables, and cat food. The tops of the cans were covered with dust, suggesting they'd been sitting there for quite a while.

"Does Jim have a pet?" he asked Lisa, looking at the cat food.

"No. He doesn't like animals."

The Bushes hadn't kept any pets, he recalled. The cans had probably belonged to a previous tenant and not to James Woods/Bush.

He went in, looking around. He heard Lisa leave the kitchen, probably to see what Kashi was doing. The walls and ceiling in here were unfinished and unpainted. The air was warm and close. There was no insulation and no heating back here, so it would be warm in the summer and cold in the winter. A typical back room tacked onto an old building. It was wired for electricity, though, because he could hear a soft humming sound. He walked past the shelves and looked at a large box freezer. The little red light was on, indicating that it was running.

He approached it, puzzled. Jim Woods/Bush kept his cans and dry goods in the kitchen. Was it reasonable, then, that he'd keep food in this freezer out here rather than in the upper compartment of the refrigerator in the kitchen, where it would be a lot more handy at mealtime?

Tom's nostrils dilated. He smelled dust, mildew, and the unmistakable tang of mouse urine. Was there also something else? Something faint but familiar?

He walked over to the freezer. There was no lock. Using the plastic bag that he still held in his hand, he gripped the handle and raised the lid.

A man sat inside the freezer, his knees up under his chin, his arms wrapped around his legs. His head rested against the inner wall. His eyes stared vacantly straight ahead. His throat was slashed, and the laceration had frozen into a gaping wound. What Tom could see of his shirt was blackened with congealed, frozen blood.

It was not the face of the electrician who had called himself Jim Woods.

Hearing a noise behind him, he turned around in time to grab Lisa by the arms. She looked over his shoulder into the freezer. "Jim! Oh my God! Jim!"

He hustled her back out into the kitchen. "Who is it, Lisa? Who is it?"

"It's Jim, oh no, oh no, it's Jim!"

"Jim Woods?"

"Yes, yes! Who would do this to him? I don't understand!"

Tom looked over the top of her head at Kashi, who'd followed Lisa into the kitchen. She stared at him, mouth open.

He passed Lisa to her and went back to the freezer.

Staring at the face, he could now see the resemblance between this man and the boy who'd lost his family to murder seventeen years ago.

This was James Bush, who'd moved from one foster home to another, his family slaughtered, his life irrevocably and horribly changed.

James Bush, who'd escaped into the forest behind his

house that night and had wandered along the highway until ending up in hospital thanks to a passing Good Samaritan. James Bush, who'd entered the child welfare system and bounced around, who'd finally taken his own fate in his hands and dropped off the grid before changing his identity to start a new life. James Bush, whose long road had ultimately led him here, crammed into a freezer in a back room with his throat slashed.

Seventeen years later, the Bushmaster had finally caught up to him.

41

The following morning Tom and Natalie were summoned to the OPP Peterborough County detachment office on Lansdowne Street. After a brief wait they were ushered into the office of Inspector Mark Roach, who sat behind his desk with a decidedly sour look on his face.

"Sit down," Roach said, without getting up.

Leaning on the corner of Roach's filing cabinet, Gavin Elliott nodded. "Thanks for coming. This won't take long."

Natalie sat down and crossed her legs. "We were hoping you could—"

"We're really not very happy you keep turning up all these bodies," Roach growled at Tom. "I'm not a hundred per cent sure what you think you're doing."

"You'd rather they went undiscovered, Mark? Or that I would just close the door and leave them there?"

"Don't get smart with me."

Gavin stirred. "We'll be adding PPS to the task force. They've assigned one of their detectives, the one who interviewed you yesterday, Tom."

"Carla Mendoza? She seemed good."

Gavin nodded. "With three active homicides and this guy on the loose in the area, we need to tighten up control."

He looked at Natalie. "As a result, we're asking you and your team to stand down on the cold case review. We'll take it from here."

"Are you sure?" Natalie folded her hands in her lap. "We could still offer invaluable assistance. A behavioural profile, for example."

"Not at this time. You and your staff are now witnesses, and it would no longer be appropriate for you to continue as investigators. The contract will be paid in full, with our thanks."

Natalie nodded slowly. "I see. All right." She stood up. "That's it, then."

"Thank you." Gavin shook her hand. "Tom?"

Tom stood up and shook his hand. He held it for an extra moment and said, "Could we talk to you for a moment? Right now?"

"Now?" Gavin glanced at Roach. "Mark and I have a few things to go over."

"It's important."

"Give me a minute," Gavin said over his shoulder.

Roach waved, turning his attention to a file folder on his desk.

Outside, with Roach's office door closed, Tom said, "Is Bell here?"

Gavin nodded. "I saw her a few minutes ago. Armour's offsite at the moment, but Pat's here."

"The four of us. In a meeting room. Right now."

"What's going on?" Natalie asked.

"I screwed up," Tom said, "but it may be fixable."

42

That evening the house was quiet. Tom sat on a high stool at the kitchen island, working on his laptop. He'd started off listening to music, but after a few minutes he'd tapped the top of the audio player and shut it off. He wasn't in the mood for it.

He was putting in time on his online private investigation basic training program. Tonight he was working his way through the section involving investigative techniques. He'd finished a module on surveillance and had just moved on to the one covering interview and interrogation.

He was struggling a little with the whole thing. The difficulty was not the material itself, of course, because it was all stuff he'd practised every day in his career for thirty-five years. His problem was finding a way to spend enough time on it to log the fifty hours required to qualify for the test. He'd heard of some guys who signed in, spent a few minutes getting into a module, then just walked away to do something else, coming back after an hour or so to move on through the next few screens. Tom was tempted, but wasn't sure he wanted to cheat the system. So he was forcing himself to read each word, hoping to learn something about the private investigation perspective that was different from his experience as a police officer.

So far, no luck. It was all pretty Mickey Mouse.

He picked up his glass and rattled the ice cubes. Empty. He got up and grabbed another can of Coke from the fridge.

As he poured the soft drink around the ice, he remembered having read on a news feed this morning that the summer meteor shower was in full swing right now. The Perseids, debris falling off a comet nicknamed the swift turtle, or something like that.

He opened the sliding glass door and went outside. There was more sound out here than indoors—crickets, frogs, and the background rumbling of a jet passing overhead in the darkness.

He looked up and, after a moment, spotted its flashing lights. Probably a flight travelling from Toronto to Montreal. He watched it for a while, then shifted his eyes around, looking for the quicker movement of a falling star.

Nothing.

He sat down on his lawn chair, put his feet up on the chunk of wood, and leaned back to rest his head against the wall.

It had been a rough day. His admission that he'd communicated with the Bushmaster on Friday night and not told anyone about it had caused a bit of an uproar. The look of disappointment in Gavin Elliott's eyes was only the beginning, as he was then obligated to submit to a lengthy interview with Pat Bell. Afterward, she made a few phone calls and reached a sketch artist who was able to come in and sit with Tom that afternoon to prepare a composite drawing of the man he knew as Jim Woods the telephone technician and electrician. The sketch went out with a news release from Media Services that made the six o'clock news.

Meanwhile, Gavin held off on terminating the Cage Intelligence contract on the understanding that the Bushmaster might contact Tom again, and that Tom would be obligated to inform Detective Constable Bell immediately, should it happen. Failure to do so would result in violation of the terms and conditions of the contract, which would leave Cage holding the bag.

The look of disappointment in Natalie's eyes was an appropriate postscript to the day.

Tom sipped, watching the sky. At least it didn't taste like root beer any more. After a while he still hadn't seen any meteors, so he drained his glass and went back inside.

He tossed the ice cubes into the sink and put the glass in the dishwasher in the laundry room. He paused for a moment to look at the small stained glass window in the laundry tub. He'd brought it in from the carport earlier to clean off the road dust. Jade was going to start building a picket fence around Pamela's garden in a few days, and the plan was to integrate the window, which stood about four feet high, into the design.

It was a nice enough thing, with an arched top and an attractive pattern of white roses, green leaves, and purple flowers of some kind. Tom could see why Pamela liked it, and he was glad he'd saved it when the windows in the church had been replaced.

He sat down and frowned at his laptop. A dialogue box had opened up on top of the training module window, and he didn't understand what it was. The training program had a chat box messaging system for online help, but this didn't look like it:

James: Hi Tom, taking a break?
Tom: |

What the hell? Tom set the Coke aside and tried to close the dialogue box. Nothing happened when he clicked the X icon at the top right-hand corner. He was about to reboot the laptop to get rid of it when he hesitated. Was it the Bushmaster? Had he hacked into Tom's computer to resume their conversation? He began to type:

Tom: Who is this?

Immediately a response began to appear in the dialogue box:

James: You know who it is.

Involuntarily, Tom looked around the kitchen. Was he under video surveillance as well as audio?

> **Tom**:   Are you surveilling me, Jim? Should I be feeling even more paranoid than usual?
> **James**: LMAO. Master of the obvious. Look, Tom, it was damned inconvenient of you to find poor little James's body like that.
> **Tom**:   Sorry to mess up your style.
> **James**: That's the spirit. Oh well, I was pretty much finished with the whole James Woods alias shit. Although it was great you thought I was Bushie boy. Gave me a few laughs.
> **Tom**:   So who are you?
> **James**: You know who I am. Anyway, fuck all that. I wanted to tell you your artist likeness really sucks. It doesn't look

anything at all like me. What a laugh.

Tom: It'll be close enough to get your ass arrested.

James: You wish. Do you really think my nose is that big?

Tom: I think you should turn yourself in while you can. Or are you setting yourself up for suicide by cop?

James: Hey hey now. Enough of that. You had negotiator training, Tom, I saw it in your file. You know you're not supposed to say stuff like that to a suspect in a potential tactical situation.

Tom: How did you see my file?

James: Don't be stupid. And boring. Gotta go. Just wanted to let you know there was one more piece of unfinished business I had to clean up, and I finally got around to taking care of it tonight.

Tom: What unfinished business?

James: Just something way down on the priority list until now. Poor Cecile. Since you're telling your cop friends everything, I suggest you tell them to look in on her.

Tom: What the hell have you done?

James: |

The cursor continued to blink next to James's name until Tom realized the Bushmaster had gone offline. He pulled his cellphone out of his pocket and, once again, made the call.

43

Peterborough city police had shut down McDonnel Street between Aylmer and Stewart, giving them a two-block crime scene to work with. Detective Constable Pat Bell met Tom at the outer perimeter at the Aylmer Street intersection. After he signed in and clipped a visitor's ID card onto the front lapel of his jacket, she led him up the block to the next corner. She stopped him a few metres outside the inner perimeter.

"This'll do. Now walk me through it once again, Faust. He said what, exactly, to you?"

"He just called her poor Cecile, and told me I should tell my cop friends to check on her."

"And that was it? Short and sweet?"

"Well, no, Pat. He started off talking about us finding the body of James Bush, that it inconvenienced him. He said I know who he is."

"And?"

"Shit, I don't know who he is. If I did, do you think we'd be standing here at one in the morning blowing gas like this?"

"Maybe he means you know him. It's someone you know."

"Yeah, apparently." Tom shoved his hands in his pockets. "Anyway, he gave me a hard time about the composite, said it didn't look anything like him. Then he said something about having read my file."

"Your file?"

"Personnel."

Bell pulled in her chin. "How the hell would he have read your personnel file? Bullshit."

"I don't know, Pat. It's what he said. Then he went on to say he'd just taken care of unfinished business and the thing about Cecile. I just don't understand why he'd kill her. She was absolutely no threat to him."

"He didn't kill her," Bell said.

Tom stared. "What?"

"He didn't kill her. He killed her common-law in the kitchen and the two punk-ass sons upstairs. Same knife work as before, gut and throat. We found Cecile Long upstairs in her bedroom, unconscious. Drugged, apparently. We'll see."

"He called her 'poor Cecile' and referred to it as unfinished business he had to clean up," Tom said. "What the hell unfinished business would the Bushmaster have with Mack Kiff?"

Bell spread her hands. "Your guess is as good as mine. Stick around. We'll want a written statement and we're going to need the laptop."

"The dialogue box disappeared when I was calling it in. I couldn't find it. It's gone."

"Did you shut it off? The laptop?"

"No."

"Then Ident'll find it." She pointed a finger at him.

"Stick around. You know the drill."

He knew the drill, all right. It would be a sleepless night for him by the time someone got around to taking him to the police station and typing up his statement for signature. After another round of interviews, no doubt. He'd be lucky to get home before dawn.

Across the street from where he was standing, city police had set up a barrier halfway up Bethune to mark the south end of the outer perimeter. He wandered up that way, bored. Nothing was happening outside the rowhouse in which Cecile lived; the coroner was still inside with a forensics team comprised of OPP and PPS crime scene investigators. They'd probably be in there for some time.

Despite the lateness of the hour, people hovered around on the other side of the wooden barricades, trying to see what was happening down at the corner. It was always the case with crime scenes in cities, Tom reflected; they drew out the curious and the morbid-minded.

They stood three or four deep, many dressed in T-shirts and loose track pants they'd probably worn to bed. Most held up cellphones, hoping for something interesting to photograph or video record.

As he approached, a few flashes went off. He wore dark blue jeans and a black linen jacket over a blue shirt open at the neck, and he knew the onlookers probably thought he was a plainclothes police officer. *Once a pig, always a pig*, as Jade had said. Instagram and Twitter would soon be flooded with posts of the police detective who wasn't.

A tingling started at the base of his neck that took the smile away. There was something . . .

He looked around. On his left was a fenced-in compound at the back of an automotive repair shop. On his right was a three-storey brick house. There were no lights on in the house and no movement at the curtains. Nothing along the sides of the house. Nothing in the compound on his left, which was filled with cars and trucks.

As he walked forward, the feeling grew. The uniformed cops on duty at the barricade watched him approach, and when he unclipped his visitor's ID and held it up, they lost interest. More cellphones flashed.

Twenty paces away, he began to scan the faces. Young people in their twenties, buzzed and curious; an old man in slippers and a bathrobe smoking a cigarette; an overweight middle-aged couple arm in arm, watching him intently; a young guy who held up a joint and took an enthusiastic drag on it; a teenaged boy with a big bottle of Orange Crush.

The usual.

There were no journalists, as they were all congregated down on McDonnel Street. Just onlookers, drawn from the surrounding houses and apartment buildings.

Over the shoulder of a young woman with a bare midriff and sandalled feet he saw a grinning face. Tom slowed, puzzled by the man's incongruous good humour. A second later, the penny dropped.

Jim Woods, a.k.a. the Bushmaster, touched an index finger to his temple in a mock salute and disappeared.

"Hey! Woods!" Tom began to run. "Come back here!"

One of the city cops stared at him while the other turned around to look at the people behind her, confused.

Tom reached the barricade and vaulted over it. "One of you, come with me! It's him!"

He pushed his way through the onlookers and ran up the street. Ahead of him he saw a running figure pelting full-tilt through the light of a street lamp. Tom ran harder.

On the far side of the intersection was a short bridge spanning Jackson Creek. Tom saw the figure swing inside the guardrail and disappear down into the darkness of the creek bed. Seconds later Tom reached the same spot and sidestepped down the narrow path, wishing he had a flashlight with him.

He made it to the bottom and began to run along the creek bed, stumbling in the darkness over unseen rocks and fallen branches. The water level was very low and the creek at this point was only a few yards across. The Bushmaster had already splashed over to the other side, so Tom followed, slipping on the moss-covered rocks. As he pounded along the muddy bank he tripped over something and turned his ankle, staggering into a tree trunk. He pushed off and kept going.

Just ahead the creek passed under Aylmer Street. Instead of ducking into the culvert, the Bushmaster clambered back up to street level and disappeared. Tom limped after him, stumbling over more unseen obstacles. Short of breath, he climbed over the guardrail and emerged onto the sidewalk a few metres north of the Brock Street intersection.

He hobbled down to the corner and looked left and right. No movement in the shadows; no one illuminated under the street lamps.

He listened in vain for the sound of running feet.

He looked behind him, in case the Bushmaster had doubled back toward the crime scene. The street was deserted.

Damn it.

His shoulders slumped. He was all alone. Neither of the city police officers had followed him from the outer perimeter of the crime scene.

It took him a while to limp back to the barricade. The cops wouldn't let him back in, but after a long argument they agreed to alert Detective Constable Bell, in case she wanted to come down to see what the hell was going on.

44

The next morning when Tom got up it was past noon. He'd spent most of the night, as he'd predicted, in a room at Peterborough police headquarters, rehashing the interview with Cecile Long a week ago Friday and his brief interactions with the Kiffs, his online contact last night with the Bushmaster, and the chase.

He'd long since grown tired of his role as police witness and pawn of the Bushmaster, and while it had felt better to have briefly been the pursuer last night, rather than the pursued, the fact that he'd lost him so quickly into the darkness of the night still rankled and embarrassed him. He hated being manipulated, threatened, and played for a fool.

He spent the afternoon mooching around the house. He cleaned his gun and left it on the kitchen island next to his laptop, within easy reach. He put in a few hours working on the PI training course. He made up a jug of orange juice from a can of frozen concentrate and drank half of it while he played a few online solitaire games and browsed the

Internet for sports news.

Jeremy showed up with another man Tom had seen around the office. The two of them swept the house and removed a total of six listening devices from wall sockets in the bedroom, living room, and kitchen.

Electrical outlets were a common place to hardwire bugs, Jeremy explained. They found a video camera hidden in the wagon wheel light fixture in the kitchen and another bug inside the receiver of the landline telephone. After running a fresh sweep, Jeremy declared the place clean.

When they were gone, Tom took a couple of aspirin and washed them down with water from the kitchen tap. It felt as though the place had been fumigated for cockroaches. The invasion of privacy was almost as upsetting physically as it was emotionally.

At suppertime he microwaved a frozen macaroni and cheese dinner. He ate half of it and put the rest in the fridge.

Early in the evening he took the orange juice and his gun outside and sat down in his lawn chair to watch the sun move behind the clouds toward the top of Pamela's house. He propped his foot up on the chunk of wood and gingerly flexed his ankle.

The paramedic who'd checked him out last night said it was only a sprain, but told him he should see a doctor anyway, in case it needed an x-ray. It was still a bit swollen this evening and a little sore, but Tom thought overall it was better than last night. He wouldn't bother having a doctor look at it.

He recognized that he was depressed and that he badly wanted a drink, but he'd resisted the urge all day and promised himself now that he wouldn't go back on it. The booze was a problem. He needed to do something about it. He—

Footsteps sounded behind him, through the opening into the carport.

He picked up the gun and got to his feet. He looked through the doorway and saw someone at the end of the car. He eased forward, the gun at his side.

"Hello, Tom? Is that you?"

He recognized the voice. It was Doreen Lacey, the reporter. He shoved the gun behind his back, inside the waistband of his jeans, and stepped into the carport.

"What can I do for you, Ms. Lacey?"

"Hi, listen, sorry to bother you." She came up the side of the car, carrying a black briefcase. "I hope you don't mind. I wanted to talk to you for a minute. Is that all right?"

She was nervous, he saw, and on edge about something.

"How did you get here? I didn't hear your van. Where's your cameraman?"

"Uh, I parked across the road. It's a hybrid car, so it's pretty quiet. Les is off today. I came by myself."

"Excuse me." He moved past her to the edge of the carport. A light green Toyota was parked on the shoulder across the road. There was no other vehicle in sight. "You're alone?"

"Yes. Is that a gun?"

He turned around. "What do you want?"

"Uh, I thought maybe I could ask you a few questions about last night."

"I have nothing to say."

"Have you seen the news coverage today?"

Tom shook his head.

"Everyone's playing the angle of a serial killer on the loose in the area. There's a lot of panic. I thought maybe you could say something to calm things down a bit."

"That's Gavin Elliott's job, not mine."

"And he's doing his best, but your name keeps coming up as the one at the centre of this whole thing."

She sighed. "Could we just sit down for a few minutes? We can go off the record if you like. I could really use a cup of coffee."

He took one last look up and down the road, then led the way into the kitchen. He closed the laptop and gestured to the high stool on the other side of the island. "I've only got regular Colombian," he said, running water from the tap into the reservoir of his single-serve coffee maker.

"That's fine." Doreen settled on the stool and put her case down on the island.

"How do you take it?"

"Black, please."

As her cup of coffee was brewing, Tom put the gun on the kitchen counter and watched her open her case. She removed a small digital recorder. She looked at it for a moment, hesitated, and then returned it to the bag.

"Off the record," he said, giving her the cup of coffee.

"I know. I thought, well, never mind. It's all background at this point, anyway, without Les to film it."

Tom watched his own cup of coffee slowly fill up. His blood pressure felt as though it was coming back down again. He'd been half-convinced that the Bushmaster had decided to show up for some kind of face-to-face meeting.

"I wanted to talk to you about, well, about you. Are you all right?"

Tom tried his coffee. Passable. "Yeah, I'm fine. Thanks for asking."

"I understand you injured your ankle."

"Just a sprain. Who told you, the paramedic?"

"I never reveal my sources." She tried to smile, but it fluttered unsuccessfully at the corners of her mouth and disappeared. "You're still recovering from the car accident, aren't you? From the concussion?"

The last time he remembered seeing her was five days ago, when he was being released from hospital. She was trying to question Natalie, and Charlie stepped in front of Les Hume to prevent him from shooting footage of Tom getting up from the wheelchair. He wasn't sure why she was interested in his health, and wondered if she might be working some kind of mental competency angle.

"I'm fine," he said.

"We ran the artist's sketch of the man police are looking for, just like everyone else did. He's the one who killed the person you found in your church, right? And he's supposed to be the one responsible for last night, as well as the murder of the family in Apsley seventeen years ago?"

"That's the theory police are investigating," Tom said. "You have to remember I'm not directly involved. I'm just a witness."

"Why is he using you in all this? Does he have something personal against you?"

"I don't know," Tom admitted.

"Is that why you have the gun? Because he's coming for you next?"

"I don't know. Doreen, what do you want?"

"I . . ."

"Look, I've recovered from the effects of the concussion. A few headaches now and again, but my mental functions are pretty much back to normal. My memory's fine, and I haven't experienced any paranoid thoughts or delusions. Is that what you're fishing around for?"

"No!" She stiffened. "Not at all. You've got it all wrong. I—" She grabbed her case and put it on her lap. "I shouldn't have come. I don't know what I was thinking."

Tom said nothing, watching her struggle with something.

"I'm sorry I bothered you." She slowly stood up.

"Stay if you want. Drink your coffee."

"No. Thanks." She walked around the end of the island, head down. As Tom got up, she stopped at the top of the stairs. "You . . ."

He waited.

"Oh, hell." She looked at him. "Sometime. Maybe when this is over. You wouldn't be interested in going out with me, would you? Maybe for dinner? Or a drink or something?"

Tom's mouth opened. He didn't know what to say. He was completely caught off guard.

"Are you seeing someone?" she blurted.

"I'm not sure. I think so. Maybe."

She nodded. "Okay, then. Rain check."

She clattered down the stairs and was gone.

He emptied out her untouched coffee in the sink and frowned at his gun, feeling more than a little foolish.

45

"Here's your laptop back," Jeremy said. "It's clean now."

"Thanks." Tom took the satchel and slung it over his shoulder.

"There was some interesting malware on it. Probably from the e-mail attachment you opened when he sent you the quote on the wiring."

"Okay." Tom looked around the office. "Where is everyone?"

Jeremy shrugged. "Toronto, mostly. Section meeting."

"Natalie?"

"Toronto." Jeremy held out Tom's cellphone. "This is also clean once again. This time I've installed a few things you need to be aware of."

Tom took the phone. "The number's still the same?"

Jeremy nodded. "Everything was wiped and re-installed. I rebuilt your contacts from the list you gave me. Now, you won't see anything different on your home screen other than the fact that a couple of apps are gone.

You didn't have too many, anyway."

"I mainly use it for phone calls and texting."

"Yeah. Your generation's still resistant to the whole convergence thing. You'll notice a little icon up on the notification bar? At the top of the screen, next to the wifi system status indicator?"

Tom frowned, trying to figure out what he meant.

"Here." Jeremy pointed, impatiently. "This icon is wifi, this next to it is something I added that keys into our security network. See? Little green box? Now over here," he moved his fingertip to the top left corner of the screen, "this little green circle? That tells you the tracing and recording app I installed is functional. Okay? You see both of these green icons, you know the phone is ready to do its job. If the guy calls you again, we'll nail his ass within thirty seconds. *If* you can keep him on the line that long."

"Will it interfere with my normal stuff?"

"No, of course not. It won't block any calls coming in unless you do it yourself, the way you normally would. Same with texting. It's okay, Tom. You're good to go."

"All right. Thanks. I—"

The phone rang, startling him. "Jesus!"

"Default ringtone. Use something else if you want, but just from what I've already put on there. Don't download a bunch of infected shit, okay?"

The call display said it was an incoming call from Jade. Tom walked away a few steps and answered it. "This is Faust."

"Yeah, it's me. I'm coming down to get the window now."

"Window?" It took him a moment to realize she was talking about the little stained glass window he'd set aside for Pamela. "Oh, right. It's in the carport. Wait. No, it's not."

"Make up your mind, Speedy."

"It's inside, in the laundry room. I was cleaning it. I'll be home in about an hour. I can bring it up to you then."

"I've got a key to your dump here, Faust. I'm perfectly capable of walking down the hill and back up again. Don't get your panties in a knot."

"Lock the door when you leave, Jade. I—" He stopped, realizing that he was talking to dead air.

46

When Tom pulled into the carport, he found the side door open. Muttering under his breath at Jade's carelessness, he got out and went inside, closing the door behind him. He trotted up the stairs into the kitchen and stopped in his tracks.

Jade stood motionless on a chair, staring at him in silent fear. A noose was looped around her neck and tied to the wagon wheel light fixture. She was gagged with a sock. Her face was battered and bruised. Her hands were tied behind her back. Her legs were quivering. She'd obviously been standing in that position for some time as they waited for him to come home, and her muscles were beginning to get tired.

The man Tom had known as Jim Woods leaned back against the far end of the kitchen island. "Hello, Tom."

"Let her go. She's not involved. This is between you and me. Let her go, and we can get this done."

"That's not how it's going to work."

"I'm going to take that off her neck." Tom stepped

forward.

"Don't move." Woods pushed away from the island, raising a wicked-looking knife. "She stays right where she is."

"Okay, all right." Tom raised his hands. "That's fine. That's fine."

Woods waved the knife around. "Recognize it, Tom? You've been looking for it for a long time, haven't you? Seventeen years."

Jade whined softly behind the gag, her eyes widening as she stared at the knife.

"Meet the classic Bushmaster survival knife." Woods held it up in front of her face. "It has a ten-inch stainless steel blade with a very nasty saw back and a metal hand guard. Kind of looks like a short sword, doesn't it? And see?" He tipped it up so that the blade went back over his shoulder. "There's even a compass built into the butt cap. Remove the cap, which I won't do right now, and you'll find a little survival kit. Got this from Crowley's store in Apsley back in the day, just walked right out the front door with it. Stupid old fool never had a clue."

"Who are you?" Tom asked.

Woods ran his free hand through his hair. "I'm disappointed. You still don't recognize me?"

Tom stared at the round face, the dimpled, clean-shaven cheeks, the short, straight brown hair beginning to recede at the temples, the long straight lips, and the large blue eyes. The eyes were flat, dead.

Woods lifted his eyebrows and smiled, and Tom suddenly saw the resemblance to Cecile Long.

"My God. Mark Long."

"About time, Tom. About time."

"Why don't we talk? Explain to me what's going on. Just let her go and we can work this out between the two of us."

Long rolled his eyes. "Standard situation defusion from Critical Incident 101, Tom. It's all online, you know that, right? 'Step one; deal with emotions.' My emotions are fine, Tom. I'm perfectly calm. 'Step two; establish communications.' Well, by golly, that's what we're doing right now. We can skip step three because the triggering event is so far in the past now it's irrelevant. Let's just move right on to step four, problem solving. How about that?"

"Okay, Mark." Tom made eye contact with Jade and nodded slightly, trying to reassure her. "If we're going to come up with solutions to our situation, maybe we could start with Jade. She's scared and her knees are going to give out pretty soon."

He held up his hands. "I'm unarmed, obviously. You don't need her. Let her go and we'll talk this through. There's no rush; we can take as long as you like, but let her go first."

"No." Long slowly extended the Bushmaster knife until the tip was under the neck of Jade's T-shirt. He rotated it slightly and jerked upward, cutting the fabric. "She stays where she is. I just stopped by to say goodbye, Tom. This won't take long."

"Where are you going?"

"Hunh." Long shook his head. "You cops are always such optimists. Ask, and the guy will answer, just like that. Well, as a matter of fact, I'm leaving the country again. This time for good."

"Again?"

"Yeah, Tom. Again. I know you made a token search for me, back then. Didn't have any luck, did you?"

"No. Where'd you go?"

"I was fifteen, Tom. Fifteen, and already looking after myself. Poor Cecile, she was such a wreck. Anyway, I could see you people would eventually get around to questioning me a little more carefully than you did the first time, so I took off. Hitchhiked to Montreal."

"Is that where you've been, all this time?"

Long rolled his eyes. "Don't ask stupid questions; it's unbecoming. No, I hung out along the harbour front and stowed away on a cargo ship. Ended up in Panama."

"Panama?"

"Yeah. Hell of a place, Tom. The things I had to do to survive, you've got no idea. Don't move."

Tom had taken a step forward. He stopped and raised his hands. "I'm a little tired, Mark. I'm still not back to full strength after the car accident. I just need to lean on something." He took another step toward the island.

Long moved the knife to Jade's neck. "Easy does it."

Tom reached the island and put his hip against it. "How did you become an electrician?"

"I didn't, not exactly. First I showed them my wet work skills. That got me in good, you'd better believe it. Half of it is having the brains to know how to off someone in complete silence, in and out, no traces left behind except the ones you leave deliberately. The other half is just having the guts to do it." Long shrugged. "I've got both."

"You were doing this down in Panama?"

Long smiled. "At first. There are a lot of different organized crime outfits down there, Tom. Did you know that? The bunch I ended up with were actually Russians. Scary people, believe me. I did a lot of different things for them. Shit, everything from cash runs to pretending to buy a condo in the Trump hotel down there. One of their favourite money laundering gigs. Anyway, wet work was my favourite."

Tom ran his palm across the top of the island. "Why did you come back?"

"I wasn't going to. You know that? I wasn't going to. I'd been keeping tabs on that doorknob Little, just keeping him onside, so to speak. Getting him to run little errands for me, like mailing condolence cards to a friend of mine. Then just on a whim I decided to see what I could find on good old Joe Kohl. Imagine how I felt when I saw that son of a bitch was back in business, just like nothing had ever happened."

"That's when you decided to come back?"

"Not right away." Long put his hand on Jade's hip. "Stop moving, dammit. You'll hang yourself, you stupid fucking donkey."

"At least untie the rope and let her sit down," Tom said.

"She can fucking well stand there and like it," Long snapped.

"All right, all right."

Long looked at his watch. "I gotta wrap this up."

"I didn't see your vehicle," Tom said.

"It's down around the corner, out of sight. I parked down there and walked back. Caught her just letting herself in. She told me you were coming, so I figured I'd hang around. Say goodbye."

"Are you going back to Panama?"

Long shook his head, smiling. "Keep pitching, Tom. Keep tossing them in there. Actually, no. Not right away. The guy I worked for, the guy who was my mentor down there, he moved on. Eastern hemisphere. I'm going to rejoin him over there." Long studied the blade in his hand for a moment. "He taught me so much stuff, it was unbelievable. How to speak Russian. Computers, the Internet. How telephones work, and how to bug them. I'm actually not a certified electrician, Tom. I would have seriously fucked up your church. But electronics, now; that's a different story."

"I don't understand why you had to kill Joe Kohl."

Long chopped the Bushmaster down on the edge of the island. He twisted it back out, causing a chip to fly onto the floor.

"I would have let sleeping dogs lie, Tom, I really would have. I made Auntie Brenda pay, the bitch, and asshole Unkie Greg, and did the girls just for the hell of it, and that would have been the end of it. Really, it would have. I didn't give a shit about James. He never knew it was me, and he wasn't worth the trouble of chasing down when he got away from me and ran. But that fucking Kohl *had* to start up again. That *fucking* bastard. First time around I thought you would take care of him for me by fitting the collar around his skinny fucking chicken neck, but *nooo*. You brilliant police officers had to fuck it up.

"Even so," he whipped the knife angrily through the air, "*even fucking so*, I was willing to let the pathetic bastard off the hook if he hadn't started screwing around all over again. Pathetic little *dick*!"

Long picked up a drinking glass from the island and threw it into the dining room, where it shattered against the wall.

"It was his fault to begin with, wasn't it?" Tom asked. "He started the trouble in your family, didn't he?"

"No." Long nudged the leg of the chair with his shoe. Jade's knees bent as the chair shifted, and the noose tightened around her neck. She snorted, blowing mucus onto the sock in her mouth. Eyes rolling, she struggled to retain her balance.

Tom straightened, ready to move, but Jade steadied herself and the pressure eased around her neck. She stared at Tom, pleading with him to help.

"It was that bitch," Long said.

"Your Aunt Brenda?"

"Yes," he hissed.

"I don't understand. Why was it her fault?"

Long curled his lip. "Are you fucking dense? Don't you get it? It wasn't enough that she was wrecking her own marriage by fucking around with that pathetic loser Kohl, but she had to drag my *mother* into it!"

He picked up another glass and threw it into the dining room after the first one. This time, it struck the window and shattered the pane. Tom could hear glass splintering and falling outside onto the lawn. Clearly, Long was losing control of his emotions.

Jade had very little time left. Tom had to do something quickly, before it was too late.

47

"Fuck!" Long shouted. "Fuck! Fuck her! Fuck them! We would have been fine! Just her and me! No fucking punk sister, just her and me! But that bitch had to bring in Dick Boy and hook him up with *my mother*! It didn't matter that I was right there! That I knew exactly what was going on! That I could hear them, when they thought I was asleep! Disgusting ugly *fucking* bastard!"

"All right, Mark. I understand." Tom took a step toward him. "I understand. You blamed your Aunt Brenda for introducing your mother to Joe Kohl. I can see why that would be very upsetting to you, at that age."

"Of course it was upsetting! Of course it was *upsetting*. Jesus! That fucking bitch Brenda. Fuck, man. She had to pay. She had to pay, man."

"So you went over there late that night, to make her pay."

"That's right. On my bike. I'll bet you guys spent all your fucking time lifting car tire prints and trying to figure out who drove in and out of there, when I had my bike stashed behind the hedge in front of the house next door. Ha!"

"So you walked into the house looking to make Brenda pay. Why did you kill your Uncle Greg?"

"Man, you don't get it. You say you understand, but you don't. I didn't go over there to kill anybody. I was just going to wave this little baby around." He waggled the Bushmaster knife. "Put the fear of God into both of them. That fucking Greg, he treated me like I didn't have a brain in my head. I wanted to impress upon that fucking idiot just exactly who he was dealing with."

"You heard him in the kitchen."

"I went in and saw it was him. I was hoping it was the bitch. But it was him, and he started giving me all this fucking bullshit, so I just lost it. I lost it, man. I let him have it, bam!" He pantomimed running his uncle through with the long knife.

"Then, to make sure he wouldn't disrespect me ever again, I slit his fat fucking throat for him. 'No more talking, *Unkie* Greg. Shut the fuck up now, *Unkie* Greg.' Asshole." He moved the knife sideways, demonstrating how he'd cut his uncle's throat.

"You went there not meaning to kill anyone, but you killed him."

"It felt so good. Sooo good. And it was the right thing to do." He looked at Tom sideways. "You never killed anyone, did you?"

"No." Tom moved forward a step. Long was about three paces from the end of the island, right in front of him now, and Jade was about the same distance away on Tom's ten o'clock. He could see peripherally that her legs were trembling again.

"Let her go, Mark. Let her get down. This is between you and me. Let her down and we can do whatever you want, okay? You and me?"

"No no, she's all right." Long grinned up at Jade. "Aren't you? Sure you are. Your buddy and I are just going to talk a little longer, then I'll put you out of your misery."

Tom edged up another step. "Gerald Little saw you, didn't he?"

Long snorted. "That fucking weasel. There I was, arranging my kills out on the lawn like precious angels—that was a good one, eh? Helped steer you toward fucking Kohl, didn't it?—when that fucking doofus pulls in his driveway and comes walking over to see what the hell's going on. Takes one look and runs back home like a scared fucking rabbit. I had to go after him and explain exactly what would happen if he told anyone what he'd seen. Then when I was all done—this was really funny, man—when I went back for my bike to go home, I pounded on his front door and shouted something like, 'Keep your fucking mouth shut, shithead!' and I could hear him yell back, 'Okay, okay, just please leave me alone!' The candy-assed fuckhead."

"You kept track of him afterward?"

"I already said that, yeah. And you. And little James, as soon as he popped back out of his hole with that weak-assed alias of his. Did you know the people he worked for were actually affiliated with mine? Same oligarch? What a laugh. Made it far too easy."

At that moment they heard the sound of a vehicle on the road outside. Tires crunched in the gravel as it rolled past the house. The sound faded and was gone.

"Let her down," Tom said. "Just let her sit on the chair and we'll talk this through."

"We'll see." Long moved sideways. "I'd like you to know. I'd like you to understand what my life has been like. I've always admired you, Tom. But I have to go. I have to get out of here now."

"Mark, I—"

Long suddenly kicked the chair out from under Jade. It skidded and tipped over but didn't completely clear her feet, which slipped over the narrow legs as she struggled to keep from dropping down. She made a keening sound through her nostrils as the noose cut into her windpipe.

Long swung the knife around and began to move on Tom.

Tom reached over the island and banged the touch-sensitive top of the CD player. It suddenly blared out loud music, drawing Long's eyes for an instant. Tom grabbed a wooden cutting board sitting next to the player and threw it.

The board struck Long in the throat, crushing his larynx. He flew backward and crashed to the floor, the Bushmaster knife clattering away.

Tom pounced on the knife and with two wild strokes cut the rope that was hanging Jade. She fell down across the chair and rolled onto the floor, turning onto her stomach. Tom sawed at the rope binding her hands together, and when they parted he kicked the chair aside and turned her over. He reached for the rope around her neck, but her fingers, now freed, were already clawing at it. Tom pulled the sock out of her mouth.

"Are you all right?"

She nodded, gasping. Her fingers continued to scrabble at the rope around her neck.

Tom stood up, the Bushmaster in his hand, and stepped over to Long, who was still lying on the floor where he'd fallen. His face was dark and he was struggling to breathe through his crushed windpipe. His hands beat feebly at his chest as he fought to get air from his gaping mouth into his starving lungs. He was suffocating.

Tom bent over and touched the tip of the knife to Long's throat. "This is how your victims felt, Mark. Terrified.

Struggling against the inevitable."

Long's hands moved toward the knife but were too weak to reach it. His eyes pleaded for help as his mouth worked soundlessly.

Tom gripped the knife with both hands and lifted the point, shifting it down below Long's ruined Adam's apple.

Long closed his eyes in acceptance.

Tom drove the point of the knife into the base of Long's neck, exactly where he'd been taught by first aid instructors to puncture when performing a tracheotomy.

48

Tom walked down a hospital corridor identical to many others he'd walked down in his life. The air was just as stale and the lights were just as unforgivingly bright. He approached a man standing outside the closed door of a room just ahead.

It was Paul Bliss. He glanced up from his cellphone, saw that it was Tom, and hastily put the phone away. "Hi, Mr. Faust."

Tom nodded at the closed door. "How's she doing?"

"She just fell asleep. It was a really rough night. They have to be careful what they give her, you know, because of her history, so it's not as strong as the stuff that's, uh, addictive. But, anyway, she's finally getting some rest."

Tom put his hand on the door but lowered it again, deciding not to go in.

"I should find the doctor," he said, "get an update. When will she be released, do you know?"

"We can sit down," Bliss said. "There's a waiting area. I'll tell you what I know." When Tom nodded, he led the way down the corridor past the nursing station to a small alcove with chairs, a table littered with magazines, and a television on the wall tuned to the CBC news channel. Thankfully, the sound was muted.

"They're going to keep her overnight again tonight," Bliss said, sitting down. "Physically, she'll be okay. There's a certain amount of laryngeal trauma, so she still can't talk very well. Her breathing's laboured, and there's bruising and swelling. But they didn't find any fractures in the cartilage, thankfully."

"That's good." Tom sat down across from him.

"It's the psychological damage we're worried about." Bliss leaned forward, folding his hands between his knees. "She's been struggling since the police talked to her when you found the body in your church. We're afraid this is going to be a major setback. The psychiatrist stopped in this morning for a few minutes and she'll see her again tomorrow for an assessment. There's an inpatient program here for stabilization and short-term treatment. I'm hoping they'll move her into that."

"You say, 'we.' You're talking as her sponsor?"

"Yes, yes. I didn't mean—I have an MSW, a Masters in social work, so I have experience in this stuff, but I'm only here as her sponsor and friend. I wouldn't dare interfere with whatever decisions they make for Jade. I just—"

"Okay," Tom interrupted, "I get it. So how long will they keep her?"

"I don't really know. It all depends. Right now we don't know if she'll stabilize or deteriorate. It'll take several days once she's inpatient, and then there's be another decision to make."

Tom listened for a moment to the quiet sounds coming down the corridor from the nursing station. He felt responsible for Jade. He'd seen her fragility and done nothing to protect her from the risk posed by Mark Long while he remained at large. He'd failed to anticipate that she would get caught in the middle of it.

He owed her.

"You're going to see her through this?" he asked Bliss.

"Yes, sir. Of course. She can stay in my building when she gets out."

Tom raised an eyebrow.

"My bowling alley? I own the building. My partner and I live upstairs, and there's a second apartment that's coming vacant next month. If she's up to it, Jade can help me renovate it and then move in. It'll give her an immediate short-term goal."

"Sounds good." Tom stood up. "You've got my number. Call me whenever there's something I can do."

"Thanks." Bliss nodded. "John and Pamela have also offered. It's probably best, though, if Jade doesn't, uh, you know, see you again. For a while, anyway."

"I understand." Tom shoved his hands in his pockets and walked away.

49

He had already passed the city limits on his way home when he remembered that he'd wanted to pick up a few things from the grocery store, so Tom worked his way over to County Road 18 and drove into Bridgenorth. He pushed a shopping cart around in the Valu-Mart, lost in thought, and he'd been there more than ten minutes before he remembered the shopping list in his back pocket. He pulled it out and forced himself to concentrate on finding what he needed.

He was bent over, comparing the prices of canned chili on the bottom shelf, when a pair of khaki-covered legs stopped next to him and a voice said, "I prefer to make mine in a slow cooker. More flavour that way."

Tom straightened. "Don't tell me you've got me under surveillance, too."

Gavin Elliott smiled. "On my way home for a couple of days. Family stuff. Stopped for a drink." He held up a bottle of pop. "How are you doing?"

"Not bad." Tom knew that Bridgenorth wasn't exactly

on the way to Orillia. He wasn't going to give his friend a hard time about it, though.

"If you've got a few minutes," Gavin said, "I can give you a bit of an update."

"Appreciate it."

"Buy your stuff. I'll be outside, across the road."

Tom paid for his purchases and took them out to his car. After loading them into the trunk, he walked through the parking lot to the sidewalk. Across the street, he saw Gavin sitting at a picnic table in front of a little shack selling ice cream cones and milkshakes. He went across and sat down.

"Want one?" Gavin held up the ice cream cone he was eating.

Tom shook his head. "How's Claire?"

"She's having surgery again tomorrow. That's why I'm going home. Some kind of complication with the plate they put in. Not uncommon, as I understand it, but she's upset."

"She's worried about missing the whole season?"

Gavin wiped his mouth with a napkin. "Yeah. The university's honouring her scholarship, thank goodness, but she's stressed about it. I keep telling her, 'academics first, sports second,' but it's like talking to a brick wall."

"Just like her old man."

Gavin smiled. "So, basically we've gotten everything we need from Long. Once he recovered, he wouldn't shut up. He talked about the Bush murders in some detail, where he's been since then, and the others. Kohl, Little, James Bush. Armour was going to press him hard on the Kiffs, who don't really fit in with the rest, but he just waved him off. 'Repaying a debt I owed Cecile for Megan,' he said. He told Armour that when he was a kid he deliberately kicked the ball out into the street so his sister would be hit by that truck. Just as matter-of-fact as you please. He said, 'I owed Cecile for that. It wrecked her, and I didn't mean for it to turn out that way.' Creepy guy."

"One of the worst I've ever come across," Tom said.

"Yeah. Me too. He says to Armour, 'It's what I do. Everyone's put on this earth for a reason, and mine's to remove people from it who shouldn't be here.' His attorney's already said Long intends to plead guilty to all charges, and he intends to invoke an NCR defence."

Tom watched a pickup truck roll past. A border collie in the back paced up and down, barking. A claim of mental disorder under section 16 of the *Criminal Code*, alleging that Long was not criminally responsible for his actions due to mental illness, would assert that Long was incapable of understanding that what he had done was morally wrong.

Because the burden of proof lay with the defence in an NCR claim, his attorney would have to request that Long be sent to a secure facility for a forensic psychiatric assessment. In order for the request to be granted, the judge would first have to review the evidence and hand down a ruling. If the decision was in favour of the request, Long would then be sent to the Centre for Addiction and Mental Health in Toronto for a sixty-day evaluation.

There were two possible outcomes. If the assessment determined that Long in fact knew his actions were morally wrong, which Tom firmly believed was the case, the judge would reconvene court for sentencing, and Long would hopefully never see the light of day again.

If, however, the assessment found that Long didn't understand his actions were morally wrong due to mental illness, meaning he was not criminally responsible, or NCR, the judge would then hold a disposition hearing in which he would hand down a detention order placing Long in a psychiatric institution for an indeterminate period of time.

His case would then pass over to the Ontario Review Board, which would hold yearly disposition hearings to assess his ongoing mental state.

Since Tom suspected that Mark Long would be diagnosed as a psychopath, and since psychopathy alone was not thought to render an offender incapable of knowing right from wrong, he expected that Long would be found criminally responsible for his actions and end up in prison, where he belonged.

"It's all part of the game," Tom said. "We do our job, then the lawyers do theirs."

Gavin nodded, swallowing the last bit of his cone. "We'll see how it goes." He wiped his mouth and balled up the napkin in his fist. "Expect to be on call for this one for a while. The Crown attorney's got your number."

"Understood." Tom knew that he would be a key witness for the Crown at each stage of the case. It was nothing new to him, of course, but it would be the first time he'd appear in court as a civilian rather than a law enforcement officer. It occurred to him that it would probably be a good idea to retain counsel himself, since the Crown attorney's office would not provide the same kind of legal guidance and protection they had when he'd testified against offenders as part of his job.

Gavin studied him closely. "What about this thing with Natalie? Are you going to stay with it?"

"Sure. Why not? It was your idea to begin with, wasn't it?"

Gavin flashed a brief smile. "You were in distress, from what I was hearing. I thought Nat could help us both." He leaned back, his eyes moving around the parking lot. "Are you comfortable with them? Cage, I mean?"

"Not really." Tom found his own eyes roving around,

looking for something or someone out of the ordinary. "It's a strange firm. Very secretive."

"Everything I've heard about them is positive. I wouldn't have reached out to her otherwise." His lips tightened. "Just the same, some of the work they do is not the sort of thing either of us went to school to study for. Watch your six, is what I'm saying."

"I will."

"Natalie's back in Toronto right now, I gather. I've left voice messages, but she hasn't returned them yet." Gavin shrugged. "Paperwork to clean up. It never ends. They're a weird bunch, though, Tom. Unpredictable."

"Eyes open, Gav. I'll watch my step."

Gavin stood up. "Gotta get moving. Stay in touch."

Tom rose, and they shook hands. "I will."

Gavin gave his hand an extra squeeze before letting go. "A church," he said, shaking his head. "Who'd a thunk it?"

Tom watched his friend get into his car and drive away without looking back.

50

When Tom arrived home, he found a black car parked in his carport. He pulled over onto the gravel shoulder across the road and got out. Someone walked out of the carport and waved.

It was Pamela.

As they hugged he said, "You're home already?"

She kissed his cheeks and pushed him out to arm's length. "You look a lot better. Yes, we wrapped up yesterday."

"That's wonderful."

"Look what I brought you, Daddy!" She stepped aside and gestured. "Ta-daaa!"

Tom stared. "A Town Car?"

"Yes, your very own replacement baby. Surprised?"

"Very!"

"Okay, hang on a sec." She fished her cellphone out of the pocket of her skirt. "I have everything right here. I'll read it to you." She tapped at the screen. "John found it for you; isn't that great? We had it shipped from Burnaby and the timing is perfect. I got home this morning, and it got here an hour later. Imagine!"

"I don't know what to say."

"Okay, here it is. Let me read this to you. All right, first of all, it was in a fleet owned by John's production company. The fleet was going to be liquidated because they were upgrading, or whatever. It's a 2011 Town Car, the Signature Limited model. Whatever that means. John says 2011 was the last year of production for the Town Car in Canada. And it's *black*, of course. It only has 5,204 kilometres on it because it wasn't used very much, so it's practically new." She grinned up at him.

"That's terrific, sweetie."

"Hold on, I'm not done yet. It has eight cylinders, AC, heated leather seats, power everything, a multi-disc CD player for your music, and a bunch of other luxury features." She grinned up at him. "I'll send you the list."

"Thank you. I want to pay you for it, though."

Her eyes narrowed. "Stop it. Stop that right now. It's a gift. Your birthday present."

"My birthday's three months away."

"Happy early birthday!" She threw her arms around him again and gave him a fierce hug.

When his breath came back he asked, "Can you stick around for a while this time?"

"You bet." She grabbed his hand and slapped the key fob for the Town Car into it. "I'm taking a month off. Maybe six weeks, depending. Then I'll have to hit the road for all the promotional stuff for the movie, but until then I'm going to look after you—" she poked him on the chest.

Tom glanced over her head at the house on the top of the hill. "I feel bad about Jade. You talked to Bliss?"

"Yes. He'll take good care of her. John thinks we should give her some space for the next little while, and I agree.

Meanwhile, I'm bringing in someone, a housekeeper."

She laughed at his scowl. "Don't worry, it's someone I know. She's great. Anyway, you know what kind of housekeeper *I* am."

"All right." He squeezed her shoulder. "You know what's best."

"Of course I do." She stepped back, looking serious. "Jade really doesn't like you."

"I know. It's mostly my fault."

"You need more practice being nice to people. Which reminds me, you seem to have made friends with Nurse Slender As A Reed."

"How do you know that?"

Pamela shrugged. "We talk on the phone."

"You *what*?"

"Relax. We're already friends on Facebook and Instagram. I have a suggestion."

Tom's shoulders dropped in defeat. When she hit full stride like this, she was an irresistible force. "What?"

"Tomorrow night, why don't you have her come up to the house for dinner? You could fire up the grill. You know how much I love your salmon, and you could do steaks for everybody else. Besides, I promised Kelly a tour of the house, and tomorrow night she's free."

"But I just did my shopping," Tom complained, waving at the rental car. "I don't have steak or salmon."

She patted his arm. "Relax, Daddy. I already ordered everything. It's all taken care of. All you have to do is grill, and Bridget will be there to help you."

"Bridget?"

"The new housekeeper, Daddy. You really need to put up your feet and relax a little. You're a bag of nerves."

He raised his hands in defeat. "All right, all right, you win. I'll relax. We'll have Kelly over for dinner tomorrow.

You're the boss."

She grabbed his hand and held it to her cheek. "I knew you'd see it my way."

51

The weather held up, staying warm with a slight cooling breeze that skirted the top of the drumlin.

Pamela's dinner party went well. She'd ordered porterhouse steaks and fresh salmon, and Tom grilled them out on the deck while Pamela and Kelly split a bottle of wine by the pool.

By mutual consent, they kept the conversation light. At table, Pamela chattered about the project she'd just finished. Tom Hanks had provided the voice for the leader of the little green aliens whose ship landed on earth to save the dogs and cats facing euthanasia in an animal shelter, and she assured them he was the nicest person she'd ever met. Stephen was incredible and Meryl Streep, who'd surprised everyone by accepting the role of Annie the Cat, was amazing.

"She gave me such great advice," Pamela said. "She's really very shy, if you can believe it. I feel like we're friends now."

Kelly devoured every word, her elbows on the table,

fork in mid-air.

Later, after loading the dishwasher and putting away the leftovers, Pamela kissed her father on the cheek. "I've got a script to read. It could be a great role, and I have to tell them next week if I'm going to take it."

"What is it?" Kelly asked.

"An adaptation of *The Turn of the Screw* by Henry James. They're offering me the part of the governess."

Kelly's mouth opened. "Wow. Didn't Deborah Kerr play her in the Jack Clayton movie?"

Pamela nodded. "*The Innocents*. You know your films! I'm not going to watch it, though. I'm just going to read the original story and go over the script three or four times." She sighed. "Colleen sent me another one that I have to read before I get back to her on this one. I don't know what to do. It's about a single mother in a big American city who runs for city council to improve conditions in her neighbourhood and ends up getting intimidated by a street gang and their crooked lawyer."

"That sounds interesting," Kelly said.

"Colleen thinks it has Oscar written all over it. Anyway, we'll see. You two behave yourselves." She headed off for the living room.

When they were alone, Kelly said, "Why don't you show me your church?"

"Are you sure? There's not much to see." Tom thought about how it looked right now. Peter Cadmon, the electrician, had finished the rewiring and it had passed inspection, so the lights, ceiling fans, outlets, and outdoor spotlights were all fully functional. Tom had started putting in the insulation and vapour barrier on the walls, but it was only partially done. He'd covered the stain on the floor with a rubber mat and had moved a work bench over it, but in general the place was still a mess.

She stood up. "Come on, it'll be fun."

Outside, as they walked to the car, they saw that the sun had set and the moon had risen above the horizon. It was full, casting a pale grey light over the hayfields on the near side of the drumlin.

"It's beautiful," Kelly said, looking at it as Tom turned out onto the road. "Buddhists believe that full moon days are very important for spiritual development. Wiccans refer to the August full moon as the wyrt moon, a time to gather herbs and healing plants to dry for the coming winter. They believe the power stored in these plants is at its peak right now."

Tom accelerated down the road. "Sounds like you know a lot about that stuff. Do you believe any of it?"

"Don't you?" she returned, her tone light and teasing.

"Full moons are good for predators and bad for prey. They bring out the wackos and fill up the jails."

He glanced over at her. "You didn't answer my question."

"Do I have spiritual beliefs? That take into account our physical environment? Absolutely."

"All right."

"Ah, the quick judgment of rational man." She smiled. "Content to live out his days within the narrow confines of his personal experience."

"You sound like my sister," Tom said.

"Oh?"

"She liked to give me the gears about having the perfect mentality for a cop."

" 'Just the facts, ma'am.' "

"Something like that."

"Do you speak to her often?"

Tom shook his head. "She passed away. Quite a while ago now."

"Oh, I'm sorry, Tom."

"It's all right." He paused, thinking about her. "She was a microbiologist, but she was always reading and talking about alternative medicine and the power of positive thinking and all that kind of stuff. Mostly to get under Dad's skin. That's why you reminded me of her." He turned right onto Seventh Line Road. "Do you belong to some kind of group?"

"You mean like a coven or a cult?" She laughed. "No. This is strictly about me, myself, and I. A quest for spiritual enlightenment. A church of one, if you will." She added, "Imagine what Aunt Nancy would say. She'd disown me."

"She's an atheist?"

"Is the Pope Catholic?"

Tom suddenly remembered Nancy's crack about True Believers and their space ship.

They drove in silence, thinking their own thoughts, until Tom parked at the side of the church and they got out. He was gratified to see that the new spotlight mounted above the archway at the front entrance had snapped on when the car rolled within range.

He unlocked the door, hesitated, held up his hand, and stepped in front of Kelly, reaching for the new light switch installed on thc wall just to the right of the door frame. The vestibule was empty. He passed through it and flicked on the switches illuminating the front portion of the church interior. His eyes darted left and right and then, instinctively, up.

Nothing.

When would he feel relaxed enough again to allow a woman to precede him through a door into a place he hadn't already cleared?

"This is gorgeous," Kelly said, moving past him. "Incredible."

"The living room will be there on the left," he said, pointing, "TV over here on the right, dining area straight ahead."

"I can see it." As she strolled forward, turning around to take it all in, motion sensors detected her movement and turned on the back portion of the interior, where the altar had once stood. "And your kitchen will be here. Laundry room on that side, and a guest room, right?" She grinned. "This is going to be great!"

He took her upstairs to the loft, showing her the master bedroom and the bathroom.

"There's a lot of work still to be done," he said, leading the way back downstairs when she'd finished admiring the view of the nave from the railing.

"When will it be ready for you to move in?"

"I'm not sure." He turned off the lights in the kitchen. "I'm hoping I can move in before winter." He shrugged. "It depends on what Cage wants me to do. I haven't heard from them in a week, which is odd, but I expect there's more work coming soon."

Back in the vestibule, Kelly saw two lawn chairs leaning against the wall. She grabbed one and said, "Let's sit outside for a while. We don't have to leave yet, do we?"

"No, of course not. Whatever you like." Tom picked up the other chair.

They went outside, around the corner of the tower away from the spotlight, and sat down.

"There may be bugs," Tom warned. "The kind that bite, I mean, not the kind that eavesdrop."

She laughed. "That's all right. I'm tough. Unless they bother you."

"I'll let you know."

They sat without speaking for a few moments, listening to the crickets and the leaves of nearby aspens stirring in the slight wind.

"It's so quiet," Kelly finally said. "You get used to the noise in the city, and it's only when you come out here that you realize what peace and quiet is really like."

"I like it." He looked over, hearing her sigh, and saw that her head was tipped back as she stared up at the night sky.

"We're looking northwest," she said. "There's Ursa Major, Polaris and Ursa Minor, Draco, and look! There's Lyra."

"You know your constellations."

"A woman of many talents." She looked at him in the darkness. "I think we can be friends, don't you?"

"I'm sure of it."

"We'll see where it all takes us, then."

He felt her fingers tap his wrist and settle over the back of his hand. He turned his hand over and grasped hers. She squeezed, and he squeezed back.

"I've had several relationships over the years," she said, "pretty much all sad and depressing, so we can talk about them another time."

"Sure," Tom said.

"How long has it been since your wife passed?"

"Linda? Sixteen years now."

"Do you miss her?"

"Every day."

"People shouldn't be forgotten," she said quietly.

"No."

They listened to the sounds of the night. A train whistle, somewhere to the south. The low drumming of the locomotive's engine in the darkness.

He thought about Cage, and the commitment he'd made, and wondered if he'd compromised his freedom somehow.

"What are you thinking about?" Kelly asked.

"Nothing important. Being free. If Cage will affect that in any way."

"I'm sure it'll be fine. You can pick and choose what you do for them, can't you?"

It was a good question. He thought about the contract he'd signed. He couldn't remember any provision that would allow him to turn down an assignment he didn't want to take. "We'll see."

It was just for a year, he reminded himself. He could walk away if he wanted to, right now, and bank a healthy chunk of change. Or he could see it through, stay in the game, exercise his mind, do what he'd spent more than half of his life doing.

Whatever he chose, he would do it from here. From this property, in the middle of this quiet place. His final home.

"Look, Tom," Kelly said, "a meteorite."

He looked up, but it was too late. Whatever had passed through the sky had already burned out and struck the earth, somewhere far away.

"Didn't see it," he said.

"Never mind." She squeezed his hand. "There'll be more."

They fell quiet again. Tom reached his free hand behind him to feel the rough stone of the tower wall. It felt warm, having retained much of the sun's energy from the day. He looked at Kelly's silhouette in profile, her head still tipped back, her lips slightly parted.

If this was going to be his last stop on the road, the place where he was going to make his final stand, then it would be nice to have someone in his life again who would be here with him. Someone who believed it was important to be alive and not dead. Someone who could explain to him things he'd lost sight of, or had ceased to understand, or had forgotten. Someone who, by their very presence, could quell the screaming fear of death he felt in his chest every night.

He flattened his palm against the wall behind him and stared at the darkness.

The warmth of the stone comforted him.

Burritt's Rapids, September 23, 2019

About the Author

Michael J. McCann lives in Oxford Station, Ontario, Canada, and writes in a small basement office in the Burritt's Rapids Community Hall. A graduate of Trent University and Queen's University, he worked for Carswell Legal Publications (Western) as Production Editor of *Criminal Reports (Third Series)* before spending fifteen years with the Canada Border Services Agency as a project officer and national program manager. He's married to author Lynn L. Clark. They have one son.

Finalist for the

2015 HAMMETT PRIZE

Best Crime Novel in North America

**Ask your local independent bookstore
to order it today!**

Sorrow Lake
Michael J. McCann
ISBN: 978-1-927884-02-7

The March and Walker Crime Novel Series

Sorrow Lake
Michael J. McCann
ISBN: 978-1-927884-02-7

Burn Country
Michael J. McCann
ISBN: 978-1-927884-09-6

Persistent Guilt
Michael J. McCann
ISBN: 978-1-927884-13-3

No Sadness of Farewell
Michael J. McCann
ISBN: 978-1-927884-15-7

Ask your local independent bookstore
to order them today!

Also by Michael J. McCann
THE
DONAGHUE AND STAINER CRIME NOVEL SERIES

Blood Passage   by Michael J. McCann
Would you believe a small boy who claims he was murdered in his
previous life? The first Donaghue and Stainer Crime Novel.
ISBN: 978-0-9877087-0-0   eBook ISBN: 978-0-9877087-1-7

Marcie's Murder   by Michael J. McCann
Donaghue's jailed on suspicion of murder while on vacation. Can
Stainer get him out in time to find the real killer before it's too late?
ISBN: 978-0-9877087-2-4   eBook ISBN: 978-0-9877087-3-1

The Fregoli Delusion   by Michael J. McCann
Their only witness has a rare disorder that renders his testimony
useless. Is Stainer wrong to believe he may actually know who the
real killer is?
ISBN: 978-0-9877087-4-8   eBook ISBN: 978-0-9877087-5-5

The Rainy Day Killer   by Michael J. McCann
A serial killer preys on unsuspecting women — when it rains. Will
Stainer's impending wedding end in murder, or will she survive to
say her vows?

ISBN: 978-0-9877087-8-6   eBook ISBN: 978-0-9877087-9-3

All he wanted was to be left alone, but THEY had other ideas

THE GHOST MAN

A Supernatural Thriller

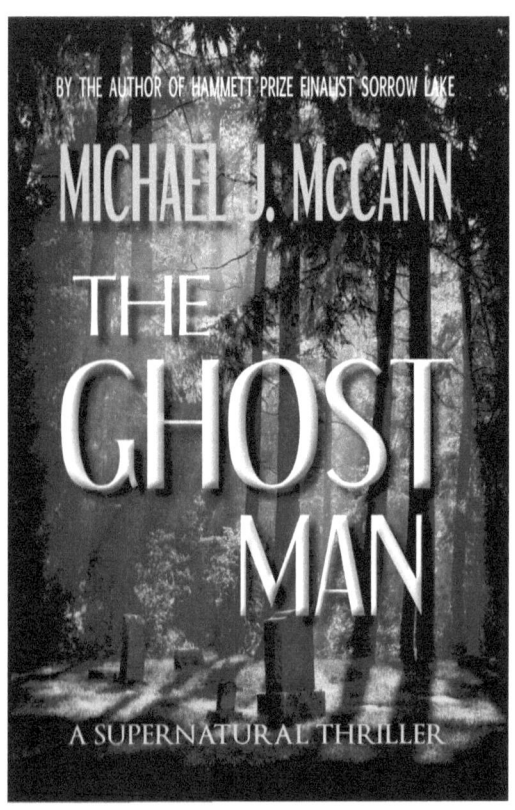

Ask your local independent bookstore to order it today!

The Ghost Man
Michael J. McCann
ISBN: 978-0-9877087-6-2

www.ingramcontent.com/pod-product-compliance
Lightning Source LLC
Chambersburg PA
CBHW031153020726
47499CB00002B/350